PERFECT BOY

HANNAH GRAY

Copyright © 2024 by Hannah Gray
All rights reserved.

Visit my website at www.authorhannahgray.com
Cover Designer: Amy Queau, Q Design
Photographer: Renie Saliba
Alternative Cover Designer: Sarah Grim Sentz,
Enchanting Romance Designs
Editor and Interior Designer: Jovana Shirley, Unforeseen Editing,
www.unforeseenediting.com

No part of this book may be reproduced or transmitted in any form or by any means, electronic or mechanical, including photocopying, recording, or by any information storage and retrieval system without the written permission of the author, except for the use of brief quotations in a book review.

This book is a work of fiction. Names, characters, places, and incidents either are products of the author's imagination or are used fictitiously. Any resemblance to actual persons, living or dead, events, or locales is entirely coincidental.

playlist

"Spin You Around (1/24)" by Morgan Wallen

"White Horse" by Chris Stapleton

"Love You Anyway" by Luke Combs

"Can't Break Up Now" by Old Dominion and Megan Moroney

"You Don't Want That Smoke" by Bailey Zimmerman

"Somebody's Problem" by Morgan Wallen

"With You I Am" by Cody Johnson

"Momma's House" by Dustin Lynch

"Last Time I Saw You" by Nicki Minaj

"Cowboys and Angels" by Dustin Lynch

"Sin So Sweet" by Warren Zeiders

"Lovin on Me" by Jack Harlow

prologue

WATSON

Growing up, I never put too much thought into getting married. I mean, yeah, I figured I probably would do it one day, but that was the extent of my thought process when it came to getting hitched. I assumed I'd tie the knot, then likely have a few kids, buy a house with a big lawn and porch, which I'd use to cook steaks on the grill. Obviously, a badass grill because, well, I'd be a husband and a dad, and that's what husbands and dads do. Maybe even have a front porch swing and a few bird feeders—and watch as the squirrels tried to steal all the shit from them. Maybe my wife would be into bird-watching. Who knows? She'd probably want an elaborate kitchen because, hopefully, she'd love to cook and bake. And I'd be able to have whatever she wanted built because I'd be in the NHL and I'd be loaded.

Those details I had thought about. Vaguely, but still … I did. But the actual wedding day itself? Never. Didn't really care, I guess. Still don't really. I knew I wasn't going to be the type of groom who wanted to decide what kinds of flowers were on tables or give a fuck about seating arrangements. Maybe I'd weigh in on the song we had our first dance to and give my two cents on the guest list, but that's about it.

I never let my actual wedding day cross my mind. Yet here I am. In my jeans and a button-down shirt at city hall on a fucking weekday afternoon. I can't say it's wrong because I never planned what it would look like to begin with. Still, I know this, right here ... wouldn't have been it.

I look at Ryann, and she continues looking anywhere but directly at me. She trembles the slightest bit because she's scared. I can practically hear the thoughts running through her head, asking herself if she's making a mistake.

She's promising me forever, and she can't even look me in the eye.

I continue to look at her, hoping to offer her some assurance—anything to let her know it's all going to be okay. That I'm here. That I'll be here as long as she allows me to be. This whole *getting married* thing, it was my idea. Maybe it was to save her. That's what I led her to believe anyway. Like I'm some knight in shining armor, showing up and saving the day or some shit.

In reality, asking her to get married was a selfish move. Because deep down, I knew this was the only way I'd get my real, true shot with the girl of my dreams. Where she'd be forced to give me a chance. To finally let her guard down and fucking see me.

Because how could she not at least try to like the dude who offered to marry her just so she wouldn't get deported back to Canada?

Exactly. I'm a fucking genius.

She might think this is temporary, but it isn't. I'm going to make her fall in love with me. There's no other option.

I want to be her husband.

And I want her to be my wife.

Not just until she gains citizenship. Nah, I want this ... forever.

1

Ryann
Two Months Earlier

Today sucks. Well, I suppose any day of the month that I have to make my car and cell phone payment does. I count the money I have in my secret stash and cringe. All the money I saved up this summer is slowly depleting. Add in the gift I just bought to send my little sister on her birthday and the shipping cost it'll take just to get it over the border to Canada? Ouch. But I work this weekend, and that'll bring in a good chunk of cash to bring my balance back up. Until more payments are due, of course. I can't complain; there's food in my stomach, a roof over my head, and I'm in a safe environment.

At least I'm meeting one of my new roommates, Sutton, for coffee in a bit. And coffee is cheap. Okay, it isn't that cheap. But it's a necessity. Practically more important than air really.

Even though I've only known Sutton for a week, I adore her. And somehow already feel this deep-rooted connection with her. We just get each other. She's sweet yet feisty. And she isn't about drama. Which is good, except when I want to gossip.

Last year, it was Lana and me in the dancers' house with a few girls who have since graduated. This year, we got two new roommates—Poppy and Sutton. The bad part? They hate each other, and it's practically like having two cats around. One a bit feral and the other the type that just comes out to eat, reminding you it's here before disappearing again. Poppy being the feral one, of course. Because trust me, her name does not match up to the sweet little pink troll from that annoying kids' movie. But I love her even if she is extra spicy.

Poppy moved in a few weeks before Sutton. Which basically means Poppy walked around, pissing on everything she could, marking her territory because she knew Sutton Savage would likely be her biggest competition when it came to dance.

While I love them both, Sutton has quickly become one of my favorite people. I even convinced her to come work with me at Peaches. When I'd told her I had a job for her, I didn't inform her right off the bat that it would be at a strip joint; rather, I let her find out with her own two eyes. I hadn't expected her to take the job. I mean, she's the freaking senator of Tennessee's daughter, and she comes from old, *old* money. And lots of it. *Loads* of it. Which is astounding, considering she doesn't even own a car or dresses and acts like a normal college kid.

I mean, even I own a car, and I'm poor. It's a pile of shit with the muffler half falling off, and it might not start every time, but still, it's a means of transportation.

When Sutton accepted the job, I was shocked. But in the best possible way. People can make fun of strippers, but what other jobs are there where you can take home stacks of money after just a few hours of work? And for the most part, I get to choose my own schedule, which usually consists of a few nights a week—or whatever my dance practice schedule allows me.

I started working at Peaches this past spring. When I had come here from Canada, I'd essentially had no money.

My mom had always put herself before her kids. Well, maybe not herself, but whatever lowlife she was dating at the time. She changed her boyfriends like underwear. But not a single one was an actual decent person. They'd use her. Abuse her. Then, they'd be gone, and she'd fall apart. Leaving me to raise myself and my little sister, Riley.

I knew when I got to Brooks, it was up to me to make it work financially. But between classes and being a dancer, it didn't leave much time for a real job. All last school year, when I wasn't in class, doing homework, or hanging out with my then boyfriend, I spent my spare time waitressing at a diner just off campus. I enjoyed it, but I wasn't making nearly enough cash because of how little I could work. Then, after a horrible but much-needed breakup with my boyfriend, another dancer introduced me to the owner of Peaches, and the rest is history.

A few shifts a week, and I can afford rent, my cell phone, and other necessities. It's not my dream job—that's for sure. But I also believe there wouldn't be anything wrong with it if it was. And to make it a little better, I love the girls I work with, and I have the best boss.

I might have lied to get my job there, just like I'd lied to cross the border and get into school at Brooks, but … I haven't been caught. Not yet anyway. And if a college campus hasn't caught on that I have a forged visa, I have a hard time believing a strip joint ever will either.

Obviously, it's not all glamorous and good times at work. And on those nights when I dread going into work, I just remind myself that I'm doing what it takes to make it through college. So that, one day, I can bring my sister across the border and take care of her like my mother never has. And if that fails, I remind myself to look on the bright side. What better workout is there than pole dancing? I can keep myself in shape for ballet while also making money. Win-win.

If it wasn't for the fact that we wear masquerade masks as a disguise from the many jocks and students who stop in from time to time, I'd be a lot more uncomfortable onstage. Heck, I've even seen some professors stop by to enjoy the show before, and I always panic that they might somehow recognize me, and that would be really freaking awkward.

Some days, by the time I get done with class and practice, the last thing I want to do is go shake my ass on a stage. And going from ballerina to exotic dancer can be tricky at times. In some weird way, it's like I live a double life. But I'm doing what I have to do to stay here in the United States.

I might have lied to get into the United States in the first place, but this is where I've always wanted to be. This is the country where I will make my dreams come true. I'm going to be a choreographer for a major dance company someday. Somewhere like Broadway. Sure, I won't be the one on the stage. But I'll be the one creating the magic. And to me, that's even better.

My sister will come to live with me, and I'll give her a life where she's never cold, hungry, or poor ever again. I'll make sure of it. And all of this lying won't be for nothing anymore. I just know it.

Nothing and no one can stop me. And unlike my mother, no boyfriend will ever dictate my life.

Because one thing I've realized is, I don't need a man in my life.

No, correction: I don't *want* a man in my life.

WATSON

"Boy, we already had practice this morning. Why the hell are you here again? I haven't declared two practices a day ... yet," Coach LaConte calls from the side of the arena, bringing me to a stop mid–butterfly slide. "Maybe I'm not running your asses hard enough. I can change that, you know."

"Trust me, you're running us plenty." I wipe my forehead and grin. "Just trying to get more conditioned, Coach." I spin around, grabbing my water bottle from the top of the goal and squirting some in my mouth. "Wanna be ready for opening game."

"No one is ever ready for opening game," he says coolly. "But you'll be damn close to it, Gentry."

LaConte has coached me enough to know how I am. Perfectionist to a fault. My own worst enemy. My own biggest critic. Competitive to the point where it's not fun. But how can I not be all of those things? I'm the goalie for a D1 hockey program. One of the best in the country. One wrong move, and I can cost my team an entire game. Hell, even a season.

And to add on the immense pressure I'm feeling, I have a spot waiting for me with the New York Rangers. But if I don't show up this season, they could easily pull the rug from under my feet and retract their offer. And it would be my own fault. After all, I'm the one who is staying in college all four years to earn a degree instead of going pro now. And if I get injured, good-bye, NHL.

The weight of the world *is* on my shoulders. And I just want to fucking hold it without collapsing.

"Did you get your workout in for the day?" he asks, stuffing his hands in his pockets.

I bob my head up and down, and he nods.

"I figured. Go home, Gentry. Go home and get ready for tomorrow's practice."

I sigh. I really did want to get another hour in before I called it a day. But if Coach tells me to do something, I do it. No matter what.

"Yes, sir," I say and start toward where he stands by the exit. "I'll see you tomorrow."

"You know it." He slaps my shoulder as I pass by. "You're a college kid, Gentry. Don't you have anything else to do besides be here every waking minute of your life?"

I stop, turning toward him. "Would you rather I chased women and partied too much?" I laugh.

"What, like Cade Huff?" he deadpans. "No, I guess not. I just don't want to see you burn yourself out on the game. It's a long road, making it to the Frozen Four. Gotta do it right." He tips his chin down. "Understood?"

I give him a nod. "Yes, sir. Have a good night."

"You too, kid." He pauses. "And for the love of God, don't go and act like Huff. Forget what I said."

"No worries there," I say with a grin before heading toward the locker room.

Every guy on my team eats, breathes, and sleeps hockey. But they also have the ability to shut it off sometimes. To think about something other than being better. Or becoming the best. I can't. I wish I could, but it isn't how I was built.

One of my roommates, Cade Huff, couldn't be more opposite of me. He fucks off *all* the time. His biggest concern is where this weekend's party is. And then there's Hunter Thompson, who is a lot like me. His family wants him to be a doctor, but he wants to make it to the pros. He has everything to prove, so he works his ass off both on and off the ice to be the best. But he's also better at compartmentalizing his life. Unlike me, where it all just meshes together.

I pull my clothes off and head to the showers. Trying to shut my mind off and think about anything else besides where I need to improve before our opening game in a few weeks.

It doesn't work. What can I say? I want to be the best. And the best doesn't sleep. Besides, when I step onto the ice in two years, wearing that Rangers jersey, I want the team to know they made the right choice, choosing me.

2

Ryann

"Heya, good-lookin'," I say to Sutton, taking the seat next to hers. "Ready to get this class over with?"

"No, I want it to last all night. Maybe into the morning hours and relive it all over again," she deadpans. "*Yes,* I want to get this shit over with. What do you think?"

"*Meeeow.*" I make a cat noise, followed by a hiss. "Someone fell on a stick today, and it went up her ass. Bend over. I'll pull it out." I nudge my elbow against hers. "What gives? You even look pissy."

"I assure you, this is just my face." She shrugs. "And nothing is wrong. This is my personality. You'll learn to love it, I promise you. Or you won't. Either way, it is what it is."

"Like how you'll learn to love Poppy, I'm sure," I tease her.

"Fuck that bitch," Sutton utters. "Not. Happening. Not until she stops being an asshole anyway." She scrunches her nose up. "How are y'all friends? I don't get it."

"You'll learn to love her, I promise." I pat her shoulder. "She's just feisty. But her heart is good."

"She doesn't have a heart. She's The Grinch. Except she doesn't have a cute dog named Max."

"Grinches need love too, babe. Be nice. Can't you at least try?"

I glance over at her, waiting for her answer. Instead, her eyes focus on something behind me. I quickly turn. Only to find that something is actually a *someone*.

My eyes land on his face before working their way downward. Bright blue eyes look down at me. His dark hair looks like he ran his fingers through it while it was wet from his shower or he just tussled with someone between the sheets before coming to class. His jawline looks like I could probably cut my hand on it.

The infamous Watson Gentry, Brooks University's goalie, stands in the aisle next to my seat. His backpack is slung lazily over his shoulder, and he's wearing a Wolves shirt that stretches across his chest in a way that has every chick in the room doing a double take. Likely salivating. Except me. Because a jock? No thanks. When it comes to those, I'm a stone-cold bitch.

Okay, even I'll admit that he's incredibly hot. But again, he's a jock. So, I can't show him that I think that. I have to stay strong. And frosty.

"Can I ... help you?" I ask, pulling my laptop from my bag. The thing is from the dinosaur ages and probably belongs in a museum at this point.

"Ryann, right?" He smiles as he says my name.

If I didn't know better, I'd swear he's nervous. But I *do* know better. And given he's one of the most popular dudes on campus, it's obviously an act. One he thinks I'll find charming and will make me want to take my clothes off and jump on top of him.

Wrong. Even though it is cute. Sort of.

"Yep. That's the name they gave me." I nod. "And you are?"

I act like I don't already know who this man is. Of course I do. *Everyone* at Brooks does. Well, except maybe for those who are hermits, like my friend Zoey. And she, the biggest hermit of them all, probably even knows of him. I play dumb though. It's always good to keep the Brooks University puck boys' egos in check. If we let them get too large, there won't be enough room on campus for the rest of us. And we're already at risk for that now as it is.

His face falls for a split second, but he quickly recovers, puffing his chest up a little higher. "Watson. Watson Gentry." He holds his hand out, like we're ninety-year-old dudes.

I glance from his face to his hand numerous times before giving it a quick shake.

If this is truly his game, it's downright awful.

Dropping my hand from his, I wait for him to leave. And when he doesn't right away, I blow out a breath and look back up at him. "Dude, what's your deal?" I come off as rude on purpose. Because it's imperative for me to keep guys like Watson Gentry away. To keep myself safe.

Flirtatious Ryann cannot come out to play right now. *Must. Stay. Strong.*

He frowns. "Uh … nothing. I just wanted to introduce myself. That's all." He swallows. "We've been in this class together for a few weeks now. Figured it was time."

"So … are you going to introduce yourself to the dozens of other people in here too?" I ask, glancing around the room and giving him a wink. I instantly regret it because he might take it as me being nice. "If so, you might want to get a head start. Might take a while."

"Nah, no need for that. I don't really care to know anyone else," he drawls slowly. Suddenly, the nervous dude I saw moments ago is gone as he stands a little taller, giving me a smirk. "It's just … I've been telling myself to say hi to the prettiest girl at Brooks for weeks now. Figured today was as good of a day as any."

I stare at him for a second before I burst out laughing. "I'll admit, that was good. Much better than the *nervous boy* act you did prior to it." I grab my textbook from my bag and set it next to my laptop. "Save yourself the trouble of acting, sweetie, and walk away. You're sniffing around the wrong tree to piss on." I wave him off. "Go on. As you were."

His head rears back, and a scowl covers his entire face. "Wait, what?"

I exhale. "Look, you seem very nice. But if you'll excuse me, the professor just walked in, and I'd rather take boring-ass notes from him than be your next attempted hookup or keeper of the hole you're looking to shove your penis in." Tilting my head to the side, I wave my hand. "Shoo, fly. Go pester someone else."

I turn my attention to the front of the room, and eventually, he stalks off. I sigh in relief because remaining cool when a guy like *that* is looking at you? Not. Easy. He had a dimple. A freaking dimple. And his eyes. Annoyingly gorgeous. But I cranked my bitch-o-meter up, and I think it scared him away. I hope it did. I can't risk falling victim to his charm.

Sutton slides her chair a little closer, and it squeaks against the floor. I sigh in relief when the professor doesn't seem to notice.

"Well, that was uncomfortable," she whispers. "Also, maybe I wanted him to introduce himself to me. Did you ever think about that before you scared him off? Huh?" She pokes her finger into my arm. "Did ya? Did ya?"

"He was looking to bone," I mutter the truth. "And I'm not interested in that."

"So? Maybe I was. Maybe I like a bone from time to time," she utters back. "Especially with guys who look like Watson *freaking* Gentry. Which, by the way, I know you knew who he was, bitch."

"Never heard of him," I reply innocently before glancing over at her and grinning. "Give him another week. I'm sure he'll circle back to our row, and you'll be his next prey." I pat her hand. "Personally, I think he looks like he would be extremely boring in bed." I'm lying. Though I'm not sure if it's for my own benefit or to make her believe that men like him have no effect on me.

"He's quiet. And polite. Those are the ones you have to look out for." She presses her lips together, glancing back at him. "I, for one, think he'd be wild in bed. I'm telling you, something about him tells me so."

"I don't know about all that." I laugh lightly. "But whatever you say, girlfriend."

I'm thankful as hell when the professor begins his lecture so Sutton is forced to stop talking.

Guys like Watson Gentry are only looking for one thing. And while the old me would have gladly taken him up on the offer, not anymore.

Even if he does look like one hell of a good time.

Last year, at this time, I was dating a Brooks football player, Denton Wells. And while everything had started off fine and he seemed like a good guy, it turned out, he was nothing but a boy with all kinds of issues. And not only did he end up being a controlling monster, but he also cheated on me for the entire six months of our relationship.

I'm not a dumb girl. At least, I never thought I was until I found myself in a situation like that. And when I found out, I obviously broke it off with him, which only led to him going ballistic. For weeks, he stalked me. Thank God he's now too busy with his new girl to bother me anymore. I've even seen him come into Peaches while I was there dancing a few times. Luckily, the mask kept me incognito, and he'd clearly never paid enough attention to my body to notice my tattoos. He might have moved on, but I have no doubt he'd still try to grab my wrist and pull me out of there if he found out.

A shiver runs down my spine as I think about that.

I ran from Canada after watching my mom get treated like shit by countless men. And then I ran right into the arms of a man much like the monsters I left behind.

Maybe I am a dumb girl after all.

But not now. After Denton and I broke up, sure, I had a little too much fun and tried to fill the void inside of me with whoever offered. But I learned the hard way that wasn't going to work.

So, sorry, Watson Gentry. Keep your dick inside your jeans and move along.

WATSON

I can't remember the last time I actually went out of my way to hit on a girl before she came on to me first. It might make me sound like a pretentious prick, but I haven't had to. Since I became the Wolves goalie, the women just come to me. Rather aggressively too. Sometimes, it's great. Other times, I'm that guy who's too nice to tell people to leave me alone even when I want to be by myself.

But ever since this class started, Ryann Denver hasn't so much as looked my way. Not once. It was time for me to properly introduce myself. Especially since I haven't been able to stop checking her out since I first saw her.

I talked myself into doing it—to finally go over to her—and then she didn't even know who the fuck I was. *Everyone* knows who I am around here. And by the look on her face, she couldn't have been more unenthused by me.

What a strange morning.

For weeks, I've noticed her. Her strawberry-blonde hair is always pulled off of her face. She sits with another girl; they giggle with each other and then leave together at the end of each class. The other girl is gorgeous too. But there's something about Ryann; it makes me stop and take a second, third, or tenth look. And I found out today … she's spicy.

I've always liked things packed with a little heat.

Go figure though; the one girl I could potentially be interested in can't stand me. And if there's one thing I hate, it's failing at anything and looking like a loser. So, I'm going to go about my life like I didn't just get rejected by a five-foot-nothing chick with an angel face, porn-star lips, and insanely hot body.

Ryann who?

Yeah, I've already forgotten her.

Kind of.

All right, not really.

Because as long as she's in the same room as I am, there's no fucking way I can ignore her presence. So, instead, I'll just be a creeper from afar.

I watch her take notes on a computer that looks like it was one of the first laptops to be made. She types mindlessly as the professor talks. I can only see the profile of her face from here, but her eyes look completely focused.

I blink a few times, forcing myself to stop staring. She made it clear she didn't want anything to do with me.

It's time to push that really weird encounter out of my brain and pretend it never happened. She sure as hell has.

3

Ryann

"I do not like where this is headed," I say under my breath as I observe our dance coach, Jolene. Her eyes sweep around the room as she gets closer to dropping a major bomb that I know I'm going to hate. One that's about to blow this whole place up.

"Not one bit."

"This is completely unorthodox, but after speaking to Coach LaConte, I've decided on something. Given that Brody was a huge part of the hockey team, we're going to team up with them and put on a show."

It's clear that Jolene is excited. And here I am, trying to cover the extremely bitchy, completely unimpressed look that resides on my face.

"Each of you will be matched up with a hockey player, and the two of you will perform a dance together! You'll have six weeks. This will give you time to come up with a routine and practice together. The main event will involve dinner, followed by a show, featuring you and the hockey player dancing!" She looks around at all of us, still beaming. "How awesome is this?!"

I rest my hands on my hips and try to stop myself from blurting out something rude. But, like always, it doesn't work. "I don't—wait, so we have to basically teach these giant men how to dance? That's what you're saying?"

Jolene offers me a calming smile, which does absolutely nothing to calm me.

"Everyone knows hockey players aren't the best ballet dancers. So, your job is going to be to make them look good! But the hockey team is so loved that having them involved will already give this fundraiser an edge. Besides, it makes sense because of who started it to begin with. But I want to add, part of this will run into their season. One thing Coach LaConte stressed is the need to keep his players healthy. So, please, nothing too strenuous in your routines. You all are the dancers; they will be the entertainment. Make them look good. Heck, it can be comical even." She pauses, gazing around. "As more information becomes available, I'll fill you in. But until then, let's get to work."

As we all move to our usual spots, I look at Sutton, and she instantly reminds me of a teapot. A teapot filled with water that's boiling on the stovetop and about to start steaming and screaming. Even her face looks red hot with anger. Most of the other bitches in here look thrilled, imagining they get to dance with a hockey player and work one-on-one with them, I'm sure. Heck, I'd be willing to bet some of them are even imagining that they could create some love story to tell their grandkids one day.

I'm the furthest thing from impressed right now. It's one thing to avoid hot, sexy jocks day to day with little contact. Ignoring them when you're forced to be partners? Damn near impossible. But I know better than to talk back to Jolene or argue why this is an awful idea. Because from an outside standpoint, it's an *amazing* idea. Of course it will bring donations in. Who doesn't want to watch some of the country's most elite college hockey players dance around the stage, pretending to be ballerinas? But still, I don't like it. Not one bit.

Jocks have a way of slithering their way into the hearts of innocent girls.

Good thing my heart turned black and shriveled up years ago.

Watson

"Coach went and lost his damn mind," Hunter says as we drive to the dance studio to be evaluated by some lady who is apparently the dance coach or teacher or something.

Earlier at practice, Coach informed us that we're taking part in a fundraiser. The good part is, it's my buddy Brody O'Brien's fundraiser, and it's a hell of a good cause. The money raised will help kids less fortunate play sports or take part in extracurricular activities that might not be so readily available to them otherwise. The bad part? Some of the selected hockey players are being paired up with chicks on the dance team, and they have to do a dance together for the fundraiser itself.

I'm no fucking dancer.

"I'll try my best to not make y'all look too bad," Cade chimes in. "It won't be an easy task, but I'll do what I can."

"Why the fuck are you excited for this, Huff? What if we have to wear tights?" Link practically whines. "I'm not wearing no nut huggers."

Cade shrugs, still grinning. "I'll wear 'em. I don't mind showing off my hogger if it brings in some extra cash for O'Brien's charity."

"If I have to look at your *hogger*, I'm bowing out of this right now. I'll make a donation to Brody's foundation when I make it to the pros," Hunter groans. "Keep it covered, Huff. Also, please ... never ... ever ... refer to your dick as a hogger."

"But that's what it is," Cade tosses back. "I don't know why y'all are complaining. Hot girls in tight leotards. And there's a dinner after. So, free food. The fuck is wrong with that?"

We all shake our heads and ignore him.

Cade's ... a lot by anyone's standards. He's hot and cold. Parties way too much. Has a *don't give a fuck about anything* attitude. And he's that flaky friend who says he's going to show up at things; sometimes, he does, and other times, he doesn't. That's just Cade Huff for you.

Hunter is the opposite. He's loyal to a fault. He's reliable, and he tends to put everyone else before himself.

They might be opposite of each other, but they are both my best friends. Link too. But Link doesn't live with us. He lives with his girlfriend, Tate.

As we pull into the parking lot, I think we're all wondering what the hell is in store for us. I don't dance. I've never danced. But I also know from overhearing them talk that ... Ryann and her friends are dancers.

If I'm lucky, maybe I'll get paired up with her. Then, she'll have to give me the time of day.

"There's my favorite son," my mom says, smiling at me on the screen.

I laugh, shaking my head. "You say that to all of us."

It's true. She's always told each of the four of us we are her favorite. It just depends on the day. My sister, Nora, is probably her favorite. She's an angel and given Mom two grandkids.

"Oh, hush. I do not." She moves the phone around, bringing it closer. "You look tired, baby. You've been working too hard again."

"You say that every time we talk," I deadpan. "You're starting to give me a complex that I look like shit." I change the subject. "How are Nora and the kids?"

Her entire face lights up when I mention my older sister.

"So good. So, so good." She smiles. "I can't believe Emmett is going to be four. And Phoebe, three." She sighs. "Just goes by too fast, I tell you. They are both so smart."

"I know." I nod. "I gotta get back home to see them sometime. They've probably forgotten who I am."

"Well, you could FaceTime them more, you know." She flashes me her signature look. The one she gives us kids when she's politely trying to deliver a message. "They love it when you do."

The only people I ever FaceTime are my sister and the kids and my mom. My mother would FaceTime me every damn day if I let her. But I limit it to a few times a week because life as a Wolf is so fucking insane sometimes that even eating dinner and getting my homework done are challenges.

"Yeah, yeah, I know," I tell her. "I will sometime this week."

"You'd better," she warns me. "Phoebe started some toddler ballet class last week." She beams. "Cutest thing I ever did see."

"I'll bet it is." I chuckle. "Well, she'd love this then." I cringe. "The hockey team has paired up with ballerinas for a fundraiser." I recoil. "I have to dance in front of everyone on a dang stage."

She covers her mouth, but I know she's laughing. Her smile goes right to her eyes, just like it always does. After my dad died, I wondered if I'd ever see her smile that big again. But eventually, she did. It just took time.

"Oh my Lord! You know I want all the pictures and videos of that."

Rolling my eyes, I nod. "No way. You'd post them all over Facebook. Or send them to your book club."

"Absolutely." She nods. "Anyway, I know you're busy, so I'll let you get going. Love you, baby."

"Love you too. Night."

"Night, honey."

Hitting the End button, I collapse back on my bed. I certainly didn't rock my audition earlier today by any means. I stepped on the dance teacher's toes at least five times. And I'm pretty sure I heard her whisper under her breath that I sucked. Then, there was Cade. Whose audition looked like he belonged on *Dancing with the Stars* or some shit, making the rest of us look terrible.

He loved that, of course.

I'll probably embarrass myself in front of the entire crowd and look like a moron, but oh well. It's for a good cause. So, being laughed at will be worth it, I suppose.

4

Ryann

The other dancers and I walk toward the studio. When I got out of work last night, I was greeted with an email stating that Jolene had chosen pairs and that we needed to come in today so she could inform everyone who they would be working with.

Yippee. Hurray. Wonderful.

There's no jock inside of the studio right now that I will allow myself to get close with. Not. One.

"Let's get this over with, ladies," I mutter, pulling the studio door open. "I really don't want Cade Huff. He's a whole fucking mess."

"He's so hot though," Lana gushes. "I love a bad boy. Remember bad-boy Brody O'Brien? The dude who started this charity? Well, before he grew a heart and fell in love, I got to ride that train." Her eyes go full doe-eyed as she speaks. "He had no clue who I was a few weeks later when we had a run-in at the coffee shop. But that one blissful half hour?" She fans herself with her hand. "I'm melting, just thinking about it. He. Was. Huge. But more than that, he surrrre knew how to use it."

"You know what else does a good job, Lana?" I whisper. "Vibrators. And I'm pretty sure they probably have a higher IQ than the hockey players we're about to work with. And they probably give a better orgasm too."

She responds, but I'm distracted by the heated exchange between Sutton and Hunter Thompson. He smirks, whispering something in her ear. And her cheeks heat. But not like she's blushing. No, homegirl is downright mad. There's a lot to unpack between the two of them, but I know she'll share when she's ready.

Just like me, she's keeping secrets. And who am I to force them out of her when I've got my own skeletons in my closet?

As some of the hockey team files in, Watson Gentry struts through the door. His hat is backward, and his gray T-shirt hugs his body in the best and most annoyingly perfect way. But the most obnoxious thing about him is the black sweatpants that make my traitorous mouth water.

He's hot. There's absolutely no denying that. And I hate that my eyes drink him in like a tall glass of icy-cold water. But given the fact that he's a puck boy, I'm sure he doesn't even remember me by now. I know how fast hockey players move. Or any jocks for that matter. Besides, if he's that hot, maybe his dick is the size of a baby carrot. Yep, I'll go with that as a deterrent. He has to have some deep, awful, major flaw. No one can be that perfect.

Stopping directly in front of me, he flashes me a dimpled grin, tipping his head toward me slightly and making my heart flutter the smallest bit. "Well, if it isn't the girl who did not want me pissing on her to mark my territory." He winks. "Ryann Denver."

And before I have a chance to even think about responding, he struts off to join his teammates, folding his arms over his chest and not sparing me a second look.

Well, I'll be damned. He did remember me.

I'm still not falling for it. All puck boys are players who are not to be trusted. I'm going to work with them and come up with a badass routine because that's what I have to do for this fundraiser and to appease Jolene. But under no circumstances will I build a friendship or have sex with whoever I get paired up with. No way.

It'll be easy. I'm not worried. Not at all.

Puck boys aren't even my weakness. I'll be fine. Everything is totally under control.

Yeah … sure it is.

WATSON

The second our names leave Jolene's lips, I watch Ryann's entire body stiffen and her eyes roll up to the sky as she huffs out a breath—clearly annoyed that she just found out she's working with me. And me? I can't wipe the grin off my face because I got the hottest dance partner here. And all that spice packed in her hot little body? I get to have my hands on that.

I'm a nice guy. A respectful man. She's going to learn to like me. After all, it'll be hard to hate each other while having practices multiple times a week. But I can't say that her attitude won't make it fun. Because it so will. I've always been drawn to fire. It keeps things interesting.

Hunter and his partner, on the other hand, really do hate each other. And when he looks at her, giving her an evil smirk, and she looks like she might actually kill him, I realize just how deep their rivalry might run. I don't really know what made him hate Sutton Savage, but whatever it is or was, it's far from buried.

Once we're dismissed and told to exchange numbers with our partner and come up with a plan, I'm shocked when Ryann's short stature comes and stands before me. She wastes no time telling me exactly how she feels. Not just by her words, but also her entire face.

"Look, I know you're some high and mighty hockey player and I'm supposed to work around your schedule, but guess what. I have a job. I have school. And I have dance. I'm also busy. Just because I don't have a willy between my legs or push a puck around the ice doesn't make my schedule less important."

"I don't really push the puck around." I shrug. "You know, goalie and all." My lip twitches, and I try my best to keep it together. "Did you just say willy?"

"Dick. Peen. Penis. Snake. Or probably baby carrot, in your case," she rattles off. "Call it whatever you want, but it doesn't make you more important than me. Got it?"

"First off, I promise you, that last thing you rattled off? Baby carrot? Fuck. No." I narrow my eyes. "Cucumber? Sure. And not the little ones either. Also, I never said having a dick makes me more important than you. You came up with that all on your own." I shake my head, looking down at her. "I get it, Tiny Dancer. You're busy. I'm busy. So, we can come up with a schedule that works for both of us."

She seems taken aback by my words, and she frowns, pointing her finger at me. "Also, some ground rules. Rule number one, I'm not sleeping with you. So, just get that out of your head now. It's not happening."

"I never said it was happening."

"You're a dude. A jock. Don't feign ignorance with me. And you know that whole thing in class the other day—you pretending like you were nervous and then acting like you'd been waiting to meet me? All. An. Act. I saw through it." She puts a hand on her hip. "Anyway, like I said, it's not happening. Ever. Rule number two, I come up with the routine. Choreography is what I'm in school for, so I'd like to be in charge. No, scratch that. I *am* in charge."

Take charge, Tiny Dancer. I find it fucking hot.

"Okay," I say, nodding. "Anything else?"

"Yeah. When we come up with a time, don't be late. I can't be waiting on you."

"Trust me, I'm never late," I assure her. "Now … can I have your number or …"

I hold my phone out to her, and she takes it before handing me her own.

She narrows her eyes. "You can, but don't be sending me dick pictures, okay?"

"Is that, like … something people do when they are partnered up?" I raise an eyebrow before typing my number in her phone while she does the same in mine.

"You're a hockey player. I know how much you guys like to snap a photo of the ol' *dick in hand* pose. You know, the one you do because you think it will make it look bigger." She hands me back my phone, and she takes her own and stuffs it into her pocket. "I don't want to see it. So, don't send it. Unless you want it posted all over campus with your number next to it."

I hold my hands up. "Deal. No *dick in hand* pictures."

Taking a step back, she jerks her chin upward. "Enjoy the rest of your day, hockey boy."

"You too, Tiny Dancer." I wave, and she slowly turns, heading out the door and away from me.

Something tells me this is going to be fun. And that my little crush I've had on her for the past few weeks won't be anything compared to how I'll feel after working with her for weeks.

Step one is to make Ryann Denver stop hating me.

Challenge accepted.

5

Ryann

I wrap my palm around the cool metal bar and extend my arm, letting my head fall back. I swing around the pole before dropping my body down and bringing it back up. It's a slow night tonight. No one is here besides old pervs and a few businessmen with their hair slicked back. It certainly isn't going to be a record-breaking shift in earnings—that's for sure.

I mindlessly move my body to the sultry beat of the song that blares through Peaches. My shift is over in twenty minutes, and I'm counting the seconds. I'm tired. After a day stacked with classes and dance practice, my feet are screaming that they hate me and need a rest. Pretty sure they want to detach from my body and go latch on to a couch potato instead of a crazy person like me.

I can't believe I'm going to be working with Watson Gentry. What a cruel message from the universe when all I'm trying to do is swear off athletes and keep to myself. Also, could the timing be worse, being paired up with him after I was a bitch when he was trying to make me his next booty call? Now, I have to spend time with him. Hopefully, after our little chat about the no sex and no dick pics, he got the message. He might play the nice, quiet guy, but I'm sure, deep down, he's just like all the other jocks here at Brooks.

I suppose I'm about to find out for sure though.

As I move on autopilot through the rest of my shift, my mind travels to my little sister. Images of her at home, all alone, and likely feeling pretty down. My mom would never lay a finger on her children, but sometimes, I think neglect can hurt just as much.

The only thing that keeps me from driving to Canada right now and staying by her side is the fact that I really do believe my being here will give her a better future. Because if I can land a gig in the city, like I'm hoping, I can get her the hell away from the place where we grew up. Canada is beautiful. And if my circumstances had been different, I don't think I would have ever wanted to leave. But that isn't my reality. And where I grew up holds so many painful memories for both Riley and me. One day, we'll get our fresh start, and it'll be in an entirely different country than where our mother is.

She and her boyfriends won't be able to hurt us anymore.

I might have forged my way into the United States, but I did it out of pure desperation. And I'd do it again too.

I snap back into the present when I spy a group of football players coming through the entrance, and I've never been so thankful to have my shift end. Sometimes, having complete strangers watch me, even if I am almost naked, is easier than having the eyes of the campus players—who I have to actually see at Brooks—raking over every inch of my body, not knowing I'm a fellow student. To them, I'm just someone to put in their spank bank.

I wonder how many times Denton came here when we were dating. At the time, I didn't even know the place existed.

I head toward the exit that leads to the break rooms and changing areas. Hudson, one of the main bodyguards at Peaches, opens the door, letting me through.

"Ryann," he mutters, giving me his best greeting.

As gorgeous as he is, he's also a little terrifying. I've also never seen the dude smile. But I've heard he's into some underground fight club shit. And looking at him, it's hard not to think he probably dominates.

"Hudson," I say, giving him a small smile. "See you next shift."

He nods. "That you will."

As he closes the door behind me, staying inside the club while I head to the changing room to get my things, my feet scream to be rubbed. Or soaked. Or anything.

But let's face it; I don't have the extra cash to go out and get a pedicure right now.

"Well, well, well," Sutton says, looking up at me as I walk through the door. She's on the couch with a blanket pulled clear up to her chin. "How was work?"

"Long." I sigh. "I'm so tired."

"Did you even eat dinner tonight?" She looks concerned. "I mean, we both know I can't cook shit and you can't cook shit. But I do have some Bagel Bites in the freezer. Oh, and chicken nuggets. Who doesn't love some nugs from time to time? And even I can't mess that up."

Collapsing next to her, I throw my head back. "Actually, that sounds good. Like, really good." As if on cue, my stomach growls. "I'd probably eat a moldy sandwich right now—that's how hungry I am."

Not like that's anything I haven't done before, I think to myself, choosing not to say the words out loud.

A senator's daughter probably doesn't need to know the things I've eaten when my mom didn't grocery shop for weeks on end.

Jumping up, she tosses me her blanket before heading toward the kitchen. "BRB, my hardworking woman. And I shall return with a home-cooked feast! Because I'm domestic like that."

Just as I hear her pulling the freezer open, followed by the beeping sounds of the oven buttons, my phone dings. Yawning, I reach in my pocket and look at the screen to see who it is.

Patrick Swayze 2.0: Tiny Dancer, don't you think it's time to schedule a practice?

I stare at the message, knowing it's from Watson. He must have put his name as that when we traded phone numbers the other day. I have yet to see him dance, but let's be real; he is *no* Patrick freaking Swayze.

Patrick Swayze 2.0: It's been a few days. You know, the less we practice, the worse I'll be. And the worse I am, the worse you'll look.

Patrick Swayze 2.0: I mean, performance-wise. You'll always look beautiful.

Me: I changed your name to Just Watson, FYI.

Just Watson: Wow. Hello to you too.

Me: Hello, Just Watson.

Me: Tomorrow. Three o'clock.

Just Watson: Works for me.

Just Watson: Oh, is that how we're leaving it? Maybe we could talk about our days?

My lips turn up the smallest bit, and I shake my head. He's persistent—I'll give him that. But everyone knows men love a game of cat and mouse. I don't want to be Watson's mouse. The mouse always gets caught. And ends up in the cat's mouth. And why does the thought of Watson's mouth make me ache?

Me: Good night, Just Watson.

Just Watson: Night, Ryann.

"Those should be done in a few minutes," Sutton says, sitting next to me. She nods toward my phone. "Who are you chatting it up with this late?"

I consider lying and telling her it's someone else. But Watson and I are dance partners; obviously, we're going to have to talk sometimes.

"Watson," I mutter, trying to look and sound unimpressed.

Just like I knew she would, she nudges my side. "Big-boy Watson Gentry." She nods slowly. "That dude looks like he's packing."

"Yeah, packing lunch that his mother put in his lunch box," I deadpan. "Good Lord. If you're so interested in his dong, why don't you hook up with him? God knows he'd jump at the opportunity. He's a Wolf." I say the words, but truth be told, I'd be a bit annoyed if they hooked up. Though I have no freaking clue why.

"That would be funny since he's best friends with my douchebag dance partner." An evil laugh escapes her. "God, I hate Hunter fucking Thompson."

I look at her face to search for any sign that she's bluffing, but I see none. Still, I pat her arm. "Eh, give it a few weeks, and you'll be falling all over him, like every other girl does."

Slapping my thigh, she scowls. "Come on, Ryann. Have a *little* freaking faith that I have a brain inside my skull, please." She shakes her head. "What is to like about him? He's a pompous asshole who is going to make it his life's mission to make this entire fundraiser hell for me."

"Hate sex." I wink. "Sounds like you two would have wonderful hate sex."

I expect her to roll her eyes, but I should know better than that. Sutton Savage is always quick with a comeback.

Wiggling her eyebrows, she scoots closer. "Guess I could say the same for you and Watson, huh?"

"Definitely not," I grumble quickly. "He's vanilla. And vanilla men don't have hate sex."

"He is so not vanilla—I can tell." She glares at me playfully. "I'm telling you, that boy probably has a closet full of whips and chains—I sense it. I can read people like a book."

I open my mouth to protest, but thank God, the microwave starts beeping, telling us the food is done. Luckily getting me out of any more talk about Watson Gentry and his possible wild and dark sex life.

There will be absolutely no sex when it comes to Watson Gentry and me. None.

But why am I suddenly thinking about him chaining me to the bed?

6

WATSON

I look at my phone. She's eight minutes late. After she told *me* to be on time. I gaze around the studio, wondering what the hell is in store for me when she walks in. It's obvious she likes to be in charge. Which is fine—for now. But if I ever get the chance to hook up with her? I'll be the one in control. But that isn't looking too promising, seeing as she's as frosty as the North Pole.

The door flies open, and in walks Ryann with her hair pulled into a bun, a huge-ass tumbler in her hand, and her bag slung over her shoulder. Dropping it down, she toes her sandals off and pulls off the Brooks sweatpants, leaving her in her black leotard, and my heart skips about five beats.

She looks up at me. "Ready?"

I try to stop staring and form a coherent sentence. She already thinks I'm a complete idiot. I don't really want her to think I can't talk when she's around too.

"Yes. I've been ready. For eight—no, nine minutes."

Walking up to me, she scrunches her nose up in an almost-playful way. "Don't be that guy, Gentry. No one likes *that* guy."

"What guy?" I frown.

"The one who fixates on things like not being on time. It's the equivalent of a Karen. You should grow your hair out and wear blouses. Instead of Karen, I shall call you Karl."

"Woman, you do realize you told me not to be late." I stare at her, completely confused. "Do you not remember telling me that?"

"Oh, I remember. And I said it because I know how jocks can be. They think their time is more important than the rest of us. To be honest, I figured I'd still beat you here."

"Well, you didn't," I toss back. "And I don't think my time is any more important than yours, Tiny Dancer. Not in the least."

She eyes me over for a second, her chest rising as she pulls in a breath. "Good." She nods. "Let's get started." As she heads to the center of the floor, she glances over her shoulder. "Oh, and the only reason why I was late is because my piece-of-shit car wouldn't start. If it wasn't for that, I would have been on time." She stops, shrugging. "Probably would have even beaten you here. Who knows?"

"You mean, you walked here?" I scowl. "Why didn't you call me? I would have picked you up."

"Oh, no, eventually, she rumbled to life. It just took a little TLC—that's all." She acts like it's no big deal. Like it happens every single day or something. "Now, let's get started. If you're ready?"

I nod, relaxing a bit. "Ready as I'll ever be, I suppose." I cringe. "I want to apologize in advance for stepping on your toes."

She gives me an unfazed look. "No worries."

I relax a little more at those two words.

That is, until she adds, "I'll just knee you in the balls every time you step on my feet."

My eyes widen, looking for any sign she's joking. Except I see none.

And for the next hour, I learn a few simple moves from her. I try not to get distracted by her pretty face or hot body, and that might be a bigger challenge than the dance moves themselves. I step on her toes at least five times, and much to my surprise, she never knees me in the balls. In fact, she's much more patient about it than I thought she would be.

Once the hour is up, she looks at me. "I think that's good for day one. But I'll warn you now: it's going to get harder. That was stuff I learned when I was six."

"Thanks for the encouragement," I say, headed to get my shoes on. "Hey … you busy after this?"

"Gentry, sweetie pie," she says in a sweet yet somehow threatening tone, "don't even consider asking me on a date. We talked about this. Not. Happening."

"We talked about me not sending dick pics," I say, putting my shoes on. "And it wouldn't be a date. But let's face it, Tiny Dancer; we're going to be working together. A lot. So, we might as well get to know each other a bit."

"And why would we do that?" she asks, her eyes narrowing slightly.

"To get more comfortable with each other, of course." I shrug, like I didn't just pull that out of my ass. "I'm sure the better we know each other, the better our dance will be."

"That's not entirely true. Do you think all actors on those cheesy jewelry commercials went to dinner before they acted all stupid with those mushy eyes? I highly doubt it," she says quickly, popping that hip out. "Also, who says I'll even like you? We could hang out, and I could find out that you are a complete dick of a human. That for sure wouldn't help our dance moves because I'd spend the entire routine wanting to punch you for being a piece of shit."

I stare at her for a minute before deciding to take another approach. "Ryann, I love my mother. I volunteer at the animal shelter downtown once or twice a month. I have a niece and nephew that call me Uncle Watty. I always return my grocery cart. And I hold the door open for people behind me." I give her a look, telling her to trust me. "I'm not a dick. I swear. Type A to a fault? Yes. Overly competitive with myself? You know it. Do I take hockey way too seriously? Yep." I hold my arms out. "But I'm not a bad guy. And if you get to know me, you'll see that."

"I don't want to get to know you," she snaps. "I've told you this already."

"Well, we're going to be working together. A lot. I want to know you." I swallow, taking a chance with my next words. "I'd like to be friends even. And before you yell at me, don't worry; I mean fully clothed friends."

She continues to examine me, seeming to seek out if I have an ulterior motive. I don't. At least, I don't think I do. But I'll admit, I want to spend more time with her. I find myself intrigued even if she is sassy.

"Fine. I get it. You're a good boy. You try to do the right thing even if it's annoying." She exhales. "But I'm still not sleeping with you. Clear?" Standing a little taller, she tilts her chin in a way to show authority or something. "I'm water—do you hear me? A liquid substance."

"What the hell does that even mean? You're water?" I scowl at the clearly crazy girl before me. "I don't get it. At all."

"You can't break me and get to the center. The center being my vagina. A block of concrete could be cracked. Glass? Easily shattered. A rock? Even that could be crushed. But water? No breaking that. And you're not breaking me down and getting in my pants. So, give it up."

"That is one weird fucking analogy," I say, thinking out loud. "But, yeah, for the last time, I get it. I'll keep my dick in my pants. Jesus Christ. If I didn't know better, I'd say you're trying to convince yourself, not me."

When she shoots me a glare, I hold my hands up. "I'm joking. Don't murder me. Now, are you going to let me take you to get something to eat or not? You just ran me ragged, and I'm hungry."

She stands there, openly considering my offer. And even though I've been pretty good at reading people my entire life, I don't have a clue what she's going to say.

"Fine. But it's not a date. I'd even offer to pay for half, but let's be honest; I'm broke. Besides, the dude should pay. Date or not."

"I couldn't agree more," I say, thankful she's going to let me pay. I'd feel pretty weird about taking her out if not. I'd also never let her pay her bill when I'm the one who insisted we go out to dinner. But then thinking about her saying she's broke makes me sad.

I jerk my head toward the exit before taking a few steps toward it. "Now, let's go. Before I pass out from my blood sugar dropping."

Reluctantly, she follows me out the door and to my truck. And even though I'd never say it out loud, for fear of scaring her away ... I know this is a huge step in getting her to possibly stop hating me.

She's so set on not having sex with me, but little does she know, I'm looking for more than just a quick hookup when it comes to her.

And someday, I'll make that clear.

Ryann

"Okay, remind me to never challenge you to a game of pool again," Watson gripes after I beat him for the second time. Holding the pool stick in one hand, he drags his other down his face. "Wow, I fucking suck. Like, really, *really* suck."

It's kind of cute, how much he's beating himself up inside. I don't think a guy like Watson Gentry is used to losing. Yet, when it comes to me, that's all he's done tonight.

"What's the matter, Gentry boy? Don't like the feeling of being beat by a girrrrl?" I try not to gloat too much, but it's impossible, so I just continue. "What's that smell? Oh, it's you! Because you stink!"

"Go on. Get it out of your system." He rolls his eyes before covering them with his hand for a second, pretending to be distraught, though I can tell he really isn't used to sucking at things.

"You're really taking this to heart, huh?" I all but snort.

We came to Club 83 and ordered a bunch of unhealthy yet delicious shit, and just when I figured he'd take me home, he asked if I wanted to play a game of pool. I think he assumed that because I'm a girl, I wouldn't be good. But little did he know, when I was a kid, our neighbor had a crappy, old pool table and would let me come over and play when I needed to escape my mom's string of boyfriends. I don't play all that often anymore. I guess I've always associated it with a bad memory, but tonight's actually been fun.

Really fun.

And what's refreshing is that Watson hasn't hit on me. Not once. Which is something I'm not used to when it comes to being around any Brooks University jocks. Even at parties, they act like complete and total dogs. I'm sure Watson usually is the same and is behaving strictly because of all of my warnings. But still … it's nice to just hang out without the pressure of feeling like I'm a piece of ass.

"I told you, I'm stupid competitive," he groans. "I'm about to go take pool lessons just so that I can beat you next time we do this." His eyes widen, giving me a serious look. "I'm not kiddin' either."

I'm not going to tell him this, but I love his Southern accent. I think about asking him where he's from, but I don't. Because then I'd sound far too interested. I'm not interested. I don't care where he's from.

Okay, maybe I do a little.

"Next time? Getting ahead of yourself, aren't you?" I raise an eyebrow, putting my stick back with the others. "This, my friend, was a onetime thing. To be honest, I just came along for the free food."

He throws his head back and grins. "Friend? Did Ryann Denver just call me her friend?" He looks around. "Pigs must be flying. Fish must be walking around on land. And hell has definitely frozen over."

"You know what I meant," I say quickly. "Just an expression."

"Uhhh-huh. Sure it is." He gives me a dimpled grin before setting his own stick back. "Well, either way, I had fun, and I'm glad you agreed to come out with me … *friend*."

"It still wasn't—"

"A date." He laughs. "Yeah, I got that."

This is annoying. I'm actually having a good time right now. With Watson freaking Gentry. I don't want to have a good time. I want to be annoyed by him. I don't want to look at him and have a goofy, stupid smile on my perfectly trained RBF. I don't want to be completely charmed.

Dancing can be a very romantic and sensual thing. And when you put a hot guy into the equation, things can get dicey. I can't complicate our partnership just because I think he's attractive. I need to keep my guard up. I don't do athletes anymore. *Literally.*

Back at our table, I take one last drink of my Sprite and look at my phone, seeing the time. "Well, I should be going. I have some homework to finish before tomorrow."

"Let me give you a ride back to your car," he says quickly.

I give him a pointed look. "Well, duh. Obviously, I'm not walking." I raise my eyebrows. "I'm not looking to be kidnapped tonight, you know."

He smiles, shaking his head. "Let's go, pool master. It's probably best we get goin' anyway. I don't think my ego can take any more losing tonight."

Before we head toward the door, I watch a group of football players file into the club. I avert my eyes anywhere besides at them because I know Denton is likely in the group. I glance up, noticing they've all made their way to the bar, and literally hold my breath. The last thing I want to do right now is run into Denton and deal with his psychotic self.

How I was ever convinced he was a good guy, I have no freaking idea. He's a slimy snake. One that I'd like to throw a rock at. No, a boulder.

For months, he's kept his distance. I've been very fortunate lately to not cross paths with him. And when I did, he was with his new girlfriend, so aside from staring at me, he left me alone. But if he saw me tonight, especially with another man, he'd have something to say for sure. I'm too tired and not in the mood to deal with Denton's shit.

Once they are all seated, I head toward the door, hoping to slip out without being—

"Ry-Ry," is called from the bar, and I know I've been spotted.

My entire body stiffens, but I push through and continue walking despite him calling my name again, refusing to take the hint that I have absolutely zero interest in catching up with his narcissistic ass. My hand reaches for the door, but Watson holds his hand out around me, pushing it open for us. Once we're outside, relief washes over me, knowing I got out of there without having to face that pompous dick. That is, until I hear the door swing open again.

"Too good to talk to me now?" comes from behind us.

My shoulders sag, and that sharp pain shoots through my chest as my nerves overtake my body, reminding me of how much control this person—this monster—has on me. An effect Denton always seems to have, making me feel like a loser. Maybe it's him. Or maybe it's the fact that he reminds me so damn much of some of my mother's exes, who I watched do unthinkable things to her, and when he's near, I turn into a defenseless, spineless person.

I turn into my mom.

"Hey, man, I think if she wanted to talk to you, she probably would have stopped when you were desperately hollering her name in the bar." Watson says the words lightly, but they are laced with something ... a threat maybe?

And when I turn around, I see Watson standing between Denton and me, almost acting like a shield.

"Gentry, do me a favor and get the fuck out of my face." Denton's voice drips with jealousy as he looks around Watson's huge stature. "I've texted you, Ry-Ry, so many fucking times the past few weeks."

"Yeah, well, your number is blocked." I try to say boldly, but they fall a little flat. Okay, a lot flat.

Denton's eyes bounce from me to Watson, and though he attempts a smirk, it's clear just how pissed off he is. I'm sure his controlling ass doesn't like seeing me with another man. And to that, I say, good. I'm not his property. I never should have been his property. But that's how relationships work, it seems. One person just acts like they own the other. And that's why I don't want anything to do with being in one again.

"What the fuck is this? You going for puck boys now?" His words drip with venom, his eyes growing dark with anger.

"Maybe." I shrug, hoping Watson knows I'm just saying what I need to say to make Denton realize I want nothing to do with him. I don't want to use Watson, but I also want to shut my ex up.

"That's really fucking sad, Ryann." He laughs bitterly, trying not to lose his cool the way I know he does. "I knew you had some fucking issues, but—"

"I'd advise you not to finish that fucking sentence, ball boy," Watson growls, stepping so close to him that their chests brush. "And if you do, I promise you'll regret it."

"Oh, yeah? And what the fuck are you going to do?" Denton coos. "This seems like a lot of work for a little bit of pussy. Though I'll admit, it is some grade-A pussy for sure."

"Ryann, go get in the truck," Watson commands before glancing over his shoulder and tossing me the keys. "Please."

Catching them in my hand, I slowly start to back away, wondering what the hell is about to happen and wishing we could just leave. Together.

"Watson … let's just go," I whisper, looking over my shoulder. "Please."

"I'll be right there," he assures me, giving me a slight head nod. "Promise."

I turn and beeline it for the truck. I've never liked violence. I guess watching too much of it as a kid will do that. I wish I could go and pull Watson to the truck and force him to leave before the situation escalates. But I saw the look in both of their eyes—they're out for blood.

Especially Watson.

I don't want to risk seeing that. But more than that, I don't want to risk being in the middle of it.

Before I make it inside the cab of the truck, I hear Denton's voice, bursting with rage. "Isn't this cute? If you're being this sweet, Gentry, well then, I'd say she's definitely shown you what she can do with those lips. Fuck, she deep-throats like a—"

Those are the only words I hear before a loud commotion starts. I don't look back. I know myself enough to know that I can't. Instead, I climb into the truck, and I bring my knees to my chest and bury my face in my hands. And I do my best to not let it take me back in time. But when I feel myself slipping back to a time when I lived at home, I know my attempt is a fail. And before I know it, everything is spinning. And the past and the future become one.

And even though my mind is somewhere else, I feel that guilt inside my chest because this fight was my fault.

And tonight, Watson has proven that he's a monster. Just like all the others. Reminding me why I have my guard up.

Watson

I'm not usually one to settle things with violence unless there is no other way. But guys like Denton, they need to be knocked around a bit to be taught to shut the fuck up. All it took was a few solid punches, and he was down. He didn't even attempt to scurry to his feet; he simply kept yelling how she's not worth it and that he could have her back in a heartbeat.

Over my dead body, asshole.

I don't give a shit that she can't stand me. If you ask me, that's an act so that she can keep me at an arm's length. Either way, I don't care. Because I'd murder that cocksucker before I ever let her go back to him. Hell, I didn't even know they'd dated until tonight. He's one of those football players who's good enough to be on the team, but not good enough to be first string or to be talked about much around campus and certainly not on the news. And if he'll say these types of things in front of me, I can't imagine how he treated her behind closed doors.

The thought alone makes me want to turn around and go beat his face into the pavement. But I refrain and head to my truck. If I wasn't with her tonight, I don't know what he would have done. Then again, I think he was only angry because she was with me. Maybe he would have left her alone if I hadn't been here. Either way, I wouldn't want to chance it.

Pulling the door to my truck open, I'm met with a sight that has my stomach turning and my heart breaking. Ryann is rocking, her face buried in her palms as she keeps her knees pulled in, making herself smaller.

Running around to the passenger side, I pull her against me. "Fuck, I'm so sorry. Are you all right?"

Her body shakes, but she doesn't respond. I don't know what happened or if this is from the altercation between Denton and me.

Fuck, that must be it. I'm such a fucking idiot.

If I had known that knocking him out would make her this upset, I would have just walked away. It would have killed me, but I would have done it.

"Shh, it's okay," I whisper, swaying her shaking body in my arms.

Not wanting anyone to see her like this, I climb into the seat, keeping her in my arms and holding her head to my chest before closing the door. It's like her body is here with me, but her mind isn't. Her eyes are squeezed shut, and she shivers against me, not even trying to wiggle from my hold.

That's how I know how bad she's hurting. She's letting me fucking hold her.

Maybe she's having a panic attack—I don't really know. But I read somewhere that when people are having panic attacks, oftentimes, compression helps. I tighten my arms around her and continue to hold her, hoping that after a while, she'll come out of it.

"I'm sorry," I whisper against her hair. "I'm so sorry."

I finally got my dream girl to go to dinner with me, and now, I went and fucked up and scared her. She thinks I'm this violent person who goes around beating the shit out of people even though that isn't true. I just couldn't fucking stand him talking shit about her. And as much as I hate to admit it, a little of it was jealousy. Because the thought of Ryann on her knees, sucking his cock, makes me crazy. No, it makes me completely lose my mind.

The worst part is, I don't know her well enough to make this better right now. I have no idea what I could do that would help. And I hate that.

I might not know what to do, but I'll sit here, just like this, for as long as I need to. This is my fault. I'm going to fix it.

Ryann

When the panic searing through my body, making it hard for me to breathe, finally begins to subside, my mind snaps back to the present. And I literally feel like I might die of embarrassment. I've managed to keep these panic attacks hidden from basically everyone in my life. They started when I was a kid, and now, I only have them every now and then. So, of course the universe would make it so that I had one when I was with Watson. Since meeting him, I've been trying to play it off like I'm some tough, badass, unaffected bitch. Welp, after what just happened, that's gone. He sees me … for me.

And the me that I am isn't strong at all. And he knows it.

Despite my cheeks flooding with heat from feeling ashamed, I don't want to move. Especially since the soft fleece of his hoodie is so comfortable. I feel like I could take a nap right here, which isn't an option. But he's warm and cozy. And, damn it, he smells so good. It's hard to pull away, but that's exactly what I need to do.

I stretch my sweatshirt over my hand and wipe my eyes before pushing off of him, making sure to not look into his eyes because then I really would die of humiliation. Or my cheeks would melt off of my face.

"You good?" he asks softly, and there isn't a single ounce of judgment in his voice. Just concern.

I nod. "I'm good. I just want to go home." I blow out a breath. "To go home and never talk about what just happened again."

Of course, he isn't going to let it go. To allow me to slip into the shadows and pretend the past however many minutes didn't actually happen. No, that would be too freaking easy.

"Ryann, I'm really sorry. If I had known that—" He stops, and I chance a peek at him to find that he's pale as a ghost. "If I had known that what I did to Denton would make you feel like this … I would have walked away. I would have walked away and gotten my ass in the truck and just taken you home." He swallows. "It would have killed me to do it, but I would have done it. And I'm so fucking sorry that I wasn't strong enough to do that."

My entire body feels how close we are. Our bodies are touching, and I feel it everywhere. My heart is racing, and I don't know if it's from what just happened or the fact that we're so close that I can smell his deodorant or cologne and feel the heat from his body.

Normally, I would call bullshit. I'd assume he does go around, beating the crap out of people, and fixes issues with violence. But there's something in his voice and the way he's looking at me right now … I believe what he's telling me.

I don't want to melt against him, so I fight it. Taking a few long blinks, I remind myself how things like this, right here, complicate everything. And that brings my brain back to its logical, smart self. Not the brain that wants to inhale Watson Gentry like a candle and cuddle his hoodie like a freaking Downy commercial.

"It's fine," I snap before reaching for the door handle. I push the door open and climb out. I need to get away from him.

Following me out of the truck, he steps toward me, gazing down. "Ryann, if he's doing something to hurt you … if *anyone* is doing something to hurt you, I want you to tell me."

I scowl up at him. "Why, Watson? What does it matter? What are you going to do, be Superman and show up and save the day? We barely know each other." I throw my hands up. "No one is hurting me. And it's not your concern if they were."

The way his eyes burn into mine tells me he's not buying anything I'm saying. And as we stand here, in this standoff, I eventually sigh.

"Watson, it's not a big deal. He's just my douchebag ex that I was dumb enough to date. He's left me alone for a long time." I stop, widening my eyes. "Until tonight. Until he saw us hanging out. Which is just another reason why I don't want to hang out with you. I don't need drama. I've lived through enough of it to last me a lifetime."

"First off, don't ever call yourself dumb. You're not," he mutters. "And what just happened in my truck … does that happen a lot?"

"No, not really," I say matter-of-factly. "Only when I have to witness dudes trying to show how big and bad they are." I blink, breaking his stare. "I appreciate the concern, but I'm fine. I've been fine. I'll always be fine. So, please … just take me back to my car so I can go home. I'm tired."

He stands there, not budging for a moment. Finally, he steps aside so I can climb back into the truck, and he walks around to the driver's side.

It might have sent me into a panic attack, but either way … Watson Gentry stuck up for me tonight. He stuck up for me and then held me like a baby after.

Maybe I had read him all wrong. But if that's true … what the hell is that going to mean for us working together?

Besides Denton and a few select friends, I've held everyone at arm's length. That stops me from being in bad positions. The way it was when I was growing up. And the way it was with Denton.

He might claim he wants to be my friend, but everyone knows that girls and guys can't really be just friends. Not without things getting complicated at least. That's a fact. Especially when the guy looks like Watson and makes my heart beat faster every time his fingers brush against my skin even if just accidentally.

I need to keep him at a distance. It's the only thing that will keep me safe.

WATSON

The ride back is silent. I attempt to make small talk, but she responds to it with one-worded answers. So, eventually, I just turn the music on and let her sit and stew. Or whatever the hell she's doing over there in my passenger seat.

I don't like the thought of knowing that Denton fucking Wells treated her badly. And I really don't like thinking about how he can still do it since he's at the same campus. The look on his face tonight, that was the look of a jealous, angry man. I don't know if he would have acted the same way if she had been alone, but I know I'm going to keep my eyes on her. And him too.

We're only a few minutes away from where her car is parked when I pull into Dairy Queen.

"What are you doing?" She scowls as I start toward the drive-through.

"My mom always says there's no bad day that can't be fixed with ice cream." I shrug. "So, I'm gettin' you some ice cream. Whatcha want, Tiny Dancer?"

"I don't want ice cream," she huffs. "Maybe I'm lactose intolerant."

"Are you?" I gaze over at her and am met with a glare.

"Well, no," she grumbles. "Maybe I just don't want ice cream."

I sigh. "It probably sounds stupid, but after my dad died, I'd bring my mom ice cream. For the first month or so, she never ate it. But after a while … she did. And then it became our inside joke in our family. That ice cream can fix everything." I stop behind the line of cars. "Obviously, I know that it can't actually fix things. But … it helps."

Her gaze softens. "I'm sorry about your dad." She pauses. "I just don't know why you're being so nice to me," she whispers. "What do you get out of it? Or what are you hoping to get? Because I meant what I said. I'm not interested in anything romantic. Not just with you, but with anyone."

"I get the pleasure of spending time with a pretty badass chick," I say, giving her a small grin. "Now, whether you like it or not, I'm getting you ice cream."

Just then, it's my turn to pull up and order. I go out on a limb and just guess what she might want. I don't know her, and I have no idea what she likes and doesn't like. But I want to make her night a little less shitty. And I don't care if I sound like a weirdo after sharing that I used to buy my mother ice cream.

"Hi, can I get one Frosted Sugar Cookie Blizzard and one Reese's Peanut Butter Cup Blizzard?" I say into the speaker.

Once the lady tells me to pull ahead, I drive to the window and pay. And when she hands me the two Blizzards, I set them in the cupholders and drive to a parking spot.

"Which one do you want?" I nod toward them and stick a spoon in each one.

"You ordered two," she says, narrowing her eyes like she's confused. "So, you must have had a specific one in mind that you wanted for yourself."

"Nah, actually." I shrug. "I just figured if I ordered two different kinds, you'd be bound to like at least one of them."

She looks from me to the ice cream, the look of shock never leaving her face. Finally, she gives me a small smile, and fuck if my heart doesn't flip. I'm a pathetic fuck when it comes to this girl.

"I like both flavors," she says softly. "You choose."

"Tiny Dancer, they'll melt before I choose the first one." I point to them. "Go on. I promise, I don't care which one you leave me. Ice cream is ice cream."

Taking the Frosted Sugar Cookie one, she tilts her head to the side. "Are you sure? You can have this one."

Grabbing the Reese's Peanut Butter Cup one, I wink. "Nah, I was hoping for this one anyway. Not a big sugar cookie fan."

Her mouth hangs open. "You were really going to eat the one you didn't want if I chose Reese's?" She looks baffled and untrusting, but then, she smiles, tilting her head and narrowing her eyes playfully. "Are you always this nice?"

"Stick around, and maybe you'll find out," I joke. "Now, eat up, and let's make this day better."

And like an obsessed fucking freak, I watch her bring the spoon to her mouth and take a bite. Sending a jolt right to my dick and making me wish my cock were that spoon.

1

WATSON

I silently give myself a pep talk. We're in the final period of our opening game, leading by just one goal. And with one period left ... now is not the time to fuck up.

As much as I love being goalie and even though I know I'd never want to play anywhere else on the ice, sometimes, the pressure of playing such a crucial position really gets to me. One miscalculation, and I can blow it for my team. The entire time the clock is running, I have to pay attention to where the puck is. And sometimes, it's mentally taxing. And I won't even mention how hard the position is on my damn body. But I train excessively and do whatever I need to do to keep my body uninjured. And I try to keep myself in tip-top shape. My team deserves the best, and so that's what I try to be.

Besides, at any given time, the New York Rangers could pull my spot if they decide I'm not worthy. When they came to me fresh out of high school, we each had some stipulations. On my end, even though they wanted me right then, I wanted to graduate college for my mother. They allowed it, but they made it clear they only wanted me if I was still in perfect condition once I got my degree. Some people think I'm nuts for not going from high school to pro when given the chance, but the truth is, I knew I wasn't ready. I needed this time at Brooks to work with someone like Coach LaConte to prepare myself for what's to come. That way, when it comes time for me to step into those bright lights and wear that Rangers jersey, I'll be the best I can be. And in my eyes, risking an injury is just a small price to pay for that.

My time at Brooks has given me what I need. Last year, I got to be the main goalie while Cam Hardy was our team captain and leading center. Watching Cam on the ice is a lot like watching Michael Jordan on the court. It's art. It's mesmerizing.

It's no wonder he's now the starting center for the Bruins. Dude's out of this world in the *raw talent* department.

The puck goes into play, and I prepare myself to go to war to stop it from getting past me. Within seconds, bodies are heading right toward me. It's a fucking balancing act, staying calm while also having adrenaline rushing through your body, making you feel like you're floating. My heart races, and my head is soaked with sweat. I'm fatigued while being wound up, all at the same time. My team has played their hearts out. I'm not about to lose it for them now.

When I see a maroon jersey getting closer, the player keeping control of the puck and moving at the speed of a goddamn cheetah, I make myself larger, hyperaware of his every move. And when he gets close enough to try to slap-shot it past me, I slide my knees together, stopping the puck before it can get into my goal.

Cheers erupt, and my heart is beating so fast that it might literally give me a heart attack. No matter how many times I do this, it always feels the same. And I always feel the same. Fucking relieved to stop another goal.

The game isn't over yet though. So, as much as I'd love to bask in my save, it's not the time. Because after a few more of those, that one will be long forgotten, just like the others.

RYANN

I can't believe I'm here, watching a damn hockey game. And somehow, I'm not even bored to death. But I won't tell Sutton that. If I do, she won't let me live it down. She'd probably call me a puck bunny. Which I am not. At all.

I'm beginning to see that maybe I had Watson pegged wrong. Perhaps he isn't just like every other male I assumed him to be. He isn't my ex, and last week was proof of that. Either way, watching him defend the goal isn't just impressive. It's kind of hot. I mean, shit, if he can move like that to stop a goal, what can he do in bed?

Stop. Thinking. About. It.

I don't need to hook up with a charming jock. I don't need to fall into bed with anyone. No more trying to fill that deep void inside of me with men. I tried that; it didn't work. Oh, how I tried. One pregnancy scare—which, thank God, was a false alarm—and a long, hard look in the mirror later, I realized happiness wasn't going to come from getting railed ten ways to Sunday. Orgasms weren't like a magic wand that could fix me. In fact, being ... *friendly* ... was only making me feel worse.

I craved that feeling you get when someone is close to you. When you feel their body against your own and their heart beating against your chest.

I wanted that so bad. I wanted to quiet the voices in my head telling me I was a girl going nowhere. That I'd made the wrong choice by forging my way into the United States. That I was an awful person for leaving my sister when she needed me so badly. That no one would ever love me because if my mother couldn't love me, who the hell would?

If I hadn't sworn off jocks and romantic relationships altogether ... Watson would definitely have a chance. If he wanted it, that is. He just doesn't seem like all the other men I've come to hate. He's ... kinder.

"Earth to Ryann," Sutton says, snapping her fingers in front of my face. "Come back from outer space and join us, would you?"

Glancing at her, I shrug. "Sorry. I was thinking about a paper I have due next week. Got sidetracked." I bump my shoulder against hers and look back at the ice. "What were you saying?"

"I was saying, you seem to be spending a lot of time staring at Watson Gentry for someone who claims to hate having him as her dance partner." She elbows my side playfully. "Don't think I missed the look on your face when he was doing those provocative little goalie stretches. You know, the ones where he pretty much fucks the ice."

I shoot her a glare. One that hopefully says she's crazy and to shut her filthy mouth.

"I was not staring. And if I was, it was because I was thinking how fucking awkward his stretches are," I deadpan, knowing I don't sound one bit convincing. "What would I possibly find hot about that?" I wave toward Watson. "Exactly. Nothing."

"Mmhmm," she drawls slowly. "Whatever. You. Say."

I roll my eyes, but the truth is, when he had his legs downward on that ice, rocking his hips to stretch himself out ...

Well, I had thoughts running through my head. Dirty. Stupid. Sexy. Thoughts. Of me, underneath him ...

Naked.

I dance with a few of the girls from the dance team at Club 83. After the game, Sutton said she needed to stay at the arena a little later to do something. Which I think really meant she secretly wanted to wait and see Hunter, her dance partner, who she is clearly low-key falling for. So, I decided to head here, where the party is, and blow off some steam by shaking my ass and loosening up.

I'm sweaty and hot. But I'm having an absolute blast as Lana, Poppy, a few others, and I all pretend that we don't know we're causing a scene with the seductive way we're dancing to "Greedy" by Tate McRae.

I throw my head back, letting my strawberry-blonde hair be a mess and not giving a shit who is or isn't watching me. I'm having fun. Who cares about how ridiculous I probably look?

I'm in my own little world, living life carelessly. That is, until every cell in my body suddenly feels a certain set of eyes on me. I don't have to look to see who would have this effect on me. Even so, I can't help myself but to search for him. But when I look around, all I see is a lot of people watching me and my friends dance, no one in particular. The hair on the back of my neck stands, and my skin prickles. And when my eyes float to the corner of the bar, I find Watson's eyes fixated on me and only me. Even from here, I can tell his gaze is darker than usual. He sips his drink, slightly tipping his chin upward when he sees me looking his way. Everything inside of me catches on fire as I think back to the thoughts I had of him earlier. Him … rolling his hips, stretching himself out. Making my mouth water, maybe even causing me to drool.

Turning my attention back to my girls, I continue dancing, pretending like he isn't there. And when the song switches to "God Is a Woman" by Ariana Grande, our dance moves only get even more seductive. We're all a little tipsy from the few drinks we had when we first arrived, and letting off steam feels pretty good. Dancing at Peaches isn't fun like this. It's work. And it's tiring.

My eyes flutter shut for a moment, and I'm met with a familiar voice in my ear and hands wrapping around my waist, instantly sending my eyes shooting open and my heart skipping a beat. And not in a good way.

"You know, baby, I really don't like the fact that you're showing off for every fucking guy in here right now," Denton's voice growls right against my ear. "But, goddamn, you've gone and made my dick hard."

His erection pokes into my ass, and I begin to pull away, feeling my stomach churn. But he only holds me tighter.

"Feel that, baby? See what you've done to me? What you *still* do to me, even after all this time?"

"Let go," I hiss, craning my neck around. "Don't make me cause a scene."

"Misty and I are done, Ryann," he mutters into my ear, and the smell of liquor on his breath assaults my nostrils. "It's time for you to come back to me. I miss you." He rubs his length harder into my ass. "Don't you feel how much I fucking miss you?"

I'm just about to kick my leg backward when a large figure stands in front of me, making a shadow over everyone before him.

"You should step the fuck away from her unless you want a repeat of last week." Watson's voice is low yet terrifying. And when my eyes move to his face, his eyes are black, and the veins in his neck are bulging. "Only this time, you'll be leaving on a fucking stretcher."

"This is between my girl and me, puck boy," Denton taunts, slurring his words, only proving he's drunk. "I suggest you walk away."

"She isn't your girl, Wells. Give it up."

"Oh, she is, Gentry. I promise you, she never stopped being my girl." He murmurs against my temple, and I want to puke. "She'll come back to me. She always does."

I attempt to elbow his stomach, but he's got me in a hold with his arms, anchoring me down like a useless weight.

Watson ignores his words before looking down at me and bending closer so that his face is inches from mine. "I'm not going to do anything to upset you, Tiny Dancer, I promise. I won't fight him. But I can't watch him do this shit, Ryann. I'm sorry, but I'm not built for it."

Holding his hand out, Watson laces his fingers with mine just as Denton's hands drop from my body, and he lets me go, but not before a slew of curse words leave his mouth.

"Go be a fucking slut, Ryann. I know whose dick you'll come crawling back for," he growls. "And guess what. I might not let you have it."

"How upsetting," I mumble, rolling my eyes.

I peek up at Watson and watch his jaw tense and his chest heave as he tries to control himself from beating the shit out of Denton. Yet he stays rooted in the same spot, all because he doesn't want to scare me.

I'm thankful that my friends don't seem to be paying attention to the three of us because when Watson leans down, bringing my mouth to his, kissing me hard and letting his tongue slip against mine, it's not something I want to try to explain later on. Especially when I don't understand it myself. And when his hands loop around my waist and he pulls me closer while his lips never leave mine, I think my soul has maybe left my body. His hand reaches around me, cupping my ass, giving it a squeeze.

When he finally releases me, his dark glare stares at Denton, who looks like he's about to erupt. "She's moved on. And if you need more proof than what I just gave you, just follow us into the restroom and watch me fuck her until she comes on my cock. The *only* cock she'll ever need."

Denton never looks at me again, but his eyes narrow to slits at Watson before he stalks off, calling something inaudible over his shoulder. For once, I finally feel like he might actually never speak to me again.

And what a relief that is.

Shyly, I look up at him. "Mind telling me what all that was?"

He leans down, talking in my ear over the music that seemingly just got louder. "The last thing I wanted to do tonight was to make you sad. It took everything inside of me not to lay him out right on this floor. But I'm not making that mistake again. I promise you that." He pulls back, shrugging as his eyebrows pull together. "Figured what I did was a safer option."

"Is that really the only reason why you did it?" I ask, staring up at him doubtfully.

"You might be dead set on not giving me a chance, but there's no fucking way I'm letting that scumbag lurk around." He continues holding me. "And maybe I just wanted an excuse to kiss you."

"You shouldn't kiss me," I say. "Not like the way you just did."

"Yeah, well, maybe you're right. But it didn't seem like you minded it too much in the moment, Tiny Dancer," he says nonchalantly. "Besides, I've wanted to do that for weeks."

I'm still completely breathless from his lips on mine. An ache between my legs the size of freaking Texas throbs, making me agitated. I've never felt that kind of electric charge from someone else's lips. It's stupid and reckless … but I want more.

"The restroom thing—why did you say that?" I raise an eyebrow, pushing the issue further even though I know the smart thing to do would be to drop it.

"Because I needed him to know that you're no longer his." He swallows. "Without beating the shit out of him like I wanted to." Releasing me, he leans forward and kisses my hair. "I'm going to go before I do something else that I'm not supposed to do. Have a good night, Ryann. See you at practice."

I stand there, wondering what exactly he meant. And as he slowly backs away, I feel my body instantly cool down. A magnetic force makes me want to follow him, but I don't. And as crazy and annoying as it is … I know I'm about to go home and imagine Watson Gentry banging me in the restroom.

And I'm going to carry those images in my head for a long dang time.

WATSON

I might have said good night to Ryann, but I'm certainly not going to leave Club 83 with Denton hanging around, waiting to bother her again. So, here I sit, in the corner of the bar, watching over her like a fucking weirdo.

I don't think he's the type that would physically hurt her. But then again, how can I know for sure? I've only ever seen him around at parties, and I didn't know he was a fucking wack job, like he's proven to be the past week. So, either way, I'm going to make sure she gets home safely. A big part of me wants to go find him and beat him senseless. What Ryann doesn't witness can't hurt her. Right?

Wrong. She'd probably find out and be mad at me. And right now, all I want is for her to agree to spend some time with me. If I go pissin' her off, that'll never happen.

"Stop fucking Ryann Denver with your eyes, would you?" Walker James says, sitting in the seat next to me. The bartender instantly slides him a beer without him even asking. Sipping it, he tips it toward me. "It's making me uncomfortable."

"You're making me uncomfortable, James," I mutter, moving my eyes from Ryann just long enough to send him a glare.

"Stay away from those damn ballerinas. They are nothing but trouble," he grumbles, taking another pull from his beer. "Trust me. Been there; done that."

"Word around campus is, you've been there and done that to most of the female population." I laugh. "Not sure you're the man I want to take advice from."

"You can't believe everything you hear, Gentry," he mutters, looking toward the group of girls Ryann is with.

From where I'm sitting, I can't tell which chick his eyes are on. But he seems distracted by whoever it is. As long as it's not Ryann, I don't really give a fuck.

"James, are you checking out Ryann?" I mumble, moving closer to him. "And if you are, I advise you to stop. Now."

Looking back at me, he gives me a slight grin. "Nah, Gentry. You're safe. I don't want your girl."

"She's not my girl." I watch her as she laughs with her friends. "Well, not yet anyway."

Walker says something back, but I don't hear what it is. I just gaze at Ryann as she hugs one of her friends good-bye and heads toward the door with a chick that I don't know.

Sliding from my stool, I clasp Walker on the shoulder. "Good game tonight, brother. Keep it up."

I head to the exit. Because she might not be my problem, but I'm going to treat her like she is anyway.

And that involves making sure her ex isn't stalking her outside.

And checking that she gets home safely too.

WATSON

If dancing with Ryann without every ounce of my blood pumping straight to my dick was hard before I kissed her, it's really fucking tricky now. The other night at Club 83, I kissed her to make a point to her ex. But when she melted against me, slipping her tongue inside my mouth, damn, it took everything inside of me to stop. And then even more to not kiss her again and take her into that restroom like I wished I could.

Unfortunately for me, she's made it extremely clear that she doesn't want anything to do with me. But I'll be a fucking dead man before I let fuckface Denton creep around her the way that he does. I'll bury that motherfucker if I have to. Just as long as Ryann doesn't see me do it, I couldn't care less.

It was so hard to not drop him right there on the dance floor. Seeing him grab her the way that he did, whispering in her ear when it was clear she didn't want him to. I saw the panic in her eyes when she heard his voice. I felt it inside of me, just watching her. How the two of them ever dated, I don't know. He's not good enough to breathe the same air as her. Let alone to have ever had the privilege of calling her his girl.

If she were my girl, she'd never have that look of sadness in her eyes again. I'd dedicate my life just to make sure of that. But that will never happen because a douchebag like Denton Wells ruined her for anyone else. And now, she thinks we're all like him. But I'm not going to let that stop me from still showing her how special she is. Even if she refuses to believe me.

Kissing her was great in the moment. But when it was over, I wanted more.

And now, here we are, dancing to the slow beat of the music. Her ass accidentally grazes against my cock every now and then, making me suck in a breath and mentally tell myself not to get hard.

It isn't helping that her neck is fully on display when she tips her chin upward. That neck is so fucking beautiful, and I'd love to have my hand cupped around it, choking her while I drove my dick so far inside of her that she'd never so much as want to look at another man again. She'd see that I had everything she needed.

"Damn it!" She groans, stepping back and dragging her hand down her face. "We keep messing up."

Her eyes have that fiery look inside of them. One that's fueled from pure aggravation. And from the expression on her face, it's obvious she's frustrated that we can't seem to get it right today. But deep down, she must know what our problem is.

She needs to be fucked. Thoroughly. She needs a release. And I really, really want to be the one to give it to her.

"Sorry," I mutter, hoping that my now-massive hard-on isn't showing through my fucking sweatpants.

I might have attempted to talk myself down—literally—but my dick had other plans. Plans that included a standing ovation for Ryann. And when her eyes float downward before widening, I know I've blown my cover.

Quickly, she looks back up, and her cheeks turn the cutest shade of red as she chews her bottom lip nervously. "No. It … it's not just you. I'm messing up too." She's flustered as shit. "Maybe we should, uh … just pick this up tomorrow. Today just isn't our day, it seems."

"My schedule with hockey and class is jam-packed tomorrow. It has to be today." I reach out, resting my hand on her waist gently. "We can get it done today; I know we can."

She drags in a breath before stepping back and away from my touch before scowling at me. "Stop. Doing. That."

"Stop doing what? Trying to be positive?"

"No!" she says, stomping her foot like a toddler. "Touching me like we're a couple! Or doing things like kissing me or pulling my body toward yours!" Her eyes are wide, and she shakes her head. "Stop doing it! Stop doing all of it!"

I could let it go. I could be the nice guy I always am and tell her I will stop if it makes her uncomfortable. I should do that and vow to be better. Only I really don't want to. I'm tired of her pretending like there's nothing between us. I'm sick of her pushing me away just because she's comparing me to her ex.

Taking a few slow steps toward her, I glare down. "Why, Tiny Dancer? Because you like it when I touch you?" I reach out, brushing a few loose strands of hair from her face. "Because you *liked* it when I kissed you, Ryann? No ... I think you fucking loved it actually."

"No, I didn't," she hisses.

"No?" I tilt my head to the side. "So, you don't want me to do it again, right? You don't think we're dancing so fucking terribly today because you're aching for me to touch you again? Like really fucking touch you?" I swallow. "I know you feel it too. Stop denying it."

"Nope. Sorry to burst your bubble, but I don't," she says through gritted teeth. "I feel *nothing*."

"Okay then." I nod, ready to call her bluff. "Let's dance. I mean, if you aren't aching for my cock to be inside of you, like I think you are, it should be easy. Right?"

She shivers but narrows her eyes. "Fine," she growls. "Let's do it. So you can see that I. Don't. Want. You."

Ryann

Every time his hands are on my body, I go and screw up. And whenever my ass brushes against him, he grows harder. I ache so badly that I can't even think straight. But if I give in now, where will that leave us? I know what happens with random hookups. They don't solve anything. Besides, we have to work together for this fundraiser. Sex will only make things awkward between us.

I can't even get through three moves without floundering. They aren't even hard moves either. It is all simple shit I learned years ago. This never happens to me. And while Watson didn't exactly bring his A game today, he's not doing as terrible as I am. Which means ... he wasn't even affected by that stupid kiss. Not the way I was anyway.

"From the top," I blurt out, but I sound much angrier and more annoyed than I anticipated.

And when I miscalculate my steps, I start to fall forward on my face. Another thing that barely ever happens to me. I don't mess up. And I certainly don't flounder.

As I brace for impact, strong arms wrap around me before I hit the floor. In the mirror, I see Watson, his arms looped around my body, his eyes fixated on mine. It's as if he hears my every thought and sees right through me.

"I can't do this today," I whisper, pulling away from his hold. "I'm going home."

"And what? You don't think we'll have the same problem next time we try this again?" His eyes narrow as he steps toward me, crowding my space and backing my ass up to the mirror. "Until we give in to what our bodies are craving, we won't be able to get this done. You know that, right?"

"I don't want a romantic relationship," I say in a low growl. "You're a nice guy. A sweet guy. You love your mom."

"And?" He scowls. "What the fuck does that have to do with shit?"

"Because after one hookup, you'll expect more. I don't want more," I argue. "I'm figuring my shit out. Alone."

Suddenly, his hand slides to the back of my neck, and he squeezes gently as he pushes my face closer to his. "I might not be as nice as you think, Ry baby." His eyes float to my lips. "I might not be nice at all actually."

"I don't care," I whisper. "I. Can't." I shake my head. "I won't."

My brain is so messed up. All from this man before me. Well, and the others who have fucked me up along the way. And when he starts to release me, I stop him, digging my fingernails into his forearms.

Here we are, in a complete standoff, waiting to see who is going to make the next move. The tension between us is so thick that I can hardly breathe. And the next thing I know … his lips are on mine. They are on mine, and I don't even pull back. My entire body is incapacitated, and I can't move.

We kiss—so hard that my lips actually feel bruised instantly. Pushing me backward, he slams my back up against the mirror. His erection drives into my stomach as his tongue caresses mine.

Reaching under my ass, he lifts me up, wrapping my legs around his waist as his lips continue to assault mine. His dick is so hard against my body that I literally moan into his mouth, unable to help myself.

My brain is fuzzy. I've lost all control of myself. Pulling back suddenly, he looks around before spotting the closet. We have this place blocked off in the schedule for an hour and a half, but still, someone could walk in at any time. Yet for some reason, that kind of turns me on even more.

Walking us into the closet, he kicks the door shut before taking a few steps and driving my back against the wall again.

"Fuck, I want to be inside of you," he growls against my mouth. "I want to fuck these mouthy lips too."

Losing all control, I reach for the hem of his shirt, desperately trying to tear it off as quickly as I can. I lift it upward with a little help from him, and I toss it on the ground before reaching between us and tugging at his sweatpants.

"So, you think I'm too nice, Ryann?" he coos, tearing his lips from mine, slapping his hands next to my head. "You don't want nice?"

"No, I don't. I don't care how good of a boy you think you are. I just want to be fucked, Watson. I want an orgasm," I breathe out. "Think you can do that? Or will your feelings get in the way?"

Sensing I'm mocking him, he slowly lets my legs fall to the ground and dips his head closer. "Let's get one thing straight, Ry baby. You know I'd love to take you on a date and all that. But you've made it damn clear that isn't what you want. So, I'll give you my cock, if you're a good girl and take it the way I want you to. Deal?" Before I can answer, his eyes darken. "And while I fuck you, I'm not going to be nice. Got it? Because it seems you don't want a nice guy."

Eagerly, I nod quickly before reaching for the band of his sweatpants again, but he grabs my wrist and slams it against the wall.

"Say please, Tiny Dancer. Beg for my cock like a good little slut, and maybe I'll give it to you."

I'm well aware that I look like a pathetic, horny, desperate girl. But the ache between my legs and the need inside my body are too much to fight. So, I give up on playing it off like I'm too cool.

"Pl-please," I moan. "Please, Watson."

Grabbing a fistful of my hair, he brings my mouth to his. "Are you going to be a nice little cock slut, Ryann?" He runs his tongue along my jaw and down my neck before returning his mouth to mine, hovering his lips above my own. "You want me to feed it to you, don't you? Every fucking inch while you drip down my thighs."

Being called a slut in everyday life? Not fun. Being called a slut just before Watson Gentry rails the shit out of me against the supply closet wall? *Hot*.

Turns out, Sutton was right. He is a dirty, dirty boy.

"Yes," I whimper.

"I'd love to have you on your knees, watching you suck my cock between those plump lips and gag on me just before I give you a drink of my cum, but we're short on time, and I really need to feel your pussy clench around me."

Pulling his own pants and briefs down, he lets them fall to the ground before kissing me again. His lips stay on mine as he peels my leotard off, taking my panties with it, and tosses them onto the floor, leaving me completely exposed.

The cool air rushes to my nipples, though I'm not sure if it's the air or Watson making them painfully hard. Either way, he takes notice and runs his tongue down my neck and over my collarbone before working his way to each nipple while his fingers slip between my legs.

"Fucking drenched," he mutters before bringing his fingers to his mouth and running them over his tongue. "Mmm. And despite how mean you are to me, so fucking sweet."

My knees are weak. My head is spinning. Whatever picture I painted in my mind of Watson was totally wrong. And I'll admit, I'm not mad about it. But no part of me is able to form a coherent thought. I'm gone.

Reaching down, he grips his length in his hand and strokes himself. The sight has me clenching my legs together and my mouth watering, desperate for him.

"Like what you see, Tiny Dancer?" he coos, his lips turning up in a knowing smirk. "I promise, you'll love having me inside of you even more."

Reaching for his length, I push his hand out of the way and begin moving my hand back and forth.

"Fuck," he grunts through gritted teeth before moving his hand between my legs and slipping his fingers inside of me. "Christ, you're so tight. Goddamn, I want to feel this tight pussy bare," he growls, a strangled groan escaping his throat. "You on the pill, Ry baby?"

"IUD," I croak out, his fingers alone bringing me closer to a climax. "Watson, I ..."

"Soak my fingers, baby. Soak my fingers and then you can drench my cock too."

Stroking him becomes less consistent as my hips rock against his fingers, and I throw my head back against the wall. My orgasm hits me like a damn Mack truck as I basically ride his hand, greedy for every second I can get out of this feeling.

"Fuck my hand, Tiny Dancer. Goddamn, you're so fucking hot when you're coming undone," he grunts. "And the fact that it's my fingers you're soaking? Makes my dick even harder."

I moan but am quickly quieted by his mouth on mine as my orgasm subsides.

"Can I fuck you raw?" his lips growl against mine. "Can I fill you full of my cum?"

I've never had sex with anyone without a condom. Yet here I am, with a man I've been so set against not getting involved with; it's our first ... and last ... time hooking up, and I want nothing more than to feel him inside of me.

"Yes," I cry out. "Please."

He suddenly stops moving and looks into my eyes, brushing his thumb across my cheek. "And know that however I treat you right now, it's not how I feel about you. I need to know that what I've said so far ... that it's okay with you. Because if it isn't, I'll stop."

I know he's referring to the *slut* word. But the truth is, the way he used it turned me on more.

"Yes," I whisper. "This isn't supposed to be love. This is supposed to be sex."

His eyes grow dark, and he slowly nods. With no warning, he quickly spins me around and shoves my entire body against the wall. My cheek pushes against it, and he plunges inside of me. I yelp out in pain, yet I'm so turned on. I still want more.

One hand grips my hip, and the other moves to my throat and applies light pressure. "Is this okay?" he mutters against my ear. "Because if this is too much, I can stop."

"Don't. Stop," I moan. "Please."

Gripping my throat harder, he thrusts himself deeper inside of me. "Such a good little slut, taking every inch of my cock and loving it," he growls before moving his hand from my hip and slapping my asscheek. "I'd love to fuck this ass, too, one day." He leans closer, growling in my ear, "I'd love to blow my load right in your ass while I finger-fucked your pussy." His hand comes down again, this time harder. "Would you like that, dirty girl?"

"Yes," I cry out, not even knowing what I'm saying.

That's nothing I've ever been into. Yet when Watson hisses the words, I find myself instantly agreeing to what he's asking of me.

He fills me to the point that I feel like I'm going to break, yet I moan, desperately not wanting him to stop. His hand continues to grip my neck, and the harder he squeezes, the wetter I seem to get.

Just when I think I can't take any more, he runs his nose between my shoulders. "Fucking Christ, you feel good."

Releasing his hold on my neck, he pulls out of me and spins me around. He lifts me up, and my legs wrap around his waist. His length pushes inside of me, and I whimper, biting his shoulder to stop myself from crying out his name.

"Fuck, baby, I feel you dripping onto my balls. How fucking bad did you want my cock today?" His hands hold my thighs as he moves in and out before they slide to my waist, gripping tightly. As he lifts me up and down, his cock brushes me in a way that has me spiraling out of control.

"So. Much," I admit in a weak, hushed whisper.

I feel my nipples harden as I drive my head further against his shoulder. A muffled scream escapes me but is muted by his skin.

"Fuck, I'm going to come so hard inside of you," he grunts, driving his face into my neck, sinking his teeth into my flesh. "You feel so fucking good."

I rake my fingernails across his back—hard—as he drives his fingertips into my sides.

"Fuck," he groans.

We both drag in shaky breaths, and I feel him coming inside of me as I squeeze his length while my own orgasm hits. Our movements become wobbly and erratic as he sucks in a breath.

"That's right; soak my cock," he utters as his body quivers. "Just like I'm soaking your pussy."

My eyes flutter shut as my orgasm takes over every inch of my being. Washing over me and leaving nothing untouched. It's like I'm being lifted to the high heavens, into the bright lights before I finally come back down. And when I do, all I want to do is take a nap. My body is completely relaxed. Every ounce of me feels satisfied and taken care of.

As he gently sets me down, he grins at me, dragging in a breath. "Ready to get back to work?"

Cheeks flushed, hair a mess … I nod. "Yeah. I guess I am."

And as I pull my clothes back on and watch him do the same, I have to wonder …

What the hell did I just do?

And why am I already imagining it happening again?

WATSON

I drive home, gripping the steering wheel so tight that I'm surprised I don't flatten the entire thing out. Less than an hour ago, I was balls deep inside my dream girl. She showed her cards tonight; she's a dirty fucking girl. And I just so happen to be pretty fucking filthy myself.

When I mentioned what I'd do to her ass, she practically came undone on my cock right then. And all the times I called her my little slut? She fucking moaned so loud that the room next door could have heard her for all I know.

Because violence scares her, I wanted to make sure choking her wouldn't put her over the edge. But when I asked if she wanted me to stop, she practically begged me not to. She fucking loved it. I can't wait to see what other things she'll love.

Because of how stubborn Ryann is, I had to make it sound like I was doing her a favor by fucking her. Like I was getting nothing out of it and it was strictly for her. She's that way; it needs to be her idea. Her terms. But the truth is, I've wanted to be inside of her for fucking weeks. But now that I have, how the hell am I supposed to settle for only doing it once? She felt so good, wrapped around me, taking every inch like a fucking champ and ready for more. She was practically dripping at the sight of my cock in my hand, greedy to get her own hands on it. And holy fuck, when she reached out, stroking me … I could have blown my load right fucking then.

I know one thing to be true: before I fucked her, she couldn't even complete a few steps of our dance because she was so wound up. I might have taken the edge off for today, but she'll need me again.

Who wouldn't want to have their dick used by the hottest chick at Brooks University? No, the hottest chick on the fucking planet.

Exactly. Sign me up. Use me, Ry baby.

I pull into my parking spot in front of the house to see everyone is home.

It used to be just Hunter, Cade, and me who lived here. But then Hunter's sister, Haley, moved in too. I like having her around. She's the furthest thing from organized, but she's a sweetheart, and she cooks.

Also, she loves my mama's candles that I keep in bulk at the house. Which is nice since no one else appreciates them.

Exiting the car, I head toward the front door and pull it open. Haley is perched on the counter, typing vigorously on her laptop with a huge bag of Nerds Clusters next to her. Those are probably the unhealthiest thing, but she is obsessed. Hunter is on the couch, scrolling on his phone. And of course, Cade is nowhere to be seen.

"What up, Watty?" Haley smiles, popping a piece of candy into her mouth. "Ballerina practice?"

An image of Ryann pushed up against the wall comes to my mind, and I feel a jolt run to my cock. But I shake my head, snapping myself out of it. "You know it."

"How's that going? Didn't you say your partner hates you?" She takes a sip of her water. "That girl Ryann, is it? She's freaking gorgeous."

I think about Ryann's teeth sinking into my shoulder, which doesn't help with softening my cock at all.

"Uh, yeah, it's going all right, I guess." I start toward the stairs, not really wanting all of my roommates to see my full-blown hard-on. "I'm going to shower. I'll be back down in a few." Walking by Hunter, I hold my hand up. "Hey."

Not looking from his screen, he jerks his chin. "Sup?"

"Showering. I'll be right back." I head upstairs to my room, noticing Cade's door is shut as I walk by.

While a lot of people tend to ignore Cade's odd tendencies, I notice them more than anyone else. When he doesn't come home. When he looks like a truck ran over him the night before. When he loses weight and sleeps in too late. So many things he does line up with the behavior of an addict or alcoholic. I know he drinks, and I know he smokes weed, but I hope to hell he isn't doing anything else. He's already been to rehab once.

Going into my room, I shut the door behind me. I look down at my sweatpants, and there's no hiding the painful bulge I got from just thinking about being with Ryann.

I just hooked up with her an hour ago. And here I am, hard and ready for round two.

And she'll want round two ... eventually. I know she will.

Until then, it's the shower. Me. And my hand. Oh, and thoughts of Ryann on her knees, sucking my cock.

Yep, that'll have to do.

Ryann

The man watching me has so much cologne on that it literally burns my nostrils, even up here, onstage, five feet away. He brushes his fingers along his chin. I'm not even sure he's blinked since he sat down. His hair is slicked back, and his suit makes him look like a man who's trying to seem more important than he actually is. But maybe he'll leave me a big, fat tip. That'll make my achy feet and the icky feeling in my belly from his stare totally worth it.

It also helps that I know even though he's looking, he can't hurt me. My boss always keeps her workers safe. If a customer shows up and tries to get handsy or is rude, the security guards are on that shit. And that person gets exiled from the club.

I move down the pole and hold on to the metal above my head, letting my ass damn near touch the ground before sliding back up. I don't make eye contact with the man in front of me because I'm afraid if I do, I'll puke.

I move on autopilot through the rest of my shift. Throwing my head back when need be, rocking my hips and thrusting my breasts to seem more into it than I really am. Whatever it takes to get through this shift and earn some coin, I'll do it.

Because my baby sister, Riley's, birthday is coming up and I spent a lot of my savings on her gift.

As I begin to walk off the stage, he follows me on the floor below.

"Hey, gorgeous," he calls, tipping his chin up before I get off the stage. "What do you say you and I get out of here? I have a suite at The Luxe tonight. Finest hotel in Georgia."

Chancing him a glance, I see that Hudson is already headed his way. Hudson is one of the biggest security guards we have. All of the women here fall over themselves just by looking at him. I'll admit, he's easy on the eyes. But he's also damn good at his job. And nobody wants to piss him off, so usually, a warning from him will do the trick for pesky clients like this one.

"No thanks," I say politely. "Have a nice night."

"Oh, come on. For ten grand, I bet we could have ourselves a good time. It'll be fun." He winks, and my stomach turns. "You know what? Let's make it twenty grand. Because I know I can have fun with those tits. And that ass? Easily worth more." He licks his lips, and I want to gag.

"No," I snap, and he grabs my ankle.

"Come on, baby. Be the needy whore you know you are and let me show you a good time."

His grip tightens, and I feel that panicky feeling settling in my gut. The one where fear begins to cripple my entire body even though I know he won't actually have the opportunity to hurt me.

Before he has a chance to say or do anything else, he's knocked down by Hudson, and I continue walking to avoid seeing any kind of confrontation. I don't need a repeat of the other night with Watson and Denton. There's always fights happening here, but as long as I don't personally know the person or am not involved … it doesn't usually affect me. Still, I try to keep my eyes from witnessing it, not wanting to take any chances on sending myself into a mental tailspin.

Unfortunately, what happened tonight happens a lot of nights. Some customers just don't know how to take no for an answer. Or they assume that just because we're dancers, we'll be down for other things. I would have nothing against anyone who took that sleazeball up on his offer because it's a free country. Except for the reason I know it isn't safe. Someone could be a rapist or a murderer. And I would never put myself in danger to that extent, nor would I want my coworkers to either. Some things just aren't worth the money.

I make my way into the back room and grab a bottle of water from the cooler before sitting down. Pressing it to my face, I take a few long, deep breaths and calm myself down. Breathing in through my nose and out through my mouth, I tell myself over and over that I'm safe.

It works. Yet here I sit, wishing Watson were holding me together.

Perfect Boy

Watson

My headphones alert me I have a call coming in. Setting the weights down, I take my phone out of my pocket and slide my thumb across the screen.

"Hey, peckerface," I say, grinning. " 'Bout time you called."

"You know, Twatty Watty, the phone works both ways. I know you're a bit of a dumbass, but you can also dial me," my brother Jameson tosses back. "What the fuck are you up to? Congrats on winning opening weekend. Wish I could have made it, but we had a show that night."

"I'd say I wish I could have been there to watch you do your thing, but you know I'd be lying," I say, cringing. "Can't be watching you lose any more brain cells, big bro. You already don't have many. You're fixin' to have none."

My brother's been a professional bull rider for three years now. When he joined the rodeo fresh out of high school, I knew why Mom was so upset and Dad was pissed. It's dangerous. And after I watched him get thrown off a bull and wind up with a bad concussion last year, I vowed I never wanted to see him do his thing again. I know he loves it, but I don't really want to watch the dude I've always looked up to die either. And my other brother, Carson, travels around the country, drag racing. Guess his name was fitting for him.

Crazy to think that out of my mom's three boys, my career will be the safest. Luckily for her, our older sister, Nora, got married and had babies right after college. If it wasn't for her, Mom would probably be beside herself.

"So, what's this Mom tells me about you putting on some tights and prancing around onstage?" I can hear the amusement in his voice. "Say it ain't so. You're a ballerina now? Giving up that goalie life? Carson is going to love this."

"Ha-ha. Laugh it up," I mutter. "No tights, asshole. And it's for a good cause. Don't you remember my buddy Brody O'Brien? Well, this is his foundation. The money we raise will go toward kids who can't afford to play sports."

"Well, fuck, Watty. Now, you've made me feel like a complete dick," he groans. "That's pretty cool though. Is your partner hot?"

"She's all right," I say, lying through my teeth. But if I tell him the truth, he'll be annoying as fuck about it.

"*All right* either means fucking ugly or that she's really hot." He laughs. "Hopefully, in your case, it's the latter." I hear someone calling his name in the background. "I gotta run, little bro. Take care of yourself."

"You too." I barely get the words out before he hangs up.

Growing up in a small town in Alabama, I suppose we had to make our own fun. When we were kids, our parents took us to our first rodeo, and Jameson didn't want to leave. Even after countless injuries—from broken bones to concussions—he won't walk away. I'm not sure if he ever will. I just hope he has the choice to instead of leaving in an ambulance for good.

And then there's Carson. From a young age, he became obsessed with drag cars. How they worked, how to make them faster, how to rebuild them. But what he really became consumed with was being behind the wheel of one. Once he got his license, he started street racing on the weekends—without my parents knowing, initially. But then he gained a lot of followers on Instagram and built a YouTube account based around racing, and now, he travels around the country, racing some of the most badass motherfuckers alive.

One being Cam's sister, Mila, who beat Carson in the finals last week.

Our parents have always wanted us to be whatever the hell we wanted to be. We lost our father to cancer a few years back, and nothing has been the same. And even though we try to be there for our mom, I think we all drown the pain in different forms of adrenaline rushes. For Jameson, on the back of a bull. For Carson, going way too fast down the asphalt. And me? On the ice. My sister though, she's just an angel who is stronger than all of us.

I don't think the pain ever subsides when you lose a parent. I guess you just learn to live with it. The grief still catches me from time to time. Reminding me that for as long as I'm on this earth, I'll never get to talk to my dad again. Or laugh with him. Or give him a hug. He's just … gone. Life seems short—until you realize some shit like that.

But that's life. And sometimes, life really is a bitch.

10

RYANN

I hole myself up in my bedroom and sit on the bed. Scooching myself until my back hits the headboard, I pull my phone out.

Half the time, my mom's phone isn't in service. It's always one of the bills that gets put on the back burner. So, it's really hard to say if I'll even be able to get through to my sister. I just have to hope that she has a boyfriend right now who insists she must have a phone number so he can reach her.

When I was growing up, it was confusing how my mom couldn't pay our electric bill, yet I could attend dance class multiple nights a week. The one good thing that came from being poor was that one of my teachers, Mrs. S, got me into a program that paid for underprivileged kids to do extracurriculars if their family couldn't afford it. That's something I find very cool about this fundraiser we're doing with the hockey team. It's for a program similar to the one that gave me the opportunity to dance my way through life.

I look at the time; it's after six at night, so I know Riley is home by now.

"Hello?" Riley's small voice says into the phone.

"*Happy birthday to you! Happy birthday to you. Happy birthday, little turd muffin. Happy birthday to you!*" I sing, knowing she's rolling her eyes but smiling at the same time. "Thirteen years old today! An official teen! Practically a dang adult these days."

"Thanks," she says, but her voice is incredibly distant. Like she doesn't really want to be on the phone with me, which is so unlike my baby sister, who could talk the ears off a snake.

"What's wrong? It's your birthday. All is supposed to be great!" I do my best to cheer her up, but I know it's no use. I get it. Birthdays aren't the magical days they are for other kids. In the Denver household, it's just another day. Only with disappointment.

"Nothing," she mutters. "I just got a letter in the mail; I get to attend a science fair at Braxton University in a few weeks."

Braxton University is only an hour and a half from our house. It's a huge university that is actually beautiful. If I hadn't been so dead set on getting as far away from my home as I could, I probably would have applied there. And avoided breaking the law with my fake-ass visa.

"What? Riley, that's amazing!" I squeal. "I know how hard those are to get an invite to. Do you know what you're doing yet for your presentation?"

"I've got a few ideas, but nothing's set in stone." When she says the words, I can tell she is already feeling a little better. She's a brainiac. And science is what makes her happiest. "I wish you could come though. Mom says she will, but ... I don't know. Besides, it costs money to get in."

"I wish I could too," I whisper, knowing damn well I'm not going to be able to travel to Canada right now. It would be too expensive. And risky as hell to cross the border. I was fortunate enough no one caught my forged visa when I came here. I can't chance it.

What surprises me is that she said Mom was going. She usually doesn't even offer.

"Well, since she said she is, maybe Mom really will go." I attempt to say the words with a smile even though she can't even see me.

"She has a new boyfriend. I've met him twice. He seems nice enough," she says evenly, like a thirty-year-old. "But you know how that goes with Mom." She pauses. "But she did get me something for my birthday. And she even took me out for pizza."

"Wow," I say, sitting up straighter in bed. "That's ... that's really good."

I feel a pang in my chest. I've gotten my hopes up in the past that my mom was going to change and start putting her kids first. It always ended in my heart breaking. I don't want that for my baby sister, but I also can tell she's happy. I don't want to be a dark cloud on her birthday.

"Now, there was a package delivered to you. And because the mail lady loves us, she promised she'd put it in a special spot while you were at school."

"What? Really?" she squeals. "What is it?! *Where* is it?"

I instruct her on where to look in the entryway of the tiny apartment building, hidden behind a shovel and some other things. The sounds of her footsteps, followed by her moving something I can only assume is the shovel, hit my ear. And when she finds the package and opens it, she screams.

"A phone? Ry? You got me a phone?" She's crying now, sobbing against the speaker. "Am I dreaming?"

"Nope, you're wide awake, babe. And, yes, I did. Because I was tired of not being able to talk to my sister." I tell her the truth.

Also, I've been so worried about her. My mom brings some seriously debatable people around our house. And my biggest fear is something happening to my Riley.

"It's all set up. It's on my plan. But before you ask me, it has social media blocks. So, yeah, no getting on the 'gram. No Facebook. At least not yet."

"I'd argue with you, but I'm too freaking excited. Thank you, Ryann. Thank you times one million." She sniffles. "This is the best day of my life."

"You're welcome. But you were so excited about the phone that you didn't even look at the card." I laugh. "I see how it is."

The sound of tissue paper being crinkled, followed by silence, floats through her phone to my ear, and suddenly, she squeaks again. "Seriously, Ry! You gave me fifty dollars too? What are you, loaded these days?"

I chuckle. "I have a job. It pays decent." I sigh. "I wish I could be there with you. But this way, maybe you can go get yourself a treat."

Normally, I'd worry that Mom didn't even get her a cake. But since she took her for pizza, maybe she did after all. I know that money and materialistic things aren't what matter most in life. But when you're a thirteen-year-old kid and the only one in your class without a cell phone ... you feel different. I don't want that for Riley.

"Thanks, Ry. I miss you so much."

I wipe a tear that spills down my cheek. "I miss you too, kid. So much. But now, we can talk or text whenever." A lump of emotion thickens in my throat, and I feel like an absolute failure for leaving my baby sister behind. "Now, go call your friends. I love you. Happiest birthday, Riley."

"Love you," she says quickly. "Oh, Ry?"

"Yeah?"

"Mom has been talking about getting your mailing address so that she can send you a letter. She said she's tried to call you from Randall's phone. That's her boyfriend. But she said you don't answer." There's a short pause. "So, she mentioned maybe sending you a letter. Is it ... is it okay if I give her your mailing address?"

That familiar anxiety fills my chest, making my head feel funny. My mom has always had that effect on me; even just being in her presence will do it. She could be sickly sweet when she wanted to, but then ... cold as ice.

"Uhh ... su-sure." I swallow. "That's fine. Love you. Go call your friends before it gets any later."

"Love you!" she singsongs before ending the call.

Even though I should be happy for making her smile, I feel empty and lost. Because I'm over here in the United States of freaking America and my sister's in Canada, and up until a few minutes ago, I was scared she hadn't been fed dinner yet.

I want my mom to turn a new leaf, but I don't trust her. Not one bit. And now, because she's giving Riley false hope, she's going to fuck my sister up.

Just like she fucked me up. Making me ... this person who can't trust anyone.

Just as I consider getting into my sweatpants and eating a pint of ice cream solo while watching one of my comfort movies, my phone dings multiple times. I expect all texts to be from Riley. Just one of them is, and it's a selfie of her blowing me a kiss. The other is from ... Watson. Asking me to freaking hang out.

Just Watson: If you're free, we should go get some pizza.

Just Watson: Or if pizza is too sexy, how about burgers? There's nothing sexy about eating a burger. Shit is gross.

Just Watson: Fine. McDonald's?

I stare at the three messages that came in a matter of five minutes. Finally, I type back.

Me: We don't do dinner. We practice our routine. And we grabbed food. ONCE.

Just Watson: We also got ice cream once. But ... who's counting?

Just Watson: Also, what would you call what we did in the supply closet, Tiny Dancer? We were practicing something. But I'm not sure it was our routine.

I curse my vagina for literally tingling when I read his message. Just the thought alone of what we did the other night turns my brain into mush. I don't want to go get a meal with this man. But I'm sad. And depressed over the fact that my sister is now a teenager and I can't be there with her. Sutton is off with Hunter. Poppy is somewhere, probably being bitchy but I love her all the same. And I have no idea where the others are. So ... as stupid as it might be, I respond.

Me: Fine. Pick me up in twenty. But just remember, there isn't and will never be anything between us. And that thing in the closet? That was just a moment of weakness. I'm back to being water.

> *Just Watson: Yes. I get it. Can't get to the center. The center meaning your vagina. See you soon.*
>
> *Just Watson: And for the love of God, don't try to take advantage of me. I have more respect for myself than that.*

I shake my head but breathe out a laugh. Looking down at myself, I'm a bit of a mess in my leggings and hooded sweatshirt. But then again, who cares? I'm not showing off for anyone. Maybe this will drive home the point that I'm not interested.

Well, in his mind and feelings. Interested in seeing his penis again? Now, that's something I might be able to get on board with even if I told him I wasn't. Because let's be honest … I'm already craving him.

I was fine swearing off sex. That was, until Watson Gentry banged me into oblivion in a supply closet.

Watson

Ryann might have agreed to come grab some dinner tonight, but she's not actually here. Physically, sure. But her mind is somewhere else. She sips her soda, her eyes looking lost even though she's trying to hide whatever it is that's bothering her.

"Do you want to talk about it?" I say as casually as I can, clasping my hands together. "Because we can."

Her eyes fly to mine, and I can tell she's mad that I asked because of the way her eyebrows shoot up.

Quickly, I put my hands up. "Hey, hey, hey. We don't have to. But I just wanted you to know that the offer is on the table. I'm a good listener. At least, my mom says I am." I wink.

She's something like a wild animal that you find injured. It might need your help, but it still doesn't trust you. One wrong move, and you'll scare it away. I need to be smart. I need to be subtle.

Well, sort of.

"No," she scoffs. "I don't want to *talk about it*. There's nothing to even talk about."

"Do you want to sneak into the restroom? Maybe that'll help you feel better," I toss out there because, well, she might just take me up on it. After all, she seems to like my dick better than me.

I watch the wheels turn in her pretty head. She's considering it, and for a split second, I get my hopes up. And so does my dick as the blood rushes to it. But I'm quickly let down when she takes a sip from her drink and shakes her head.

"No. That was one lapse in judgment. That's all."

I push my back up against the booth, smirking like an idiot. "Hmm, well, if I remember right, you had two lapses in judgment. Because, well ... not only did you soak my fingers, but you soaked my cock too." I shrug. "Just to clarify. You know, facts and all."

Her eyes narrow in a harsh glare, and she scrunches her button nose up a little higher. "Yeah, well, what can I say? I was desperate. It had been four months." She tilts her chin up in defiance. "The touch of a feather would have probably had me coming."

Holy fuck. Did she just say coming? That's hot.

And now, suddenly, I want a giant feather to drag down her neck, between her tits, and straight to her pussy. And the fucking image of it won't. Go. Away.

She's so set on hating me, and for some reason, I find it hot. Really hot. Because deep down, I know she's still thinking about that supply closet. Just like I am.

But then another thought hits me. She hadn't had sex in four months. That means, whatever she had with Denton, well, it wasn't a fresh break.

"Four months? Is that how long it's been since you and Denton split?" I ask. Because, well, curiosity is what killed the cat. But that cat probably died, knowing the answer to his question at the very least.

"Nope," she says, her lips forming a flat line. "We split up six months ago. But then I decided to drown my sorrows in one-night stands and alcohol." She leans forward, giving me an unapologetic look. "Still interested in me now, nice, good boy Watson? Now that you know I have a ... friendly side?"

"Who said I'm interested?"

She laughs, but it's more of an annoyed tone. "You didn't have to."

"What can I say? A man wants what he wants." I wink. "Also, I don't care if you had a friendly side or not. I mean, it makes me jealous, sure. But YOLO, right? Also, I thought you'd found out the other night that I'm really not all that nice," I say, dropping my voice lower. "But I guess I should remind you just how not nice I can be." I stare at her. "If that's what you're into."

"You lightly choked me and called me a slut," she deadpans. "You're nice, trust me. Heck, your mom probably does your laundry still. She probably uses fabric softener."

"Everyone should use fabric softener." I scoff. "And I'll take you in the restroom right now and choke you over the sink, to the point where you'll be begging for air. All while your pussy quivers around me because you secretly fucking. Love. It." I shrug. "Try me, Tiny Dancer. If you want rough? Let's get fucking rough. I've got a whole drawer full of things that can be as painful as they are fun."

Her face is full of shock, which doesn't surprise me one bit. Everything in my life is and has always been structured. But sex? Fuck no. When it comes to that, I want anything but vanilla. Even though I'd still take vanilla sex with Ryann fucking Denver any day of the week.

"Holy shit, Sutton was right," she barely whispers.

Before I can ask her what the hell she means, her phone dings. She grabs it, her brows instantly pulling together, and I swear I see her eyes fill with tears.

This entire night, she's been off. Her jokes are more like stabs. And it's obvious that she's hurting. I just have no idea what from. But if it's her ex, I'm about at my wits' end with that motherfucker.

"Everything all right?" I ask just as she sets her phone down.

"Yeah, it's fine," she grumbles. "My sister, it's her thirteenth birthday today." She gives a sarcastic smile. "She's officially a teenager."

I know that Ryann came here from Canada, so I'm sure it isn't easy for her to get back home to visit. My parents are in Alabama, and that still seems so damn far away.

"And you're missing her?" I guess. "Can't be easy, being in a whole other country. Are y'all close?"

"Okay, Dr. Phil." She rolls her eyes. "You're not my shrink. Calm down."

"Why do you do that?" I stop mid-sentence when the waitress drops our meals off, and we both thank her. But just as Ryann stabs her fork into her calzone, I hold my eyes to hers. "Why do you get so defensive when I'm just trying to make conversation with you?"

"Why bother making conversation with me?" She shakes her head. "What's the point?"

"Because I want to." I say the four words evenly. Because, well, they are the truth. I want to know her. I want to know everything about her. And I think the fact that she wants me to know absolutely nothing only fires that want even more.

She sets her fork down and sighs. "Look, Watson. Contrary to what I thought … you actually seem like a good guy." She waves her hand toward my chest. "All squishy and warm in there. But what happened between us was just a natural thing. I needed a release, and your hands were on my bod. Bam, some closet sex was born." She stops, inhaling. "Nothing is going to transpire between us. I need you to know that. We can dance together. And sometimes, if you want to chill like we are right now, that's fine. But that's it. You don't own me. You'll never own me. So, please, stop looking at me the way that you do."

"I don't want to own you, Ryann," I mutter. "I'm just trying to be your friend."

"Friends don't do what we did in closets. And they don't flirt or say filthy things during dinner. So, let's get better at this friend stuff from here on out, yeah?" She gives me a questionable look.

It's not the answer I want, but I guess, for now, it's the answer I need to accept.

"So, if we're just friends, why are you so weird about opening up to me? You'd tell Sutton about your life and things that are bothering you, wouldn't you?"

She laughs lightly, so lightly that I barely hear it. "You'd be surprised by how much I *don't* share with Sutton. Or anyone for that matter." When she sees the surprise on my face, she continues, "I love Sutton. Like, totally love and adore her. But some things are just better left unsaid. I'm not going to complicate everyone else's life by sharing my shit." She shakes her head. "There's no point in dragging others into my mess."

By now, I'm so fucking confused about what she's even talking about. But the last thing I want to do is freak her out by showing it. So, instead, I grab a slice of pizza and bring it to my mouth.

Before she opens up to me, she needs to trust me first. I'll get to know her; it's just going to take time.

Unlucky for her, time is all I have.

"All right," I mutter. "You don't have to tell me anything. But I'll tell you whatever you want to know."

Her eyes narrow, almost in a testing way, like she doesn't believe me. "Whatever I want to know? Like ... sky is the limit?"

"Yep." I nod. "Do your worst."

"Where are you from? You have a Southern accent, but it's different from the people I've met who are from here in Georgia."

"Alabama." I take a sip from my soda. "Born and raised."

"Does that make you a cowboy?" she asks, giving me an amused grin.

"I grew up on a farm, and my family always had some horses. My brothers and I grew up riding them." I shrug. "So, yeah, I guess it does."

"Riley—my little sister—loves horses." She sighs. "I'm terrified of them."

"Why's that?" I ask, trying not to seem too interested. She seems to hate when I care too much.

She finishes chewing her food, wiping her mouth with a napkin. "Because they are *ginormous*. And strong. And ... scary."

"They are also really beautiful, intelligent creatures." I inhale, debating my next words before they come out. "You should go back home with me sometime; I'll teach you how to ride one. I'll put you on Daisy. She's the sweetest, laziest horse we have." I laugh. "Besides, she's so chunky that I don't think she could possibly throw you off."

I fully expect her to scowl at me and rattle some snarky remark off to tell me no. But instead, she takes a sip from her drink and gives me the smallest smile.

"Daisy sounds nice," she mutters, the corner of her lips turning up.

Maybe I'm getting somewhere after all.

"What's your plan after Brooks?" She tucks a strand of hair behind her ear. "Are you hoping to go pro?"

I stiffen slightly. I never want to come across like I'm bragging. And telling people that I have a secured spot in the NHL always seems cocky to say. But she asked, so I'm going to tell her.

"As long as I don't get injured, I have a spot with the New York Rangers after I graduate." I nod once. "What about you? What's your plan after college? Will you keep dancing?"

She sighs. "I don't want to keep dancing, but I want to stay in the dance world." Her eyes light up. "I'd love to work as a choreographer for Broadway shows. That's the real dream. To live in New York City and take it on." She looks like she's daydreaming about the day this all happens, smiling subtly before she snaps back to reality.

"But we're talking about you tonight, not me. So, I want to know, when you came up to me in class that day, was that nervous thing an act?" She tilts her head to the side. "You don't really seem like the type of guy who gets nervous." Her eyes widen, like she's realizing something. "Also, why haven't you been in class since that day? Do you hate rejection so much that you dropped the class?" She looks amused.

"First off, no. I didn't drop because you rejected my ass. Though I'll admit, that sucked. But no. Because of hockey practice, I switched to the online course."

"That's an option?" She gawks openly at me before rolling her eyes. "Wait, let me guess ... puck boys only?"

"Sorry." I cringe.

"Whatevs." She huffs. "Okay, back to my other question. Were you actually nervous, or was it some weird thing you do to try to get girls?"

"No. I'm not a nervous guy," I drawl. "But you, Ryann Denver, make me really fucking nervous. So, no, it wasn't an act." I smirk. "When you acted like you didn't know who I was, were you bluffing?"

She leans forward slightly, giving me a playful grin.

"I'll never tell," she whispers before pretending to zip her mouth with her fingers.

Well played, Tiny Dancer. Well played.

I pull up in front of Ryann's house and put the truck in park.

Dropping her off and not kissing her is torture. Now that I've been with her, it's hard to fight the urge to want to pull her against me. But I know that would freak her out, and I don't want to scare her away. Not yet.

When I was fourteen, my parents rescued a horse that had been not only abused, but extremely malnourished too. We named him Storm. Because he was wild and so unpredictable. But Jameson was dead set on training him and making him his own horse. Storm didn't trust any of us. And if we went into the stable, he'd lose his shit and charge on instinct. It took time and a lot of patience, but he learned to trust all of us. And I'll never forget the day when we all went on a trail ride and Jameson rode Storm.

It was when it all changed. It was when Storm saw us as family and not just another person who would hurt him.

One day, Ryann will look at me that same way. So, if I need to be patient, that's what I'll do.

She deserves that.

"Thank you for dinner," she whispers, glancing over at me with one hand on the door.

"You're welcome. Anytime"—I smile—"*friend.*"

She pushes the door open, but then stops. "I'm sorry I'm so bitchy. I'm, uh … not really used to many people in my life being good." Her eyes meet mine again. "I get the feeling you're good though. And … I just hope I'm not wrong." She swallows. "I don't trust anyone. But, well, I feel like I can trust you. A little tiny bit."

"I promise, I am exactly who I say I am," I say, keeping my voice low. "I'm sorry you missed your sister's birthday."

Like a zombie, she simply nods mindlessly. Like she's traveled somewhere far away even if she's still right here. "Me too. See you in a few days for practice?"

I nod. "Yes, ma'am. Have a good night."

Slowly, she gets out of my truck and closes the door. As I watch her walk to her house, waving to me once more before going inside, I wish so badly I could get her to trust me. To open up to me and let me help her.

But just like Storm, Ryann is wild. And wild needs to do things on their own time.

And terms.

Something Ryann doesn't know is, I'm not going anywhere.

Ryann

"I really can't believe our performances are just a little over a week away," Lana says from my bed, watching me as I curl my hair. "I caught a glimpse of Sutton and Hunter's dance. Oh. My. God. Ryann, they are probably going to win the entire thing." She sighs, putting her hand on her cheek. "Soulmates. Total goals."

I can't tell her the truth. That they were fake dating, and then things turned ... complicated. That's what happens when you have sex. It makes things complicated and weird. Just take me and Watson, for example. We slept together weeks ago, and my body still tingles when he touches me during our routine. But we've done really good at keeping things professional and not winding up back in the supply closet again. But, holy hell, it's been hard.

"If Princess Poppy hears you, your ass is toast," I tease her, knowing she's terrified of Poppy. And that Poppy hates Sutton.

Her eyes widen a smidgen before her face relaxes again. "Yeah, but I don't really get her beef with Sutton. I mean ... Sutton is really nice." She holds her hand out, examining her nails. "Maybe Poppy secretly wants Hunter." Her eyes flash to mine, and a smile spreads across her face. "Oh my gosh, that's probably it. Wouldn't that be something?"

"Uh … sure," I mutter, knowing damn well it wouldn't matter if Poppy stripped down naked in front of Hunter because that boy is all in on Sutton Savage. It's written all over his face.

I finish curling my hair and give it a spray to keep it in place. Tonight, Lana is dragging me out to this speed-dating event that Club 83 is putting on. I, by no means, want or need a man. Nor do I want to talk to countless random people for an hour of my life. But she begged me to go with her, and she's one of those friends who is always there when I need her. Going is the least I can do. And besides, maybe it'll take my mind off my dance partner. I'm not interested in completely throwing myself at random dudes just to feel something tonight. But a hot make-out session? I could get on board with that.

After giving myself a spritz of the best scent ever, Sol de Janeiro Cheirosa, I apply a little more lipstick and give myself one last look before standing and puffing my hair up a bit with my fingers. "Ready," I chime.

She looks up from her nails, and her eyes grow wide. "Hot damn, bitch. How the hell am I supposed to get a guy tonight when you show up like that?" She sticks her lip out, pouting as she stands up. "Can't you put a garbage bag on?"

"Not a chance, babe." I wink. "Besides, have you looked at yourself? You'll be swimming in a pool of dude drool, showing up like that." I walk behind her and swat her butt. "Let's go get this over with."

I'm far from the prettiest girl in any room. But with my hair curled, my face done up, I feel pretty tonight.

Though I might have gone a little too extreme. After all, my eye makeup is smokier and more dramatic than usual. Add in that my forest-green dress is short and tight. Probably *too* short and *too* tight. But nights like this are meant for sexy clothes. So, here I am.

Following me out of my room, she grabs my arm and giggles. "This is going to be so fun."

"Oh, it'll be something all right," I utter.

Watson

"Why is this place so fucking packed on a weeknight?" Hunter frowns as we find a parking spot outside of Club 83.

"Fuck if I know. I say we skip it and go get pizza," I mutter, sweeping my gaze around at the dozens of cars.

"Fuck that, we're already here. And I'm too hungry to go any farther off campus," Link suddenly chimes in from the backseat.

I'm surprised he even heard our conversation; he's been so obsessed with his cell phone and texting Tate since he got in with us after practice.

Turning the truck off, Hunter jerks his chin toward the building before opening his door. "Let's roll then. If there's any food left in there."

We all pile out, following him toward the entrance.

He looks around the full parking lot once more. "Place is loaded to the rafters, I swear."

When we get to the door, we all see the hot-pink paper taped to it. "Speed-dating night?" I mutter, reading the sign. "What the fuck is that?"

"Pretty sure it's when you go around and talk to random people every few minutes until you find one that you would swipe right on if you were on Tinder." Hunter shrugs. "Sounds fucking weird. What if you talk to someone for five minutes, and they seem cool, so you leave with them, and a few hours later, you're tied up in their basement?" He stops, pulling the door open and glancing back at us. "And not in a good way either."

We walk into Club 83, and it's packed with people, shoulder to shoulder. Right away, I'm regretting not just running to the grocery store and grabbing a few steaks to cook up.

Somehow, by the grace of whatever bar god there is, we find three empty stools next to each other at the end of the U-shaped bar.

Link points toward where all the tables are perfectly set up. "Look at that dude in the floral shirt. You're telling me he isn't a fucking creep? He just smelled his fingers."

"My uncle Stewart smells his fingers." I shrug. "To my knowledge, he hasn't killed anyone yet. Then again, I've also never seen where he lives."

Hunter's lips form a flat line, and his eyes widen. "Note to self: don't attend Watson's family Thanksgiving unless I want to be slathered up like a turkey and chopped up by his creepy, finger-smelling uncle."

I laugh lightly, bringing the beer to my lips that the bartender dropped off. That's one of the perks of being a Wolf. I don't have to ask for shit. It's just given to me even if I maybe don't want it.

I mean, heck, I planned on drinking water tonight.

When she stops in front of us again, we put in our order for some burgers and a few appetizers. Hunter and Link dive into a conversation about our upcoming game, but I can't hear what they are even saying. Not really. Because my eyes have found *her*.

Ryann is perched at a small, round high-top table for two. From here, I can see her legs. Too much of her legs, and I know every other motherfucker in here can see them too. Her strawberry-blonde hair hangs in loose waves. Her lips are painted bright red. Like a cherry I want to taste.

A chick wearing tall black boots and a black leather skirt and white tank top stands in front of the crowd, holding a clipboard up. Once she seems to gain everyone's attention, she yells out that they are going to start the speed dates. And when I see the line of dudes wrapped around the other side of Club 83, I feel my jaw tense, just knowing all of those fuckers will be sitting across from Ryann at some point tonight.

Without thinking twice, I stand up.

"Where are you going?" Hunter calls from behind me.

Looking over my shoulder, I smirk. "I'm going on a date."

Ryann

Some days, I'm not all that thankful for a lot of things. Some days, I'm an ungrateful little bitch. But today, I'm thankful that speed dating means I only have to talk to the same dude for five minutes. But I'll be honest; each date has been the longest five minutes of my entire life. I mean, dear Lord, where are these people coming from?

I don't even know who the worst has been. It could be the one who told me my dress reminded him of his mother. I mean, ew. Or maybe the one who picked his nose in front of me. And if either of those wasn't the worst, the dude who told me my eyes were too large and my freckles were weird could certainly be in the running.

So far, Hector, the nerdy-looking dude who loves Captain America and Starbucks, could possibly be the best one yet.

"Ryann?" A tall, extremely thin man, wearing a name tag that says *Hue*, repeats my name. "Ryann? Did you hear me?"

I force myself to focus on poor, sweet, innocent Hue. "Sorry, what were you saying?"

He opens his mouth to speak, and as if God actually does love me or something ... the sound of the timer rings through the air, and I try my best to hide my smile.

Hue frowns, so I offer him a soft smile. "It was nice to meet you, Hue. Good luck on your dates."

"Thanks," he mutters before taking off, completely and utterly annoyed with me. And I guess I don't blame him.

As I wait for my next suitor, let's call him, I pull my phone out. But just as I start to scroll through my newsfeed, a deep voice sends my eyes flying upward.

"Ryann, is it?" Watson grins, pointing at my name tag. "How very nice to meet you."

"*You're* speed dating?" I gawk at him.

Pulling the chair out, he slides into it and gives me a confused look. "I'm sorry. I don't believe we've met." He holds his hand out. "Name's Watson Gentry."

I take his hand, and he grips it in his and gives it a tiny shake.

"So, Ryann, how's your night going? Filled with lots of dates, I see." He tries to hide the amused grin. "Lots of … interesting … dates."

"Oh, you could say that," I mutter. "And what about you? How've your dates been?" I say as he releases my hand. Tilting my head, I narrow my eyes. "Meet anyone interesting?"

Leaning in closer, he smirks. "This will be my first and last one, babe." He eyes me over. "So, no need to be jealous, Ry baby."

The audacity of this dude. "Why would I be jealous? You're just my dance partner."

"Your dance partner who you love to take advantage of in supply closets," he drawls.

"Oh, right." I roll my eyes. "I *totally* took advantage of you. You didn't leap at the chance to have sex with me or anything."

Out of all the men who have sat across from me tonight, he's the hottest by far. With his gray henley shirt stretched across his chest, hugging his biceps as he leans forward. His short, dark hair and sharp jawline. My mind can't help but travel back to the time we had sex.

But a quick hookup happens one time. Not two, three, or even four times.

"Oh, I definitely leaped at the opportunity." He drops his voice lower. "You were all wound up, frustrated and in need of a release. Who would I be to not give you that?"

I refrain from squirming in my seat. Just thinking back to how uptight I was while we were dancing, messing my moves up, all because every single time his hands touched me … my body would catch on fire.

"Watson," I hiss. "Stop. It's been weeks. And we've worked together without anything getting complicated or messy. And then you pull this shit." I shake my head. "Just go. And we'll pretend this little encounter didn't happen next time we practice."

"Or I could leave and you could come with me," Watson says, jerking his head toward the table next to us. "The dude coming here next is wearing white sunglasses on his head."

"And?" I shrug. "So?"

"White sunglasses equals total douchebag," he deadpans. "Obviously."

"My ex wears white sun—" I stop myself before saying it, hiding my grin with my palm.

"Exactly my point," he mutters. "They should call them tool-glasses. Because I assure you, those are the only people who buy them." When the timer goes off and the white-sunglasses man makes his way to my table, staring down at Watson, Watson keeps his eyes on me.

"I'm not leaving with you," I tell him, keeping my tone low and relaxing in my seat. "Sorry to disappoint you."

His gaze holds mine, calling my bluff. Of course I want this night to be over. And, yeah, I'd love to leave with him right now. But it's taken me weeks to stop picturing him naked every time we see each other. If I leave with him right now, I know what will happen. We'll end up hooking up. And that isn't what I need.

He isn't what I need.

Waving my hand, I smile at my next date and look down at his name tag. "Hi there ... Ryan. I'm ... Ryann too." I look back at his face. "Watson was just leaving. Weren't you, Watson?" I look at him, widening my eyes. "See you at practice, Gentry."

Reluctantly, he stands. But not before pointing to Ryan's sunglasses. "Sweet glasses, man." He nods, giving him a cheesy thumbs-up. "Super badass."

Sparing me one last look, he heads to the bar.

And he doesn't leave there until the hour of speed dating is over. And then he gives me a knowing smirk when Lana and I head out. As if knowing I was bored to death and could have fallen asleep countless times.

And wishing like hell I had just left with him when I had the chance.

RYANN

"I don't understand," I say, feeling my chest cave in as I stare across the table at my boss. The truth is, those words are a lie. Of course I understand.

I knew this day was coming. I mean, I hoped it never would, but the chances were high of being caught.

I just hoped it would be later. Much, much later.

In her hand is a group of papers, all stapled together. And apparently, after a lengthy audit was done at Peaches, they found something. Something bad. Something about me.

My fake visa.

I always assumed that Brooks would be the one to find out the truth before anywhere else ever did. I mean, I thought they were supposed to ensure that all paperwork was correct. But here I am, in the United States, attending college. Fake visa and all. Yet a strip club is the place I was caught.

So didn't see that coming.

"Ryann, save it. Don't bullshit a bullshitter," my boss, Ginger, says, leveling me with a look that sends her eyebrows shooting upward. "Be straight. Be up front. And maybe I can try to help you." Her face softens, and she leans forward, setting the papers down. "It's just you and me. You can talk to me."

Obviously, I'm ashamed. I've lied to this woman who has been nothing but good to me for months. I feel like a total loser, but I suppose that comes with being a criminal.

"I'm sorry," I whisper, looking down at my hands. "I lied to you. I've been lying to everyone."

"And why is that?"

I suck in a breath through my nose, blowing it out through my mouth. It's an attempt to calm myself down, but it doesn't work. At all.

"I came to the United States with a fake visa. And ... somehow ... it got me in."

Her eyebrows pull together. "I ... I just don't understand. Why would you do that? Why not just get a real one? Why risk your entire future when you had to know you'd be caught eventually?"

I need to say the words. To open up and explain why I would do such an awful, stupid thing. It's the only way she'll see me as a human being. But, goddamn it, the words don't come easy. There's nothing I hate more in this world than feeling vulnerable. And sharing my secrets with her, telling her my past ... that's exactly how I'll feel.

Naked. Vulnerable. *Pathetic.*

"I couldn't go get an actual visa," I finally say. My voice so low that I barely hear myself. "I have criminal charges that prevent me from being able to."

Forget my cheeks being red. No, my entire face is on fire. Admitting this to anyone would be humiliating. But my boss? The freaking lady who gave me a job so I could afford to buy a car? Keep my cell phone on? Send my sister a phone and a little cash for her birthday? I could do all of that because of this lady. And now, I'm sitting before her, telling her that I'm a criminal.

"What charges, Ryann?" she asks, her voice soft. "If you don't mind me asking."

As much as I don't want to tell her, I know I have to. I don't want her to look at me like a thug or someone who just did bad things for no good reason. I always had my reasons even if that still doesn't make it right.

"One is from stealing a few packages of ramen noodles, a loaf of bread, and some peanut butter when I was thirteen." I look down at the floor again, my fingernails digging into the flesh of my palm. "My sister was five at the time. We were so broke. And she was so hungry." I stop, wiping the back of my hand over my eyes. "I didn't know what else to do. She needed to eat."

"Ryann, I'm so sorry," she says before stopping. "You said charges. Are there more?"

I reach up, mindlessly raking my hand through my hair. I try to not let my brain travel back to the day I'm about to explain, but it's hard.

"When I was sixteen, my mom's boyfriend at the time was beating the crap out of her. That wasn't anything unusual." I laugh sadly as thick tears gather in my eyes, blurring my vision. "She really knew how to pick 'em." I exhale quickly, wiping my cheeks. "But this time … I really thought he was going to kill her. He just wouldn't stop. And then … he was screaming that my sister and I were next. Me? I could take it. My sister? She was still little. Too little. And young."

My mind goes to that day, and I remember peeking out of my and Riley's bedroom. I had given her my headphones and some music to distract her months before this. I was tired of her having to listen to the same bullshit down the hall every night. But when I peered out, my mom's body was so weak. So … battered.

"The thing about him that I didn't know was, he was a police officer. He had connections. Lots and lots of connections." I look at her to find her eyes staring straight at me. "I grabbed a fifteen-pound weight that I had in my room for lifting, ran out of my bedroom, and hit him with it. Right in the back of his head." I'm crying harder now. Completely out of control. "He almost died. And I had to call an ambulance." My body rocks as I think back to the day. "Spent six months in juvenile hall and got more red flags on my record."

I remember thinking he was dead. The feeling settling in my stomach that I had physically killed someone. And that for the rest of my life, I would be a murderer.

That's when the panic attacks began, though I don't know why it wasn't sooner, given how many times I had watched my mom get the shit beaten out of her.

She's quiet. Too quiet. And I know it's because my stupid, miserable story has gone and made her feel bad. That's not why I told her. I told her because I needed her to know that I'm not just an awful person, going around and stealing things and beating the shit out of people. I had my reasons.

"Ryann, I am so sorry." She grabs a tissue and hands it to me before taking a second and blotting her own tears. "This isn't fair. You have to know that."

I shrug. "Life isn't fair. But no one believed that it wasn't my fault then. They certainly won't now. Now that I've lied to get here. Forged my way into this country." I sniffle. "Officials will be alerted, and I'll be deported."

"You don't know that!" she scolds me like I'm a little kid. "You need to fight. And explain everything to them. They are going to understand, Ryann. Just have some faith, okay?"

God bless her because she really does believe that it's as simple as just telling my sad, pathetic story and getting a visa handed to me. Life doesn't work that way.

Before I can answer, she sighs, looking up at the ceiling before her eyes find mine again. "The man who did the audit was extremely nice. He said typically, when he finds something like this, within a few weeks, you can expect to hear from someone that they've discovered you're here illegally. And then, because of the process, another few weeks for deportation."

I nod somberly before standing up. "So, what? Am I done working here then?"

"To my understanding, until you've been legally found guilty, you've done nothing wrong. So, until they tell me otherwise, you've got your job." She shrugs. "When someone gets charged with theft, they aren't guilty until proven so. So, I'm treating this the same way. Deal?"

"Deal," I mutter.

She stands, giving me the smallest smile. "Besides, you're one of my best dancers and favorite employees. I'm not ready to lose you just yet."

Coming from behind her desk, she throws her arms around me and pulls me against her. "It's going to be okay, Ry. I know it."

I don't answer because, honestly, I don't think it is going to be okay. I think it's going to be the opposite.

I'm going back to Canada. And I will likely never be able to come over here again. All the dreams I had for New York City ... gone.

After she releases me, I walk out of her office, knowing I need to think of something. And fast.

13

WATSON

Ryann *is in a bad mood.* Maybe it's because this is our last practice before dress rehearsal, and then the fundraiser is this weekend, and she's worried I'm not ready. I have no idea. But ever since we started practicing today, she's been short with me.

Since we hooked up weeks ago, it hasn't been easy to be around her. Probably because I wish I could kiss her anytime I feel like it and she's dead set on not letting me get too close. Whatever it is, it's frustrating as hell. It's like she's put a wall between us, and that makes dancing together pretty damn strange.

She looked so bored during her dates the other night. If she had looked like she was into someone, I probably would have lost my shit. But it was almost comical, watching her trying to stay awake date after date. Being too damn stubborn to just join me at the bar.

During one of her moves—a move she usually does with ease—when she leaps into my arms and I spin her around, she tumbles to the ground.

"Damn it!" she growls. But before I can help her up, her palm slaps against the wooden floor. "I can't do this right now!" Bringing her knees to her chest, she drives her face into her legs. "Watson, I appreciate how hard you've worked, but I can't do this fundraiser with you. It's an important day, and I'm going to ruin it." She exhales. "Who knows if I'll even be here by then anyway?"

Kneeling down next to her, I run my hand over her hair. "What are you talking about, Tiny Dancer? Why the fuck would you think you'd ruin the fundraiser?" I frown down at her. "And what is that supposed to mean? If you'll even be here? Where else would you be?"

"Nothing," she mutters. "It means nothing."

Going out on a limb and preparing myself to be headbutted or kneed in the balls, I tuck my hands under her and lift her against me. Sitting on the floor and scooching my back to the mirrored wall, I hold her in my arms. Shocked that she isn't kicking and screaming to get away. But when I see her face, I realize she's crying.

"Twice now," she croaks. "Twice, you've seen me lose my shit. That's twice more than any other human being alive."

"What's going on, Ry?" I whisper against her head. "I promise, you can talk to me."

"Why do you act like we're friends? I barely even know you! We've danced together." She sniffles. "And, yeah, we hooked up, sure. But aside from that and the few times we've hung out … I don't know you." She peeks up at me. "And you don't know me."

"I know enough," I say lowly.

She's quiet. But I wait patiently, hoping she'll open up. It seems like a far-fetched thing to hope for, seeing as she never wants to open up to me at all. It's like staring up at the sky and waiting for a shooting star to fall. You never know when it'll happen, but eventually, it has to.

All stars burn out at some point.

And finally … she speaks. "I'm probably going to get deported back to Canada in a few weeks," her voice barely squeaks. "And part of me thinks I should just do myself a favor and go back right now. Before I'm forced to against my will."

I'm stunned. Out of all the things I imagined might come from her pretty lips, that wasn't it. But I try to hide my shock and just keep myself calm and my voice level.

"I don't understand," I say softly. "Why would you get deported?"

"Because I lied to get here." She looks down, ashamed. "I weaseled myself into Brooks with a fake visa."

Holy fuck. This is some serious shit. My entire body tenses, but I try to hide the sheer shock on my face.

Slowly, I brush some loose strands of hair away from her forehead. "How did you find out that you were caught?"

"My work," she says, holding her eyes to mine. "At Peaches."

"The *strip* club?" This time, I can't hide how I'm feeling. "You work at the strip club?"

I've been there once. And honestly, places like that aren't my cup of tea. The men act entitled, and so many of them are creeps. So, when I was there, I never really looked around much.

"Go on and judge me," she snaps. "But working there has allowed me to have a car, a phone, and buy my baby sister a phone too."

"I'm not judging," I answer quickly. "I'm just … surprised. I had no idea."

"You are judging, but it's fine." She shrugs her shoulders. "Unless you grew up so poor that you had to steal dinner for your family or were taught to dine and dash by your own mom … you don't get a say. I do what I need to do to survive. And I'll do it again when it comes time to go back to living with my mother. That's life."

"I'm sorry." Two words—that's all I can bring my mouth to say. I don't have any answers for her. There's no way I can help.

Glancing at the clock, she quickly scurries off of me. "The next group is going to be here in less than ten minutes. Let's run through it one more time from the top."

As she smooths her hair, I look up at her. "Ryann—"

"Get up. Let's dance." She walks to the center of the floor, standing taller. "We had a nice moment. I told you a secret. Now, please, don't ruin it." When I simply stare at her, she tilts her chin up and straightens herself out. "I will be fine. I always am."

I don't want her to just be fine.

And I sure as fuck don't want her leaving the country.

Ryann

"I'll see you at rehearsal at the end of the week," I call out, hiking my bag over my shoulder and hightailing it to my car. Hoping like hell I'm still here by the end of the week.

My boss said it would be weeks before I heard from the immigration office. But who really knows?

"Ryann, wait." Watson comes jogging behind me, grabbing my elbow and spinning me around.

Tugging me against him, he wraps his arms around me in the warmest hug.

"It's going to be all right," his deep voice mumbles against my forehead. "I promise."

Involuntarily, I suck in a breath. My lungs burn, and my eyes sting with tears threatening to spill out. My mom isn't a bad person. But affection never really was her thing. I can't remember a time when another human being pulled me against them and told me everything would be okay. Emotions flood through me, but I keep myself under control. I'm just exhausted. And emotional. That's all this is. It has absolutely nothing to do with the strong set of arms holding me close.

Not one bit.

I let myself bask in his hold for a moment longer before stepping back. "Have a good rest of your week. I'll see you at rehearsal."

He looks unsure. And, dare I say ... worried.

But eventually, he gives me a slight nod. "See you then."

Headed to my car, I feel his eyes on me still. The way he was looking at me in the studio, I could tell he desperately wanted to be able to say the right thing. Or help if he could. But he can't. Besides, we aren't even friends.

I think honesty is the way to go on this one. Play the part of the poor little girl who did what she had to do to survive. I don't have to play it; it's who I am. So, that's what I'll do. Once the dance fundraiser is over, I'm going to go straight to the United States immigration office and admit what I did. And beg for a second chance.

God, I hope they'll grant me it.

There is nothing wrong with Canada. But Canada isn't my dream. New York City is. A better life for me and my sister. Being able to provide for her in a way my mom can't.

I messed up. But I'm ready to make it right.

14

RYANN

"For the love of all things, please, no one pull a muscle," Jolene shouts, pointing to all the dancers. "We're days away from the biggest fundraiser we've ever done. Everything needs to go perfectly! Not to mention *The Nutcracker* for those of you who were cast." Her eyes sweep across all of us once more. "Now. Is. Not. The. Time. For. Mess-ups!"

"Famous last words," Sutton mutters, looking like she's been run over by a car.

The bags under her eyes are hard not to notice. And she's grumpier than usual. I guess that's what happens when you fake date your enemy and end up falling in love.

They'll work it out. I hope.

I hide a yawn, not wanting Jolene to yell at me for not getting enough rest. I was up way too late last night, researching this whole deportation crap. Even reading stories. And I'll admit … I sort of wish I hadn't done that.

When we auditioned for *The Nutcracker*, it was back in the first week of school, before Sutton transferred here. I have no doubt that if she had been there, she would have been chosen for the Sugar Plum Fairy instead of me.

I'm a little envious that she doesn't have the extra few practices a week to get ready for it now that the holidays are getting closer.

I glance up at the clock. *Just five more minutes*. I'm ready to get out of here and take a short nap before my afternoon class.

A pounding at the door has every head turning to look who it is. And when we all see Watson, Jolene shoots him daggers.

"Mr. Gentry, can I help you?" She moves her head back and forth. "As you can see, we're still in the middle of practice. So, this'd better be good."

He gives her one of his signature sweet, boyish grins. His dimple pops out, making most bitches in here weak in the knees. Even Jolene seems to soften instantly. Me? I cross my arms and narrow my eyes, wondering what in the hell he could be up to.

"So sorry, Miss Jolene," he drawls smoothly. "You're looking beautiful today. Y'all are." He waves at the entire room, and I hear a few girls literally squeal.

When his eyes land on me, I cringe, knowing he's here for me.

"Ryann and I talked about changing one of our moves. And, uh … I just wanted to ask her about that." He gives Jolene an apologetic look. "I'm so sorry to interrupt. With hockey, my schedule is stacked, so I figured I'd run over here while I had a minute." He smiles. "You know, since we're so close to the fundraiser and all."

"You don't have a phone?" Jolene grumbles. "And why change anything this close to the performance? Are you guys trying to give me a heart attack?"

"No, ma'am." He shakes his head. "It's something super small. Swear it."

Jolene's eyes shift from Watson to me before going back to him. "Fine. Go." She waves her hand. "But don't you dare interrupt a practice again, Mr. Gentry. Or I'll be talking to Coach LaConte."

"No, ma'am, I won't," he tells her before his eyes land on mine.

I give him a confused look, but eventually, I grab my things and follow him out the door.

"What in the ever-loving God are you doing here? She's going to have my—"

"Let's get married," he blurts out when we get outside.

I look around for Ashton Kutcher, wondering if I'm being punked. Or perhaps I heard him wrong. Yeah, that has to be it.

"Come again?" I gawk at him.

"I'd love to. But the studio's occupied right now, so it'd be hard to sneak into the closet," he teases.

I punch him in the stomach, and he keels over.

"Jesus Christ, you're so dang feisty, woman!" He stands up, shaking his head. "What I was saying is … let's get married."

"And why the hell would we do that?" I scowl. "Have you lost your mind?"

He steps toward me, taking my hands in his. "Because you need a green card. And, hey, I'm sort of over getting attention from all the single ... and taken women on campus. You'd be doing me a favor, really." He gives me a small grin. "What do you say?"

"You're mocking me, right? My whole *needing a green card* thing? You're making it a joke?" I shrug, pulling my hands from his. "Well, sorry to be a party pooper, but joke's over."

I start to turn, but he grabs my arm, forcing me to look at him.

"I'm not joking. I one thousand percent mean what I'm saying." He moves his hand to my wrist, enveloping it with his fingers. "What do you have to lose, Ryann?"

"Marriage is a big deal," I whisper, gawking at him like he's insane. And right now, I kind of think he might be. "I mean, not really to me. Because I've never even given it a thought. But to guys like you? It's everything." I narrow my eyes slightly. "Don't you get that?"

"Why haven't you given it a thought?" he asks softly.

"Because I don't believe in all of that *happily ever after* marriage crap." I shrug lazily. "I never have."

"Well, that's sad, Ryann." He's so relaxed, and I don't understand how he could be. "But just because you refused to be my friend, basically used my dick for an orgasm, and hate the sight of me—that doesn't mean I don't consider you a friend of mine. Because I do." He pauses. "I like you, Ryann. You're badass. And to be honest, I'd be pretty fucking honored to have you as my wife. If you'll have me, that is."

"This is ... crazy," I say, thinking out loud. "Don't you get how crazy this all is?"

"Maybe it is. Maybe I'm fucking nuts. But if it keeps you here and you get to keep chasing your dreams, I'm okay with that." He shrugs. "Look, I have to go to practice. Just think about it, okay?"

As he starts to turn, my voice stops him. "Watson?"

"Yeah, Tiny Dancer?"

"You actually mean this? You'd really do this for me?" I take a step closer. "Even though you hardly know me?"

"Hell yeah, I would. And I know you enough." He reaches down, brushing his thumb against my chin and tilting my head upward. "I want to help you, Ryann. Take my help."

My heart is beating so fast. I have no idea what I'm about to say. I know in the long run, this decision is probably going to bite me in the ass. But I can't help but do what my brain is telling me.

"I'll marry you," I croak. "As long as you're sure. I mean, obviously, we'll be getting a divorce at some point. But … this is your first marriage. Are you sure you want to waste it on me?"

"Damn straight, I do. Wouldn't want my first wife to be anyone else, Tiny Dancer." He winks, dropping his hand. "Meet me at the courthouse at three o'clock."

My mouth hangs open. "As in, like … *today?*"

Walking backward, he gives me a dimpled grin. "Hey, the sooner we get you wifed up, the sooner you can get that green card, right?" Jerking his chin upward, he holds his hand up. "See ya soon, wifey."

I watch as he turns around, strutting casually to his truck before climbing in and driving away.

Like he didn't just ask me to marry him.

Like he isn't risking his entire future just to keep me here.

My whole life, I've been trained to look for the worst in people. But I'm not sure there's anything bad inside of that man.

And here I am, using him to stay.

Watson Gentry offered to marry me. Maybe I've lost my mind … because I said yes.

Watson

I keep glancing in my rearview mirror, seeing Ryann rooted in the same spot I left her moments ago until she's just a blip in my mirror. Then, I turn down the street and can no longer see her.

I was up all night, trying to come up with a plan. Something, *anything*, to keep her here. This is risky. Not only with the law, but my heart too. I've had a thing for that girl since the moment we shared a class together and I watched her float through the room, catching the attention of literally everyone. But this? Getting married? I'm fucking done for.

She isn't the Hallmark type of girl. She doesn't do touchy-feely shit. But being married is a big deal. It'll force her to spend time with me without constantly pushing me away. And at the end of it, once she gets her visa, if she still doesn't want me the way I want her, I'll let her go. Until then, once she's my wife, I'm pulling out all the stops to make her fall in love with me.

I know it's crazy. And, yeah, my mother might kill me, but I'm willing to take the risk. Because Ryann is one of those girls. The kind you can't help but fall for because she's so damn enthralling. She's talented. She's sassy.

She's funny. Smart. And she really doesn't give a shit what anyone else thinks of her. Everything about her pulls me in and keeps me there.

She's everything I've ever wanted. And in a few hours, she's going to be my wife.

I just hope she doesn't change her mind first.

15

Ryann

I look at myself in the mirror. The best I could do with this short of notice is a white romper with a delicate lace overlay from my wardrobe. My hair is curled in long strawberry-blonde waves that fall down my back, and I pulled half of it up into a twist. The wedding might be far from genuine, but we'll need proof that it happened. I don't want to give away the fact that it's a sham just by looking like crap. I at least need to make myself look decent. I need to look like a bride.

What a great love story this could be. Boy marries girl to save her. They fall hopelessly in love and live happily ever after. But I've known my entire life that fairy tales like that are a big, fat lie. Something created to make life suck a little less for all the sad souls.

I'm thankful that no one is home to question why I am semi-dressed up on a Thursday afternoon.

My hands feel cold, but I know it's just the nerves taking over my body. My mind is traveling a million miles a second, and I can hardly form a real thought.

Am I really going to marry a guy I've slept with once and hardly know? Yep, I guess I am.

I drag in a long, shaky breath and slowly let it out.

I've never thought about my wedding day, really. But I never imagined I'd be marrying a Brooks Wolf for a visa either.

It's time to go get married.

I park in the parking lot across the street from the courthouse. I check my reflection in the mirror one last time before pushing my door open. It creaks and sounds like it might fall off, but that's not nearly as awful of a sound as when I close it and the entire thing rattles. It serves me well though. Having a car isn't something I'll ever take for granted. I can go where I want to go.

Unless it breaks down, of course.

I lean against my car, looking around for Watson. I arrived here a few minutes early. I guess I couldn't stand to just sit in my house any longer. But when I hit the side of my phone to light the screen up, showing it's five minutes past three, my stomach churns. He's never late.

He probably changed his mind.

It would be for the best if he did. I mean, this is illegal. And stupid. Not to mention really crazy. Even though I know that, my heart sinks at the thought that maybe he's backing out. And truthfully, I think it's because he's always been someone I could trust, and if he decided against this marriage, I'd be disappointed that he stood me up without an explanation.

I continue standing here, trying to stop my heart from pounding so hard. He's ghosting me, and then I'll have to dance with him in front of hundreds of people in a few freaking days. This is a disaster.

Turning, I reach for my door handle. But before I can pull it open, Watson's truck comes speeding into the parking lot, quickly pulling into the spot right next to mine.

Swiftly, he climbs out, jogging around the front of the truck to get to me. "I'm so sorry. I got stuck in construction, and then my phone died, so I couldn't call to let you know." He sighs. "I was afraid you'd leave when I didn't show up."

"I was about to," I say, chewing my bottom lip anxiously. "I thought … I figured you had changed your mind." I try to smile, but nothing happens. "And I wouldn't have blamed you. I know this is insane."

Coming closer, he surprises me when he takes my hands in his. "I didn't change my mind, Ryann."

He gives me a small, reassuring smile before dropping my hands and heading to the passenger side of his truck. Pulling out two boxes, he holds the larger one up first.

"Before I give you this, please know that I have no clue what I'm doing when it comes to jewelry. I'd never bought it before. So, if it's ugly and you hate it, that's fine because we can take it back and you can choose something you want."

When he pushes the box my way, I stare down at it, embarrassed to actually take it from him.

"I ... I didn't get you anything," I croak, my cheeks boiling. "I didn't even remember a ring. Shit. Were we supposed to get rings?" I feel myself shrinking, feeling an inch tall. "I'm so dumb. We're about to get married. Of course we need rings."

"Ryann," he says, dipping his head a little lower. "Please, take it. I didn't expect anything. I know I sprang this on you at the last minute." A look of sadness briefly touches his face, disappearing just as fast as it came, but still, it was there. I saw it. "I know I'm not what you want. And that's fine. I can't force you to give me a chance. But you mean a lot to me. And I still want to make this day special for you. You deserve that much."

My entire chest squeezes as I glance from him to the box, feeling terrible that he thinks the reason I wouldn't give him a chance is because he isn't what I want. That's not it at all. I'm just trying—I've been trying—to protect myself. And my heart. And here he is, completely selfless and willing to marry me just so I can stay.

Finally, I reach out and slowly take it from him. I hold the large velvet box it in my hands, wondering what on earth it could be. No one has ever given me jewelry before.

Opening it, I look down at the necklace. It's white gold with a black diamond pendant that is surrounded by white diamonds. It's beautiful. Too beautiful for someone like me. And I'm sure it wasn't cheap either.

"Watson, this is too much. You didn't have to get me anything." I chew the inside of my cheek nervously. Maybe it's because I don't receive gifts often—or at all—so when I do, I don't know how to act. "Thank you."

As I stare at it, I feel Watson as he shifts around on his feet nervously. "The dude at the jewelry store was trying to talk me into pearls. But I don't know. You just don't seem like the type of girl who would want pearls."

"I hate pearls," I whisper, looking up at him. Emotions unexpectedly sear through my body, bringing tears to my eyes, clouding my vision. "It's really, really beautiful."

Taking it from the box, he spins me around gently. When his hand grazes my neck, pushing my hair out of the way, I'm embarrassed by the instant goose bumps I get. Securing the necklace around my neck, he takes my hair in his hands before smoothing it back to where it was. When he's finished, I slowly turn toward him.

"Thank you, Watson," I say, peering up at him. "Really. Thank you."

"Anything for you." He shrugs, giving me a tiny smile.

And I know he means it. He's too good for me. Too good for anyone who isn't pure perfection.

Grabbing the empty box, he takes it to his truck. He's over there for a moment, and I'm wondering what he is doing. And when he returns, both boxes he held a minute ago are gone.

Slowly, he slides down onto one knee and opens his hand. In it lies a thin wedding band, made up of black diamonds.

"Ryann, I know you don't like me all that much. And I get that you think what happened between us weeks ago was a mistake. But it wasn't a mistake to me. Not at all. And I want to get to know you. I want to know everything about you, even the shit you keep hidden." He stops, swallowing. "I know enough to know that even though you claim you didn't have a dream wedding day, if you did, this wouldn't be it. And I know I'm not the man of your dreams. I've come to accept that. But if you'd do me the honor of being my wife, even if it's just for a short time, I'd consider myself the luckiest bastard in the universe."

More tears build in my eyes before rolling down my cheeks. He's so kind. So thoughtful. So selfless. And it isn't that he's not my dream guy. If I had one, I'm sure he'd be it. I've just been so consumed with trying to push him away; that way, I couldn't get hurt. If I let him in, I know I'd fall—hard. And that's not something I want to do right now.

I did not expect him to do all of this. I guess I should have because it's Watson and he lives to make others happy. But on this day, I guess I just figured we'd go inside, take care of business, and then that would be it. I never foresaw him showering me with the most beautiful gifts or getting down on one knee. Yet here he is.

He really is full of surprises.

I stare in complete awe. Whatever this man is made of, it's something I never knew even existed.

Holding my hand out, I nod. "I would be honored to be your fake wife, Watson Gentry." I smile. "I consider myself pretty lucky for it too."

He seems surprised by my words. Then again, why wouldn't he be? For weeks, I've done my very best to keep him at arm's length, not wanting a repeat of the closet situation because I didn't want to allow myself to get hurt again.

When he slides the ring onto my finger, my entire body feels it. Every nerve ending ignites. And every part of me is aware of his existence.

Slowly, he pushes himself to stand. Pulling a chain from under his shirt, he reaches around to unclasp it and pulls something from it. He hands me a dark silver-colored band, and his face grows somber. "That was my dad's wedding band. I was lucky enough to be the one who got it out of the four of us kids." He nods toward his hand. "Use this in there."

Looking down at his hand, my eyes float to his, and I feel a knot in my stomach. "Watson, that ring means ... everything to you and your family. Don't waste it on me."

"It's not a waste, Ryann." His expression grows even more serious. "Trust me, this isn't a day I would ever want to forget." Jerking his head across the road, he smiles. "Let's go get hitched. Before you go and change your mind."

And when he holds his hand out, I take it. And the crazy part is ... it doesn't even feel wrong.

Ryann

Over an hour later, here we are, about to be hitched.

Upon arrival, we learned that we needed two witnesses for anyone to marry us. Neither of us were planning to tell anyone about this arrangement right away, so asking someone like Sutton or one of Watson's closest friends was off the table.

Watson's younger brother, Carson, just so happened to be nearby because, apparently, he's some drag racer who has a race twenty minutes from Brooks tomorrow night. The two of them had planned to meet up at some point while he was in Georgia, but twenty minutes after Watson made the call—the awkward, shocking *I need you to be my witness* call—Carson strutted in.

And, wow, it seemed good-looking men ran in the family. Because, like Watson, he was insanely attractive.

They whispered for a few minutes. I could tell Carson was confused, but he didn't try to talk Watson out of it. Which I appreciated, but also kind of wished he had at the same time.

I'm so scared that Watson is going to wake up tomorrow and hate himself for doing this. And regret it. Regret me.

And I called the only person I knew who wouldn't judge me. Okay, she might judge me, but I knew she wouldn't talk me out of it. And given the fact that she was an absolute hermit ... I knew she wouldn't tell anyone.

I called Zoey.

I'd met Zoey last year when I was waiting tables. She's some sort of math major. She tried to explain what she's studying, but it was over my head. We don't hang out much, but I like her. And more importantly, given some things I learned about her last year at the diner, I know she'll keep this secret.

Her chestnut-brown hair falls below her shoulders, and her blunt bangs give her a bit of an edgy look, though I don't think that was done purposely.

"I now pronounce you husband and wife," the older lady in the business suit says, keeping her face extremely emotionless. "You may now kiss the bride."

My eyes widen, and Watson looks noticeably uneasy. We kissed that day at Club 83. Only because he was trying to get it through Denton's tough skull that I had moved on. And on the day we hooked up in the closet. And that was only because we were both sex-crazed in the moment. But this ... this is different. It's intimate, and it's in front of people.

And for some reason, it feels like our first kiss. I guess it is in some way because it's our first kiss as husband and wife. But it makes me feel ... exposed.

As if feeling the woman's stare, Watson leans down. Cupping my face with his hand, he brings his lips to mine. My eyes flutter shut, and I let myself travel to a place where we aren't two people who just committed a crime. But instead, just two people kissing. As he kisses me, my entire body floods with butterflies. And when he finally pulls back and I force my eyes to open back up, I find myself wishing it could have lasted longer.

"Our first kiss as husband and wife, babe." He winks, as if trying to lighten my mood and play it off like everything is normal. Nothing to see here. "Hope I did okay."

I nod quickly. "Uh, you did ... yeah. It was good."

As if reading me like a book, knowing I'm hot and bothered, he smirks. "Good, Tiny Dancer. There will be more of that later."

No. Well, maybe. No, there can't be ... can there?

Taking my hand, he gives it a squeeze. "Ready to go, wifey?"

I bob my head up and down, far too quickly and looking like I probably just snorted a line of coke. "Yep. I'm ready to go." I practically bounce, just needing to get out of this building and away from this lady's stare. Judging us. Trying to figure out if this is real or not.

"Not so fast. I need you to sign your marriage certificate," she mutters, glancing at Carson and Zoey. "The witnesses need to sign too. So, if there's anything fishy, now would be the time to speak."

"Fishy? I've never even met this chick who is now my sister-in-law," Carson says, grinning like a complete idiot. "If she's hiding any dead bodies, trust me, I wouldn't know."

The woman scowls at him, straightening her posture, and Watson smacks his brother's arm playfully before chuckling.

"That's my brother for you. Always has been a joker."

Shaking his head, he grabs a pen from the small table and looks over the paper. After he signs, it's my turn and then Zoey's and Carson's.

And when she takes the paper, holding it up to make sure it's all set, she narrows her eyes at us once more. "Congratulations." And then she walks away.

I'm someone's wife. And I have a husband.

Holy shitballs. This isn't how I thought my day would go when I woke up this morning. That's for damn sure.

16

WATSON

My brother is so confused. But luckily, he hasn't asked too many questions. Not yet anyway. I'm sure when we're completely alone, he'll bombard me with them. For now, he's too busy hitting on the nerdy girl who showed up to be Ryann's witness to bother me and Ryann about this shotgun wedding. My brother can't help but be a flirt. It's just who he is. Even if she is the furthest thing from his type.

After the ceremony, they were both going to take off, assuming we'd want to be alone. To do ... newlywed stuff, I suppose. Which, obviously, I would have fucking loved that.

But Ryann was quick to tell them to tag along to dinner. Giving them the excuse that, "We'll have our whole life together now that we're hitched."

I know the real reason she wants them here though.

When I kissed her and she melted against me like fucking butter on a hot stove, I knew her body wanted more. And I know damn well she's afraid if we end up alone, we'll have another *supply closet* incident. Little does she know, that's bound to happen at some point. Only, this time, I'd love to have her in my bed. How could I not? I mean, fuck, now that we're legally bound together, she can't date, hook up, or kiss anyone but me.

And fucking right, I'm going to make sure she knows that.

It's not a sin if we're married. After all, husbands and wives are supposed to fuck.

"So, how did y'all meet?" Carson says, leaning back in the booth and tossing his arm behind Zoey. Which makes her squirm and turn bright red. My brother, of course, eats that up. "Also, why didn't you mention her before?"

At the same time I say, "We had a class together," she answers, "We were partnered up for a dance fundraiser."

And when we each try to change our answer, we both switch and come out opposite again.

"We briefly met in class, but when we really got to know each other was when we were paired together for dance," Ryann says sweetly, looking over at me. "Wouldn't you agree, *babe*? That our encounter in class wasn't all that romantic?"

"She was obsessed with me," I toss back with a shrug. "Came over just to introduce herself. Thought I was the handsomest man in the class."

Rolling her eyes, she smacks my shoulder with the back of her hand. "Mmhmm. That's exactly how it went." She shakes her head, looking at my brother and Zoey. "Whatever helps you sleep at night, big guy."

"Wait, Jameson told me he asked about your dance partner a few weeks ago." He smirks at Ryann. "Jamie said you were either really hot or really ugly. And just like we both thought"—he licks his finger, making a sizzling sound—"smokin' hot."

"You know she's my wife, right?" I shoot him a warning glare. "You can't check my wife out. And you sure as hell can't call her smokin' hot."

"Just calling it like I see it." He winks. "Have you told Mom? She must know, right?" His eyes widen. "Fuck, she's fixin' to be one pissed-off woman for not getting an invite to the wedding though."

"Nah, it just happened so fast." I glance over at Ryann, hoping the next words out of my mouth won't freak her out. "Figured we'd go see her real soon. Tell the news to her face-to-face. And hope that she's all right with it."

"And if she isn't? Then what? Y'all get divorced?" he jokes.

"At that point, assuming it's in the next few months, they could still get an annulment. People who get drunkenly married in Vegas do it all the time," Zoey mutters, and we all stare at her. She simply takes a sip from her Coke and looks down. "I've heard that anyway."

I feel so guilty, knowing my mom will be sad that I didn't tell her beforehand. I knew she'd have talked me out of it because she would think we weren't ready since she wouldn't know the real truth behind why we were doing it. She would have urged me to date Ryann for a few years and then see where we were at. I didn't want to have to go against my mother's wishes, so I just didn't say anything. Clearly, now, I need to tell her what's going on. Especially since a caseworker could look deeper into our marriage and see it's a sham. We need to sell it to our friends and family that we are in love. We don't want to be a walking red flag.

"Just buy her a bunch of new candles and those melty things she puts in those warmers she's obsessed with that get hot." Carson laughs. "The things Dad used to say we were going to burn the house down with."

"And she'd always say, 'Well, at least it'll smell good,'" I add, feeling a pang in my chest, wondering what the hell my dad would think of what I've done.

He's been gone for a few years now, and we all still miss him like crazy. Carson will at least talk about my dad. Whereas Jameson will change the subject and do anything to avoid even talking about him. I guess everyone has their own way of coping. Jameson's is shutting everything out. Mine is to do everything in my power to be the best in hopes that he'd be proud. Our sister is similar to me. And Carson, well, he just acts like nothing bothers him.

"So, what time's the big race start tomorrow?" I ask, fully planning to use the rehearsal for the fundraiser as my excuse to get out of going to his race.

I've seen him crash a few too many times already. One time, he needed surgery on his legs and had to spend a week in the hospital. If I could avoid seeing that again, that'd be great.

"Starts around nine tomorrow night." He sighs. "Usually, I've got the car loaded up, and I'm headed home by then, but it's an *under the lights* type of shit. Given the car count, they're saying it could go till at least two a.m."

"We'd come, but we have rehearsal." I do my damnedest to sound bummed. "Next time."

"What? No way am I missing this! I've never watched any kind of racing before," Ryann's quick to say, shaking her head. "Let's go! We'll be done with rehearsals long before the race starts."

"Yeah, but ... you heard him. It's going to go into the morning hours. We need to rest. Big fundraiser and all."

Scowling at me, she finally cracks a grin. "Okay, old man, we will have literally all day to rest tomorrow."

When I say nothing, just give her a stare, she pokes me in the stomach. "Don't be a party pooper." She bats her eyelashes. "Besides, this is our honeymoon, *babe*. And the woman should be the one to choose what to do on the honeymoon, right?"

"Yeah, and how romantic will it be to spend it on the side of an abandon road, watching drag racing?" I deadpan.

I don't hate racing, but it's also not what I do in my spare time.

That's hockey.

I can tell Ryann really wants to go, and that alone is enough for me to say to hell with it and take her. Blowing out a breath, I rest my head back.

"All right. Fiiiiine. We'll go." Leaning toward her, I bring my lips to her ear. "What are you going to do for me though, wifey?"

She squirms at my touch, biting her lip.

Once I move away from her, she looks at Zoey. "You heard him; we're going racing! And, yes, you are so going too!"

"I am?" She widens her eyes.

My brother, being the charming bastard that he is gives her a grin. "Hell yeah, you are, Freckles."

She chews her bottom lip nervously. She's a cute girl, but it's clear she hasn't had much interaction with guys like Carson. Maybe none with guys at all actually.

"All right, so it's decided then." Ryann smiles. "We're going racing!"

"No, sis, I'm going racing. You're going to watch me do my thing." Carson winks, and Ryann rolls her eyes, but still smiles.

I chose Carson as my witness because I knew he wouldn't give me shit. He just flies by the seat of his pants through life, and he never gets wound up. Well, unless it's at the racetrack. But when my friends find out? Or my mother? Hell, even Jameson? Yeah, that won't go over so easy, I'm sure.

Even as I look at Ryann, thinking about the fact that she's now my wife … I don't feel like it was the wrong choice.

She deserves everything she's ever wanted. And if marrying her helps her get it, I'll gladly wear this ring.

Ryann

"Where are you off to?" Poppy asks when she sees me looking out the front window, waiting for Watson to pull in at any second.

Even though he didn't really want to go to his brother's race, he agreed to go for me. I've never seen anything like street racing, and I'm intrigued.

"Just out for a bit," I say just as Watson's truck pulls into the driveway and I reach for the doorknob.

Glancing out the window, Poppy gives me a sly smile. "Maybe you're not so annoyed with your dance partner these days, huh?"

"We're friends," I gripe. "See you later!" I close the door, not giving her a chance to say or ask anything else.

We all had dress rehearsal today, and it's hard to believe that after tomorrow, we won't be dancing with the hockey players anymore. I think I might miss it; we've had a lot of fun—even if some of it was pure torture.

I start toward his truck, and he waves. Even through the tinted windows, I can see him beaming at me. Just like he always does. And when I climb up into the truck, I suddenly feel bashful. Like I did at rehearsal earlier.

Even though the marriage isn't real, it still made everything between us shift. How could it not change our dynamic? It's hard not to look at the man as a martyr when he did such a selfless thing for me.

"Hey, wifey." He winks as I pull my seat belt on. "Ready for some drag racing?"

I nod, unable to stop the smile that spreads across my face. "I think so. Are we picking up Zoey?"

He cringes. "Uh … I think she's already with my brother." He glances over at me. "Sorry, looks like you're stuck with me alone tonight."

"Oh boy." I giggle.

But something inside of me flutters when I realize we'll be all alone. If we start to have sex randomly, how will the line dividing this marriage between a fake one and a real one not blur? I don't want it to blur. I need it to stay crisp and bold.

Putting the truck in reverse, he backs out of the driveway and speeds down the street. Even in the passenger seat, I inhale his scent. He always smells so dang yummy.

We might have danced together for the past however many weeks, hooked up in a closet, and gone out a few times as sort of friends, but we're still basically strangers. I don't know his favorite color or what his first pet's name was. Or if he even had pets, growing up. Maybe he's like me and never had the luxury of a furry friend. I don't know if he prefers dogs to cats or summer to winter. Heck, I only know his middle name is Matthew because the officiant said it during our ceremony.

I'm married to a man who seems perfect. But I don't know him. And he certainly doesn't know me. Not enough to do what he did.

After visiting Carson, his pit crew, and Zoey for a bit, Watson and I make our way to the fence and stand against it, waiting for the race to begin. I didn't want to leave Zoey, but Carson was pretty determined that she stay close by him and his crew tonight, and she didn't object. In fact, she seemed more than ok with it. I don't really know what to expect out of this night. A part of me is nervous. I've only ever seen races on short videos, never in person.

"Have you ever wanted to do this?" I ask him, turning my head toward him.

"Race?" He shakes his head. "Nah, no way. Being on the ice is more than enough adrenaline for me." He laughs. "My brother, he lives for this. Been like that his whole life. Even when he was a kid, nothing was ever fast enough for Carson."

"Is he your only sibling?" I blush. "How insane is it that we're married and I have to ask you that?"

"Totally normal," he says jokingly. "And, no, I have two brothers and a sister. Nora is the oldest. Then Jameson, Carson, and me."

"Aww, the baby," I coo, reaching up and giving his cheek a tiny pinch. "Baby Watty."

"Very funny," he drawls in that damn Southern accent that I've come to find some strange comfort in. "What about you? I know you have a little sister. Is it just the two of you?"

"As far as I know. Then again, neither of us knows our dad, and our mom trades boyfriends more than I hear the infamous Cade Huff used to trade women. So, the jury is still out," I attempt to joke, but quickly wonder why the heck I blurted that out. "But, yes, it's just Riley and me."

As soon as he opens his mouth to answer, the sound of engines roars through the air, making it impossible to talk. Moments later, two cars fly by us, and when I lean forward to see them cross the finish line, their parachutes come out.

"Care to make this night interesting, husband?" I wink.

"I'm listening," he drawls. "Whatcha got in mind?"

"I'm too broke to bet much. How about a dollar each race? We each pick who we think is going to win."

"If you don't want to bet money, we could bet something else." He shrugs. "Might make it more interesting."

My mouth hangs open. "Are you trying to make a sex exchange with me?"

"Maybe," he says casually. "Maybe you owe me a kiss every time I win?"

Though he says the words smoothly, I can tell he's worried that I'll be mad.

Quickly, he nudges me in the side lightly. "I'm just kidding. A dollar is fine."

Taking a breath, I tilt my head upward. "If I kiss you for every race you win, what do I get when I win?" I narrow my eyes, tapping my finger against my chin.

He leans his forearms against the fence and grins. "What do you want?"

"You have to take off an article of clothing every time I win," I say slyly and watch his eyes widen.

He brings his lips to my ear, and his deep voice is as smooth as butter. "You know, wifey, if you want me naked, all you have to do is ask."

Rolling my eyes, I elbow his stomach. "You wish." I shake my head.

Who wouldn't want to see Watson Gentry naked? It's like art. But beefy and delicious.

"And what if we choose the same one?" He raises an eyebrow. "You're not leaving me with the shitty cars, wifey."

"Fine then. How about this? On the ones where we choose the same car, no one wins."

"You're on." He tips his chin up, taking my bet. "You're going down though."

After the first two cars race down the track, the car I chose wins the first race, so he peels off his hoodie. I almost feel bad because it's a little chilly tonight. A part of me is bummed when my car wins because for some reason ... I'm ready for him to kiss me. But me being me, I can't just say that.

The next two rounds, we choose the same car, so no one wins. But when the fourth goes down and Watson's car wins, my heart races in anticipation.

"A bet is a bet," he says, completely amused.

Butterflies go wild inside my stomach as he steps back slowly, moving behind me. As he spins me around and backs me up to the fence, he puts one hand on my hip, and he cups my cheek with the other. When he dips his head closer, my eyes flutter shut as I wait for his lips to be on mine. My heart thunders in my ear, and even though other cars fly by us, all I can focus on is his presence.

His lips mold against mine. At first, he kisses me slowly and gently. But when I slip the tip of my tongue into his mouth, he kisses me harder before pulling my bottom lip between his teeth. Everything inside of me tingles, and I can't stop from moaning into his mouth.

Pulling his head back slightly, he looks down at me. "Not sure that counts since I kissed you. I think you were supposed to kiss me."

His eyes twinkle, but before he can step back, I push to my tiptoes and press my lips to his. My mouth attacks his, and I can't even try to play it cool. Every single fiber of my being is awakened, and my entire body shivers with pure need.

Pulling back, I gaze up at him. "There. Am I paid up now?"

Slowly, he nods, keeping his hand on my hip. "Yep. That'll do it."

When we hear more cars approaching the starting line, I spin toward the track and lean my body against the fence. And when he crowds behind me, I feel a bulge in his jeans press against my ass. I want to wiggle against it, but I refrain.

He points toward the starting line. Through a cloud of smoke due to burnouts, two cars roll toward the line. "That's Carson in the left lane," he says, his deep voice close to my ear, making my entire soul vibrate. "But ... he's racing Mila Hardy."

"A girl racer?" My mouth hangs open, and my eyes stay fixated on the black car. "Say no more. I'm going with her. She might suck for all I know, but she's still a badass in my eyes."

"Oh, she definitely doesn't suck. She beat Carson a few weeks ago in the finals. No one wants to draw her name when it comes time for chip draws because if you do, there's a pretty good chance your ass is done racing for the night."

"Well, shit. I sort of wish I said three articles of clothing for this one. Since it seems you'll be the one paying up," I say playfully.

As the cars rev their engines, waiting for go time, he cups his hands over my ears.

They go zooming by us, and it's such a close race that I don't even know who won. When he takes his hands from my ears, I crane my neck and look at him.

"Mila's and Carson's cars are really loud. I just didn't want your ears to hurt." He shrugs.

Before I can respond, the announcer comes over the speaker, informing us that Carson picked up the win, sending Mila Hardy home.

"Damn," he says, grinning ear to ear. "My brother just took out the best driver and the fastest car on the premises. Looks like he's in for one hell of a long night."

"Guess that means we're in for a long night, too, then. Right?" Turning slowly, I jerk my chin up at him. "And I guess I need to pay up, huh?"

"Honestly, if you kiss me like you just did, I'll have a hard time not wanting to fuck you right against this fence," he mutters. "I know you felt what you did to me, Tiny Dancer. My dick might actually fall off if I kiss you again. Or I'll wind up leaving this race and bringing you back to my truck."

"It's not like Carson will know if we left for a short time ... right?" I say the words shyly, but my voice is strangled and breathy.

His gaze darkens, and he dips his head lower. "Don't tease me if you don't mean it, Tiny Dancer."

I keep my eyes absorbed in his for a moment before ducking out of his hold. As I walk toward the parking lot, I look back at him with a teasing smirk.

Maybe I told myself we wouldn't hook up again. But let's be honest ... I can't stop it from happening.

WATSON

I didn't expect for our little bet to lead to this. But here we are, in the backseat of my truck, making out like sixteen-year-olds as Ryann straddles me, my aching cock pressing into her thigh.

I'm glad I parked away from all the other vehicles in the corner of the parking lot. When I did it, it was strictly so that no one smashed their door against mine. But I had no idea it would end up being the best decision I'd made all day.

She's topless, grinding on me, and her nipples are hard, begging for me to suck on them. I pull my lips from hers and lift her higher so that her tits are right in my face.

"You're so fucking perfect, baby," I growl before driving my head between them.

I run my tongue along her flesh before working my way to each one. Releasing each with a popping sound. She moans, wiggling around on my dick, being the needy little thing she is.

Climbing off of me, she sits on her knees in the seat next to mine. Unbuttoning my jeans, she pulls them down, along with my briefs, just far enough for my cock to spring free. Wasting no time at all, she bends forward, bringing my cock into her hot little mouth.

"Fuck. Yes," I bite out, my hand tangling in her hair and gripping tighter. "Be a good wife and suck your husband's cock." I guide her head down, feeling her throat flex as she takes me deeper. "That's it. Good girl. Take me. Take every inch."

With my free hand, I reach between her legs and push it down the front of her jeans. She's soaked. I guess deep-throating her husband turns her on.

As I work a finger and then two in and out of her, she moans against my dick and stops sucking me abruptly.

"If you stop sucking my cock, I won't let you come on my fingers, Tiny Dancer," I growl, stopping my fingers from moving.

Quickly, she drags me back inside of her, letting me slide against her wet tongue.

"Good girl," I grunt before I start working my fingers inside of her again. "Such. A. Good. Fucking. Girl."

My left hand works faster in and out of her while my right hand grips her hair as she bobs up and down, moaning every now and then, making it hard for me not to blow my load right now.

When I feel her start to grip my fingers and her mouth momentarily stops moving, I thrust my hips up and down, fucking her mouth as she comes on my hand.

"That's it, baby. Give it to me just like I'm going to give it to you."

My balls tingle, and soon, I'm pouring myself down her throat. My entire body shudders, just like hers.

Throwing my head back on the seat, I squeeze my eyes shut because I'm damn near blacking out.

When I finally come to, I grin over at her. "Goddamn, wifey. You trying to kill me?"

She simply shrugs, smirking as she wipes her mouth. "Maybe. What's your life insurance policy like?" She winks. "Kidding. Kidding."

Pulling my jeans back on, I suck in a few breaths, my chest heaving.

I'm now not only addicted to Ryann. I'm addicted to her lips wrapped around my cock too.

18

Ryann

Watson and I stand behind the curtain, my hand in his as we wait for it to be our turn. My heart's pumping like crazy, and when I look over at him, I can tell he's nervous. Which is something I've never seen when he's on the ice.

We haven't talked about last night, though every time I think about it, my body feels jittery. Something about doing what we did, in an open parking lot, where people could see us … so freaking hot.

Squeezing his hand in mine, I smile. "You're going to do great. Time to show 'em what you got, Gentry." I wink just before the music comes on and the curtain rolls up.

Morgan Wallen's smooth voice floats through the air as his new version of "Spin You Around" plays, and we start to dance. It's such a beautiful tune with the perfect melody for our performance, though I'm pretty sure we're the only pair dancing to a country song.

Unlike Cade and Poppy's song, ours is much more romantic. Just like Sutton and Hunter's is going to be. It isn't a bad thing. But this dance, well, it's our first dance as husband and wife.

The first time we're dancing as newlyweds, and it's for a fundraiser in front of thousands of people. All of whom don't even know we're married.

He looks so handsome tonight. And even though he's a big, brooding hockey player, he's absolutely killing his performance. I might have initially complained when I learned I had to work with a puck boy, but it's obvious Watson can master any skill he sets his mind to.

For the next few minutes, my entire body feels like it's floating in the clouds. We move seamlessly across the stage, and his eyes remain on mine for the entire thing. And when the song comes to an end, I twirl into his arms, and he holds me before dipping me down. The curtain is closed when his lips hover over mine. He's so close. All I'd have to do is move my head an inch upward, and our lips would touch.

It's like a magnetic force is pulling me toward him. And I so badly want to stop fighting it and just kiss him. After all, he is my husband, for God's sake.

Jolene's loud clapping brings us both back to reality, and he slowly pulls me to stand straight up.

My legs are shaky, and I don't know if it's from the performance or from Watson's lips being so close to mine.

"Good job," I whisper, my palm patting his chest. "Proud of you, Gentry."

"Thanks, *Mrs. Gentry*." He grins before taking my hand and leading me off the stage.

Watson

What started as a really good night ended up being awful. Shortly after Hunter and Sutton's performance, she collapsed. It turns out, she has asthma and had a severe attack that landed her in the hospital.

Ryann is pale as a ghost, her makeup now smudged all over her face from crying. She's scared. That girl is her best friend.

She sits in the waiting room chair, her legs tucked under her with my Brooks hoodie on. I could tell she was freezing in her leotard thing, and I couldn't stand the sight of her shivering, so I grabbed my sweatshirt from my truck and put it on her.

I throw my arm around her and pull her toward me, thankful that we are sitting on one of those chair benches rather than a regular chair, where there would be an armrest between us. She melts against me, tucking herself into my side, and I hear her sniffle.

"Hey," I whisper, looking down at her. "She's going to be okay, I promise."

She nods slowly, but the tears only flow more. Burying her face into my side, she shakes. There's nothing I can do to make this better. Her best friend is unconscious, being kept alive by machines, while we all wait out here to see what is going to happen. All I can do is hold her and tell her it's going to be all right.

Even if I don't know if it really is going to be all right. And our marriage is fake, but I still want to do my part as her husband and somehow take her pain away. Maybe she didn't mean those vows, but I did.

It's been hours since we got here, and I'll sit here as long as Ryann wants to. But I hope I can get her to go home and at least try to get some rest at some point. She'll need it.

Ryann

I'm so tired, but my mind just won't shut off. Yet my body, well, the thing is completely done for. I suppose a performance like the one Watson and I did and then watching your best friend's body go lifeless in front of you will do that though. I know I need to sleep, but I can't leave. She hasn't woken up yet.

I remain snuggled against Watson. He feels so good. Too good really. I mean, are fake husbands really supposed to feel this cozy? I think not.

"Hey," Watson mutters against the top of my head. "I think it would be good for you to go home, just for a little while. I promise, as soon as she wakes up, someone will call us. I'll make sure of it."

I shake my head gently. "No, I can't leave." My voice cuts out, my throat burning with every word that comes from my lips. "What if ..." I stop, sucking in a breath.

"What if she doesn't wake up?" he says, finishing my sentence. "She will, Ryann. She's strong."

"You don't know that," I croak out. "No one knows that."

"Look at me," his deep voice says. And when I don't look at him, he repeats his words. "Ryann, look at me. Please."

Craning my neck, I look up at him, my vision blurry from the tears.

His hand cups my cheek. "You know your friend better than anyone. Do you think Sutton is going to give up without a fight?" He gives me the smallest smile. "Because, from what I hear, she's a pretty tough, badass chick. After all, her last name is Savage."

I sniffle. "She is."

"But when she does wake up, she won't want her best friend looking like a zombie, sitting next to her. Or smelling like an unwashed ass," he whispers. "Let me drive you home. Or back to my place even. And you can get a few hours of sleep, take a shower, get some food, and then I'll bring you back after."

His eyes stare into my soul, like he's promising me it's all going to be okay without saying the words. And for the craziest unknown reason, I believe him. Instantly feeling like maybe, just maybe, it really is going to be all right.

"Okay," I whisper and slowly stand up.

And this time, it's me who reaches for his hand.

I wake from a deep sleep, but my eyes refuse to open. I have no idea where I am, what time it is—hell, I don't even know what day it is. All I know is, I feel like I could go back to sleep and stay asleep for ten days.

I wonder what Sutton's plans are for today. The thought barely crosses my mind when my eyes fly open and I shoot up in bed.

"Shit. Shit. Shit," I curse, rubbing the sleep from my eyes.

When my hand drops down, making contact with a rock-hard abdomen, I quickly remember where I am.

Watson's house. In his bed. With him.

And apparently, he's shirtless.

I reach for my phone, my eyes bugging out when I see the time. It's eleven in the morning. We got here at three a.m., and I never anticipated I'd sleep an hour. Let alone eight.

I open my messages, finding only a single one from Lana, telling me she just left the hospital and there's no change. Sutton is in a coma and hasn't woken up. My stomach drops. Each minute she doesn't wake up probably reduces the chances she ever will.

I look over at Watson. His head is turned to the side. The light flooding through the window dances across his face, showing off his stubble. His sharp jawline is just another annoyingly perfect characteristic of his. Something that makes him even more stupid hot.

His body is completely chiseled, and even though it's probably rude, I openly stare. He's my husband. I'm allowed to check out my husband, right?

I know that every time we kiss or hook up, it only complicates things more. It'll make it harder to sign those divorce papers. Which is inevitable. How could it not be when we only got married to save my ass? But, on the other hand, the night in the backseat of his truck … it felt so good. It felt right.

Honestly, nothing about it felt wrong.

When he starts to stir, I quickly scooch my body out of the bed and grab my sneakers from the floor. After pulling them onto my feet, I attempt to smooth my hair down, which is completely useless.

"Morning," he drawls before yawning.

I glance over my shoulder, and even though I hate myself for it, I can't stop the stupid grin that spreads across my face just from seeing his sleepy smile. A sight I could surely get used to. "Morning."

"Were you able to get some rest?" he asks softly.

I nod weakly. "I was."

"Good. I'll jump in the shower, and then we'll grab some breakfast." He looks at the time. "Scratch that. Lunch. I can't eat breakfast past nine a.m."

"I should go back to the—" I start to say, but he cuts me off.

"I know you want to go back to the hospital. And I don't blame you. But you haven't eaten anything since before our performance, and as your husband, it's my duty to make sure you don't wither away to nothing."

"I'll never wither away to nothing." I laugh. "Have you seen my ass?"

"Yeah, I have. And thank God for that. If it did, the world would be a less beautiful place." He winks. "For real. Fake husband or not, I can appreciate a nice ass."

That only makes me laugh harder, but there's something about the interaction that also makes me feel warm inside. It shouldn't. There's nothing real between us, but I can't help but feel *something*.

"I need to shower and change my clothes." I look down at the baggie T-shirt and huge sweatpants he let me borrow last night. "I look like I'm about to mug someone."

"Hey, you know what?" he says, jumping up and walking toward a small closet. "I got these for my mom the other day, but I haven't seen her to give them to her. Take them, Tiny Dancer." He holds out a pair of black joggers with *Wolves* written down one leg.

"No, no," I say, quickly shaking my head. "I don't want to take your mom's gift." I can't help but laugh, snorting a little bit. "I love that you bought your mother sweatpants."

"What can I say? I love my mom. And she loves Wolves gear." He holds them closer to me. "Take them, Ryann. I'll grab her another pair sometime."

When he widens his eyes, I know he's not going to give up, so I take them from him. "Thank you, Watson. I feel like all I've been doing is thanking you lately. You're too nice to me."

"My dad lived by the motto, *Happy wife, happy life*," he tosses back. "Then again, he sure pissed my mom off a lot. He loved to buy old cars he'd claim he was going to restore, but we all knew he never would." He shakes his head. "Loved bringing home stray animals too. Just another thing she said made her mad, but deep down, she loved all the pitiful animals he lugged home."

I could listen to him talk about his father for hours. There's so much love there. Same with when he speaks about his mother.

"It sounds like he was a pretty cool man." I smile. I want to say more. I want to tell him I'm sorry and that he must miss him so much. But since I suck at feelings and talking about them in general, I don't. "And your mom, she sounds amazing."

"He was." He nods. "And, yeah, she sure is," he says as he heads toward his dresser. Reaching around, he pulls out a sweatshirt and tosses it to me. "This is way too small for me. I've had it since I was fifteen. My parents brought me here to a hockey game, and by the end of it, I was so obsessed with the team that I made them stop at the gift shop before we left that night. It's a little worn out, and it'll be a little big, sure. But it'll work."

"Are you sure you want me to have it?" I whisper, truly touched that he's offering it to me. "I mean ... if you've kept it this long, it must mean something to you."

"I'm sure. What kind of husband would I be if I didn't make sure my wife was warm? Besides, it'll look better on you anyway." He grins.

"Thank you." I chew the inside of my cheek. "What was your first pet? I mean, I know your dad brought home strays and all." I blurt the words out.

By the look on his face, I instantly know he's confused, but even so, he answers, "Muffin. She was a yellow Lab. We got her when I was two." His eyes crinkle at the sides a little as he smiles. "Why?"

"I was just curious, I guess. I don't know. I suppose I thought it was something a married couple should know about each other. That's all."

"True." He nods. "Well then, what was your first pet?"

"I've never had one," I say with a shrug. "I did pretend I had a pet for all of fourth grade though. In my head, I'd make-believe I had a French bulldog. I've always wanted one since I was a kid."

"Maybe one day, you will have one." He smiles.

I avert my eyes to look around his room and not at him. Last night, I was too exhausted to do anything besides crash on his bed, so I didn't investigate much.

It's neat in here. Too neat, considering I'm a whole mess most of the time. I let my laundry pile up until I'm down to a few articles of clothing. A few framed pictures are scattered on his desk. One of him, Carson, and another guy I assume is Jameson because of how much he looks like the other two. And another of him, the two boys, a girl, and two adults who must be his parents.

I pick it up, not thinking. "This must be your family?"

Coming next to me, he nods. "Yep. Me, my sister, my brothers, and my mom and dad." He elbows me lightly. "Or should I say, your in-laws?"

My eyes grow wide as I set the frame down. "Wow. Really weird when you put it like that." I exhale. "So, what is your mom like? And your dad … what was he like?"

Plopping down at the edge of his bed, he watches me as I continue scanning his room. In an attempt to learn more about the man I married.

"My mom is the sweetest person you could ever meet. Until you cross her family." He cringes while chuckling. "And then, wow, mama bear mode activated." He shakes his head. "But she loves candles, reading, and her two cats, Waldo and Rocket. And my dad, he was the toughest dude I'd ever met. But when it came to my mom, he was the biggest softy."

Suddenly, he pushes himself up off the bed. "I'll get the shower running for you. Sometimes, it takes a minute for the water to heat up."

Swallowing hoarsely, I follow behind him, holding tightly on to the clothes he gave me. When he heads into the bathroom, I stop in the doorway, pressing my back to the frame while he brings the shower to life. After a moment, he sticks his hand in before pulling it out and walking toward me.

"It's warm." He stops, standing in the doorway, facing me. His body is so close that my nerves begin buzzing.

There's this … tension between us that I'm sure we both feel. And when his eyes float down to my lips, I feel my heart racing, and I swear I hear my blood pumping in my ears.

"Watson," I whisper, barely hearing myself.

"Yeah?" he mutters, his eyes hooded.

I stand a little taller, brushing my lips against his. His hand goes to the back of my neck, gripping me at the nape as our mouths continue to collide. I'm just about to reach for his sweatpants when a loud voice stops me.

"Yo, Watson, you home?" the deep voice calls from downstairs.

"Cade," Watson mumbles, cringing. "I'd better go see what he needs."

He stays where he is, only making my heart beat faster.

"Okay," I breathe out, nodding.

Slowly, he backs away and heads down the stairs. And when he's out of sight, I close the door and rest my head against it.

Once again, I couldn't stop myself from wanting more.

Watson

I sit across from Ryann at the café just off campus. Less than an hour ago, Cade unknowingly cockblocked me. From the way she gazed up at me before her lips grazed against mine, I could tell she was thinking the same filthy thoughts I was.

"I can't believe you don't like breakfast past nine a.m." She shakes her head at me. "You'll never know the joy of driving with your friends in the afternoon to a place that serves breakfast all day and stuffing your face with pancakes."

As soon as the words leave her lips, the waitress is at our table. She has to be in her mid- to late-thirties, and she has a little too much eyeliner on. "Ryann, I'm guessing you want your usual?"

I look at Ryann, wondering how the waitress knows her name or knows what she wants to eat.

"Yes, ma'am." Ryann smiles. "I'll do a coffee with some milk too. I feel like I've been hit by a truck." She looks around. "Is Zoey working?"

"Nah, she's off today." She finishes jotting down the order before her eyes move to mine. "And what about you, handsome? What can I get you?"

I look at Ryann and wince. "I'm kind of nervous about this, but … I'll get Ryann's usual." I pause, my lips turning up. "Even though I know it's likely from the breakfast menu."

"Hell yeah, it is," Ryann chimes. "Only the best meal ever. Right, Mal?"

"If you say so." Mal shrugs, completely unimpressed. "And to drink?"

"I'll do everything exactly the same as Ryann," I tell her, and she slowly walks away.

"So, I'm guessing Zoey works here?" I ask. "And since you have a regular order, you must come here a lot?"

Mal returns and sets our coffees down, passing us each a little cup of milk before walking off again.

"Yeah, she's worked here for a while. I used to work here too. That's how I met Zoey." She reaches for the container of sugar packets; she pulls out a few and rips them open. "I actually loved working here."

"If you loved it, why did you stop?" I ask.

I hate the fact that she strips for a living now, but it isn't like I can ask her to quit her job. That would make me a controlling prick. And just from things she's said, I know she doesn't want to be controlled. I'm scared to even voice how I feel about her employment at Peaches. I know how many teammates go there, and it makes me fucking fume inside.

"I wasn't making enough money here," she says evenly. "And when I was approached to work at Peaches, I jumped on it." She sighs. "Then again, this place never found out my visa wasn't real. Guess I should have just stayed here, huh?"

"Does it bother you?" I blurt the words out before I have time to even stop myself. "Dancing in front of people you don't know? Knowing they are turned on, watching your body move?" I swallow, cringing. "Because I'll be honest, Ryann. I really, *really* hate it."

She continues to twirl a spoon mindlessly in her coffee, looking down at it before glancing back to me. "When you come from what I did, a job is a job. I can separate the negative aspects of it and understand I'm doing it just to provide for myself. Well, myself and to help Riley."

"Do you send money back home to her?"

"I try to," she says softly. "The biggest thing was getting her a phone. And now that she has that, I feel a bit better, being so far away. She can call or text me if she needs anything."

"What's she like?"

"Nerdy." She laughs. "She loves science. She's way smarter than I will ever be. She even got invited to take part in a science fair at a university."

"Wow, that's awesome." I can sense that it's hard for her to be away from her sister. "Are you going to it?"

"The science fair? I wish." She frowns. "No, I mean, I'd love to, but crossing the border wouldn't exactly be a good idea right now. But I'm going to send her flowers. That'll make her smile."

"Speaking of crossing the border and all that, when do you think you'll hear something about this whole green card stuff?" I shift around. "How's it work? Does someone just show up at your house or something?"

"No idea," she says with a shrug. "From what my boss said, the man who did the audit was extremely nice and told her the office is quite backed up. So, it might take weeks before anyone reaches out to me." She swallows. "Which is good, I guess. Because they said our marriage paperwork would take a few days to process."

"You know, we're going to have to tell people the truth, right?" I give her an amused look. "You'll have to admit you married my sorry ass to more than just Zoey."

"Oh, yeah? Why's that?" she says playfully. "Maybe you're my dirty little secret."

"Because once your immigration officer—or whatever they are called—finds out you're now married to a good little boy from Alabama, they'll want proof that it's not a sham." I wink. "Guess you're going to have to learn to like me, huh?"

She sighs, tilting her head to the side. "Watson, I do like you. You make it sound like I'm a grumpy bitch who hates your guts. If that were the case, I don't think we would have done what we did in the backseat of your truck, would we?"

"All right, let me rephrase that. You have to like me enough to act like we're married in public and continue to let me make you come." I shrug. "Think you can do that?"

Her cheeks turn red just as the sun comes out from behind the clouds and shines through the café window, illuminating her entire face.

Fuck, my wife is gorgeous.

"I think I can handle it," she says, chewing her lip.

I know right away she's got some dirty thoughts running through her head. I hope she does anyway. I think about reaching under the table and brushing my hand across her knee, but the waitress appears with a shit ton of plates on her tray. Slowly, she sets them down on our table, and my eyes bug out of my head at the amount of food.

"Breakfast for lunch," I mutter, staring at the pancakes, bacon, and home fries sprawled out in front of me.

"Breakfast for lunch," she singsongs, nodding her head before grabbing a fork. "Look at us, doing married couple things." She winks. "Better go get that front porch swing and adopt a dog named Wilson."

"Wilson?" I frown.

She shrugs. "I don't know. Sounds domesticated."

I look at her and eventually laugh. I know as soon as we finish eating, she'll be ready to go back to the hospital to check how Sutton is doing. But until then, I'm just going to soak in getting to know her.

And I guess I kind of like the feeling that she needs me right now. I could get used to that.

19

Watson

My happy bubble of me and Ryann getting along and actually acting sort of like a couple is over. This day has been a fucking disaster, and I'm ready for it to end.

A few days ago, we learned that Cade had been struggling with addiction. And even though I'd had my suspicions, it was a whole different story. I wish my intuition had been wrong. Unfortunately, all the signs I had seen but turned a blind eye to were right all along.

A few hours ago, his parents came here and took him to rehab, and he wouldn't even say good-bye to any of us. I guess I can't blame him. We're the ones who told Coach that we were worried.

And then, to add on to the chaos, minutes after he left, Haley blurted out that she's pregnant with his baby.

Yeah, it's been a weird fucking day.

For hours, Haley didn't come out of her room after dropping that bomb and running in there. I needed her to know I was here for her because I couldn't imagine what she was going through. Or how scared she must be.

I hadn't even known she and Cade were into each other. Then again … Cade's into everyone. At least he was before she moved in with us.

Yep, I'm an idiot for missing the signs.

So, just when things were looking better because Sutton was recovered and out of the hospital, this shit happened with Cade. Putting everything back into chaos.

When I couldn't stand the thought of Haley alone in her room anymore, I finally knocked on the door to check on her before going into her room. And then something happened. Something I hadn't expected. I told her that Ryann and I were married. I just left out the details of what had led to us getting married.

I guess I knew I could trust her not to tell anyone. Not like I want to keep it a secret anyway.

We've been married for a few weeks now, but because she's been practicing for her next performance and I've been so busy with school and hockey, we've only hung out a few times. And I think that's just her way of covering her bases in case we need to prove that we actually have spent some time together. I can tell that, deep down, she's trying to still keep me at arm's length. Which really, really sucks.

Now that I've told Haley, I feel like I have to tell Hunter. But not until I talk to Ryann first. After all, Hunter is dating Ryann's best friend. I need to make sure she's okay with people knowing. And I want to apologize for telling Haley before asking if it was all right. We're in this together. I can't go making decisions like when to let the cat out of the bag on my own. Especially since trusting people is so hard for her. I don't want to give her any reason to believe I'm not her safe space.

Pulling out my phone, I bring up her contact. But before I type a message, I remember she told me yesterday that she's working the afternoon shift and gets out at ten tonight.

Guess I'm going to Peaches.

I've been here one other time, and even though it's probably an unpopular opinion for a dude to say, it's just not my scene. I think it's badass she took a job she doesn't love just to provide for herself and her sister, but I'll be honest … I fucking hate that she works here. But it's not my place to decide what she does with her body. Even if I wish it were.

And even if I wish my eyes were the only ones looking at it.

It's nine forty-five, and even though she's almost out of work, I head inside and take a seat at the bar. My eyes search the different stages, looking for where she might be. It doesn't take me long to find her, and when my gaze lands on my wife, a jolt goes straight to my dick, and that fucker is rock hard within seconds.

Then, I remember how many others are probably watching her, feeling the same way. It would be hard not to when she's pure perfection. Absolutely the fucking sexiest creature on this planet. I grind my back teeth together, feeling my blood boil as I glance around at the others looking her way.

"Porn Star Dancing" by My Darkest Days blares through the club. There's a dozen or so other dancers, but everyone but her disappears. Her strawberry-blonde hair is in wild curls. And the black thong and nearly sheer bra she's wearing don't leave much to the imagination. I shift in my seat as my dick strains against my zipper.

Every now and then, she moves wrong, and I swear her body tenses up, like something is hurting her. But she recovers so quickly that I can't tell for sure.

Her legs part as she slides to the floor before moving back up. I look down the bar, and every set of eyes is on her.

My fucking wife.

Ryann

"Porn Star Dancing" comes to an end, and "Good for You" by Selena Gomez begins. This is my last five minutes of my shift. I'm in the homestretch now.

My sciatic nerve is screaming. I've had trouble with it since I was thirteen, when dancing became more of a way of life than a hobby. A few days ago, in dance practice, I pulled something, bringing it to agony yet again. After ice and lots of Motrin the past few days, I thought I was fine. But about twenty minutes ago, it started acting up again. Which is the absolute worst timing because *The Nutcracker* isn't that far away now, and I have a huge part in it.

Like a zombie on autopilot, I go through the motions to show the customers in here what they came to Peaches for. Mentally, I'm checked out. I'm tired, and my leg hurts. But it's been pretty busy tonight, so at least I'm making some cash to numb the pain.

When the song comes to an end and I read ten o'clock on the wall, I sigh in relief. Walking toward the exit, I whimper as pain shoots from my asscheek to down my leg. Grabbing my leg with one hand, I push the door open with the other.

"Ryann," a deep voice yells from behind me, and when I turn, I see Watson standing behind Hudson, who is blocking him from coming in through the door.

"Hey, let him through." I continue rubbing my leg, hoping the pain will subside.

"You know him?" Hudson barks over his shoulder.

"She's my fucking wife, asshole. And she's in pain," Watson growls. "Let me through."

My mouth hangs open, as I'm shocked by the words Watson just blurted out. Hudson cranes his neck to glance at me, giving me a look that's asking if this dude is crazy or if I'm actually married.

Nodding slowly, I blow out a breath. "Yes, Hudson. It's fine. Let him through."

He looks not only unsure, but pissed off too. I have to hand it to Watson; not many people stand up to Hudson. He's too intimidating. Hudson glares at him for a moment but finally steps to the side. But not before grabbing Watson's arm.

"Call me asshole again, and your teeth will meet the pavement outside," he growls.

"Keep me from my wife again, and I'll break your fucking arms off." Watson shrugs, and I'm shocked when Hudson doesn't lay him out right here.

Watson rushes toward me, putting his hands on my sides. "You're hurt."

I breathe out a laugh, trying to cover my wince. "Calm down, big guy. I'm fine." I pat my leg. "Just my sciatic nerve—that's all. It's bothered me forever; it comes and goes."

Unconvinced, he looks me up and down before scooping me up.

"What in the world are you doing?" I scowl. "Put me down."

"Where're your things? I'll take you home. We can come get your car tomorrow."

"In there." I point to the vacant changing room. "I don't have my car. It wouldn't start."

Walking into the room, he kicks the door shut, locking it behind him. "So, what? Were you going to walk home?" He glares at me. "Please say you weren't going to fucking walk home this late at night, alone, Ryann." His eyes darken. "Because that would make me really, really mad."

"No," I deadpan. "I was going to hitchhike." When his face turns as red as a tomato, I laugh, poking his stomach. "I'm kidding. One of the girls told me if I needed a ride, she'd give me one. Calm your pickle."

Speaking of pickles, I can feel his dick pressing into the side of my hip. As if realizing it, he shifts around.

"Ooh, did Watson Gentry get a chub from watching the dancers tonight?" I tease him as he sets me down on the plush chaise lounge.

The sweet look that usually rests on his face is gone. Leaving behind that primal, crazy look, like the one I saw in the supply closet that day.

"I only saw one of them, Tiny Dancer. And, yeah, that one made my dick really fucking hard."

"Tina's boobs were only covered with pasties. And those things are as perky as they are huge. So, that must be who put you in this"—I gaze down at the bulge in his jeans—"position."

"If by position you mean what made my cock hard as stone … it was my wife." His gaze sweeps over me. "Just being honest."

"Yeah … right," I squeak.

He kneels down before me, and his hand splays against where the pain was shooting from just moments ago. Yet, now, it's slowly fading away.

"Ryann, I don't give a fuck if Tina's tits were in my face and she was begging for me to take my cock out and fuck them. I'd still be looking at you." He gently massages my leg. "How the fuck would I not look at you?" He growls the words. "But I hate the fact that every motherfucker out there was looking at you too. Looking at *my* wife."

I suck in a breath. Breathless from his touch. My brain feels fuzzy as his hand works against my skin.

"Don't," I whisper. "We can't do that now." I clear my throat. "We shouldn't do it at all. It will just complicate things. More than they already are."

"Do what?" he rasps, his pupils growing bigger. "You mean, I can't bury my cock between your legs? Or feel you dripping down my thighs?" His fingertips glide higher. "Why not, Tiny Dancer? I can feel the heat radiating from between your legs."

"Because … it will make things weird between us. You know, when it comes time to … end this."

My words seem to hurt him, but he regains his smooth composure right away.

"You know, baby, until we're divorced, the only cock you're allowed to fuck is mine. The only tongue allowed to lick your pussy is mine. And the only dick you're allowed to suck is mine."

My body turns to jelly, and he continues to massage my leg.

"Does this hurt?" he mutters, and I shake my head, which makes him widen his eyes. "Don't lie."

My body trembles, and everything inside of me aches. "It hurts a little. But it also feels kind of nice."

"I'd love to fuck you right now, Ryann. And my cock is begging to be inside of you, letting you soak me because I know you're so fucking wet." He leans forward, pressing his lips to my forehead. "But you're hurting. And we can't have that. You have your performance coming up."

Standing, he looks around the room until his eyes land on the lockers. "Which one is yours?"

"Number thirteen," I say and start to stand.

"Stay there. I'll get your clothes," his deep voice commands me, and for whatever reason, I listen.

Opening the unlocked locker, he grabs my bag and brings it to me. One at a time, he pulls my high heels off, setting them to the side. His eyes stay on mine, his pupils huge. I'm a prisoner of his touch, unable to move, talk, or even think.

Reaching inside the bag, he takes my leggings out and brings them to my feet. Slowly pulling them onto my ankles and up my legs. Reaching around me, he tugs me forward onto my feet. As he yanks them over my ass, his fingertips glide over my asscheeks, and I swear I moan.

Leaning down, he finds my oversize crewneck sweatshirt in my bag, and he pulls it out. "Arms up," he whispers.

Even though I'm fully capable of dressing myself, I play along because there's something so comforting about him taking care of me.

Pulling the sweatshirt over me, he untucks my hair and brushes it away from my face. Grabbing my sandals from the bag, he pushes me back to sitting and puts them on my feet before running his fingertips up my ankles, under my leggings. Goose bumps cover my body, and every part of me aches for him.

When he's finished, he takes my high heels to my locker, closing it behind him. Returning to me, he looks down, his eyes hooded.

"Ready?" he croaks, his voice tortured.

"Yeah," I say—or I try to. But the word barely squeaks out.

When he holds his hand out, I take it and stand. I don't want to just take his hand. I want his hands all over me. I need him so badly right now. But instead, I settle for a kiss on my forehead before I follow him out the door.

Unsure of what the night holds.

Ten minutes later, we pull in front of the building that houses a swimming pool used for the Brooks University swim team, as well as a gym, I think. The dancers don't use this building for our workouts. Instead, we use a smaller one that's located on the opposite side of campus.

"Working out tonight?" I give him a look, scrunching my nose up. "I don't know if you saw me back there, but I've done my workout for the day. It's called working the pole."

"There's a pretty nice hot tub in there," he says, holding his key card up. "And this place should be vacant this time of night."

Soaking in a hot tub sounds so nice right now, but I frown. "I don't have my suit with me."

Pushing his door open, he grins. "Live a little, wifey. Wear that thong and bra. It'll make things more interesting."

I glance down, knowing what I'm wearing under this oversize sweatshirt, and I cringe. "Watson … I just got done with my shift at Peaches. You saw my bra and underwear. They literally show my nipples and my entire ass. What if someone walks in?"

"They won't," he assures me. "I've come here enough on nights when my back is bothering me to know that after nine, this place is a ghost town. Besides, where the hot tub is in the building, we'll be able to see out the window if anyone pulls in. Bring a towel out on the pool deck just in case."

"I don't have a towel!" I whine. "This is a terrible idea."

"They have them in there. Now, would you get your ass out already?" He hops out.

Slowly, I do the same, unsure if this is even a good idea. But the thought of relaxing in a spa with the jets going is too good to turn down. Especially with the way my body feels.

"If we get busted, I'm blaming you!" I say, chasing after him and tucking my arm around his. "What if there's a janitor and he sees my ass and nips?!"

"Then, he'll die a happy man." He shrugs, grinning down at me before we reach the door and I unhook myself from him. Pulling it open, he nods. "Ladies first."

Walking inside, I gaze around at the ginormous pool. "Holy shit. This is nuts."

Stepping inside and letting the door close behind him, he looks around. "I'm surprised you've never been here before. The spa and workout room are for athletes only. And you're on the dance team."

"I don't think we rank as high as the hockey and football team," I grumble. "Or the swimmers, apparently."

Reaching down, he bops his finger on my nose and winks. "Well, my wife can come here anytime she pleases. I'll give you my spare key card."

Stepping around me, he walks to the corner of the room. Reaching inside a bin, he grabs two blue towels. As he walks toward a dim corner of the building, I follow behind and see a large spa. Wasting no time, he pulls his hoodie and shirt over his head, leaving him in his jeans only. And my mouth waters as I take him in as he kicks off his shoes and socks.

"Like what you see, Tiny Dancer?" He smirks before unbuttoning his jeans and pulling them down, leaving him only in his briefs.

My brain turns to mush.

As he struts toward me, I let my eyes rake over every single inch of his muscled body. My knees feel weak. But the good news is, the pain in my leg seemingly disappears.

My fake husband looks good enough to eat. And I kind of want a taste.

Stopping inches from me, he reaches for the hem of my sweatshirt. But when his eyes narrow on the front, he scowls. "How the fuck did I not notice this at Peaches?" he growls. "You're wearing a Brooks football sweatshirt? For real?"

I bite my lip nervously. It was a gift from Denton back when we were dating. And it's not like I have boatloads of clothes in my closet. So, I'm not about to throw away a perfectly good sweatshirt just because my douche of an ex gave me it. It's still in good shape.

I shrug. "Yeah. Why? It isn't like it has Wells on the back or something."

"It's a good fucking thing too."

He takes the center of the hem and pulls. After a few seconds, it tears, and he continues ripping it until the front is completely torn. He pushes it off my shoulders, and as it falls to the floor, he looks satisfied.

"That belongs in the fucking trash," he grumbles. "Denton's a fucking loser, Ryann. Don't wear his shit. Not while you're my wife."

My mouth hangs open, and I stomp my foot. "Watson! What the hell?! Now, what am I going to wear home?"

"*My* shirt, Tiny Dancer. Because I'm your fucking husband."

When he kneels, pulling my shoes off, my head grows fuzzy. After he rolls my leggings off me, he sets them to the side. But not before leaning forward and pressing a kiss to my thigh and gazing up at me.

"You're too beautiful to wear Denton's shirt, Ryann. He wasn't worthy of you then. He certainly isn't now."

Slowly standing up, he turns away from me and steps into the spa. The steam rolls from it and into the air, clouding the vision of him. And seconds later, I'm right behind, climbing in a spot on the opposite side. Because if I get too close to my husband, I'm going to end up jumping his bones. Which would be good and all, but this is a public place.

We sit in silence, the tension between us so thick that it's hard to breathe. I wonder if he feels it too. There's no way he doesn't. Especially when it feels like my entire body is on fire.

A person can only hold so much willpower inside of them before they give in to temptation. Watson is my temptation.

Right now … my husband is what I want.

WATSON

Fuck. The way Ryann's tits are practically begging me to play with them is making my dick so hard that even in this hot tub, I can't relax. I reach down to adjust myself, and it doesn't help a bit. The things this woman does to me, it's unreal.

I want her so badly that it's all I can think about. I was so close to fucking her at Peaches, but I didn't want to do it there. The next time we have sex, it'll be our first time as a married couple. It should be special. It should be perfect.

Then again, I'm so desperate to have her pussy wrapped around my greedy cock that I don't know if I can wait. Especially when I know she wants it just as badly. It's not hard to tell with the way her body shook when I peeled her leggings down. Or how her nipples pebbled when I undressed her. I wanted nothing more than to bury my face between her legs and let her soak my tongue. But somehow, I got myself together and didn't eat her like a cupcake.

"You're so far away," I drawl slowly, looking at her through the steam. "I'm lonely over here without you."

"Then, what's stopping you, Gentry?" she coos, her eyes glimmering with mischief.

Swimming toward her, I stop just before I reach her legs. Reaching for her thighs, I swallow. "How's your leg feeling?"

"Surprisingly better." Her voice is raspier than usual, and gradually, she puts her hands over mine.

Moving my palms upward, I stop when my fingertips are touching the sides of her asscheeks. Leaning forward, I bring my lips to hers and kiss her.

She doesn't hesitate at all. Her mouth is desperate for mine, and I slip my tongue inside. Like the greedy girl she is, she sucks it into her mouth, and fuck if that doesn't make me imagine her sucking on my cock too.

I part her legs and brush my hand between them. Pushing her thong to the side, I slip one finger and then two inside, pumping them in and out slowly at first, working faster as my thumb circles her clit.

"Watson," she cries, a strangled moan.

"My baby is so fucking needy," I growl against her lips before removing my hand and bringing her to the edge of her seat. The head of my cock brushes the soaked fabric of her thong, begging to be inside of her.

"You're so fucking hot, Ryann," I snarl against her lips. "Jesus Christ, you make my cock so hard."

I look above her, and a sly smile takes over my face when I see a small hook on the wall. Unclasping her bra, I reach for her hands and tangle the bra around them like a makeshift restraint. I pull the fabric tighter, keeping her wrists together snugly. "Hands up, baby."

She puts her hands above her head, and I waste no time hooking the fabric to the small metal hook, keeping her arms straight up.

"I'm going to fuck you, and you're going to keep your arms just like that," I murmur against her neck. "And if you make a sound ... I'll have to punish you."

At my words, a soft, strangled moan leaves her lips, and I tilt my head to the side.

"Strike one, baby. If I didn't know better, I'd think you wanted to be punished." Reaching between her legs, I yank her thong down, tossing it on the floor.

Grabbing her thighs, I pull her legs around my waist. All at once, I plunge inside of her. And when I begin thrusting in and out of her, she tips her head back, her breathing growing heavy, and she moans louder.

"Bad girl," I growl. "I see what you're doing. Making noise, just hoping to be punished. Well, baby, what I should have said was, I'll punish you by not letting you come. I'll get you really, really close, and then before your pussy has a chance to clench around my cock, I'll pull out." I lean forward, biting down on her shoulder. "So, Ry baby, are you going to be quiet? Are you going to be allowed to get off on my dick or not?"

Sluggishly, she nods, not breathing a sound.

"Good," I mutter before I grip her hips and thrust in and out of her again.

She bites down on her lower lip so hard that I'm shocked I don't see blood dripping from her pretty mouth.

The water sloshes around as I fuck her over and over again, knowing we're both on the edge of letting go. And she stays quiet, never making a sound.

Of course, I wouldn't let her *not* come. But she doesn't need to know that.

"Someone can swim in my cum tomorrow, Ry baby. I don't give a fuck. I'm going to come inside my wife's sweet fucking pussy and fill you so fucking full. Reminding you that you fucking belong to me."

Gripping the back of her head with one hand, I push our mouths together just as I feel her squeeze around me. She doesn't full-on moan, but she squeaks a little as she drags in a breath.

Our rocking becomes slower and our kisses messier as we both drag in shaky breaths. As her eyes flutter open, I reach above her head and untie her hands. But not before kissing her one last time.

"Good girl," I breathe out. "Now, let's soak this leg of yours. Seeing as I probably just made it worse."

She smirks up at me, her makeup smudged and her hair a mess.

"You're kind of hot when you act all dominant." She splashes me lightly. "Just a tad."

"Yeah? Well, trust me, that's just a glimpse, baby," I say seriously.

Because to be honest, there are so many more things I want to do to this girl. And I will.

I pull in front of Ryann's house, and she instantly unbuckles her seat belt, but doesn't get out right away. And I'm thankful for it too. Because I'm not ready to say good-bye to her for the night.

"I need to get something off my chest. It's been really bothering me," she says softly. "I know I said before I was sorry for acting like a bitch. But I really owe you an apology. I judged you just because you're a jock, and that wasn't fair." She turns to face me, tilting her head slightly. "Guess I need to learn that not everyone is like my crazy, cheating ex." She tenses. "Or my mom's piece-of-shit exes."

Reaching over, I brush a wet strand of hair away from her face. When I do, her head leans against my hand, making me cup her cheek. It's a small gesture, but to me, it means everything. It means that maybe she is learning to trust me.

"It's all right. But I am curious about that. How long did y'all date?"

"Too long," she utters. "Six months."

"Was he always so … controlling?" My fist curls up as I think about how he was talking to and about her. "If you don't mind me asking."

"For the first month or so, no. Not at all. But then, he just got super jealous. And he always thought I was cheating on him. Or he'd accuse me of flirting with his friends." She sighs. "It's crazy, you know; when I was growing up, my mom was always bringing home these awful men. Some were just complete losers. Some used her. And others, well, they knocked her around." Her hands stay folded together in her lap. "As bad as it sounds, I've always thought of her as a stupid woman for putting up with what she did. Turns out, I'm like her." Her eyes widen as she sees the look on my face. "Denton never hit me or anything. He was just very, very controlling." She tries to lighten the mood with a laugh. "And a complete toolbag."

I relax a little, but I know he sure as hell emotionally abused her. Thanks to him and her mother's stellar life choices, she feels like she won't ever fully trust me. Or anyone for that matter. I didn't really get it before. I was frustrated that she had this wall up, never letting me so much as chip away at it. Now, I understand. Her wall keeps her safe.

I don't care if she has her heart locked up like Alcatraz; I'm getting through.

As if needing to change the subject, she waves her hand. "What about you? Any crazy exes who are going to be coming for me now that I'm your wife and all?"

"Nah," I say with a shake of my head. "I've only had one serious girlfriend. Rosie. And that was back in high school."

"What happened with her?"

"She was going to college in Cali, and I was coming here." I shrug. "She said I could follow her to Cali or we'd break up."

"And here you are," she whispers.

"And here I am." I nod. "Brooks has been my dream school since I came here that first time for that hockey game as a kid. If I'd followed her to California, I would have resented her for making me choose."

"Did you ... love her?" She looks down for a second before moving her eyes back to mine.

"I don't know," I tell her honestly. "I guess I've never known how to tell when you love someone. All I know is, when my mom walked into a room, my dad's entire face would light up. He'd do anything to make her happy. And if my mom had made him choose between her and his dream, he would have chosen my mom. She was his dream." I swallow. "So, even if I loved Rosie, I didn't love her enough. Because when it came time to choose between Cali or Brooks, I didn't flinch."

"What your parents had sounds beautiful. Like ... a fairy tale." She smiles. "I'm sure you'll find that one day. Because you, Watson Gentry, will make your real wife very happy when it happens." Reaching for the door, she pushes it open. "Thanks for everything tonight. The orgasm. The Dr. Phil chat. All of it. I, uh ... I actually had the best time. And my leg feels pretty good."

As she hops down, I reach into my backseat and grab something. "Ryann."

"Yeah?"

Tossing her the jersey with my last name and number on the back of it, I wink. "We have our next game in a few days. And while I love having you in the stands, I expect my wife to wear my number on her back."

Catching it, she holds it up across her front. "I guess that would make sense, huh?" She looks down at my sweatshirt she's now wearing. "Oh shit. I forgot I had this on. Since, you know, you ruined my other one and all. I'll wash it and give it back to you tomorrow."

"Nah, you keep it." I wink. "Just don't say I never gave you anything. Oh, and please, for the love of all things, don't ever wear any clothing with Brooks football on it again. Deal?"

"Pfft. Never gave me anything? So far, you've given me a necklace, a ring, two sweatshirts—one which was very sentimental—a pair of joggers, and a jersey." She looks thoughtful. "Did I forget anything?"

"The orgasms." I nod. "You forgot the orgasms."

"Ahh … yes. Debatably the most important part." She laughs before it dies in her throat. "Wait, if I'm wearing your jersey … should I, uh … tell Sutton? I feel like she'll think it's strange if I show up, wearing this with no explanation."

I grimace. I was so caught up in wanting her that I forgot the entire reason for needing to see her tonight. To tell her that I told Haley about us. After we hooked up in the hot tub, I told her about Cade and how upset I was. But I failed to mention my talk with Haley. She needs to know.

Pushing my own door open, I jog around to where she's standing by the passenger side.

Stepping back, she closes the door and looks up at me. "What's going on?"

"Don't be mad. But … I sort of told Haley that we got married." I cringe. "I'm really sorry. She was just having a hard time with Cade being sent away to rehab. They have some … things going on between them. Things I'll tell you all about when I can. But when I went to see her after, she was so upset, and I guess I just blurted it out." I stare down at her, her back pressed to the truck. "How mad are you?"

Slowly, she gives me a soft smile. "I'm not mad, Watson. Thank you for telling me the truth." One hand holds my jersey while the other floats to my abdomen. "As for Sutton, Hunter, and everyone else, I'd say it's time to pull the Band-Aid off and tell them the truth." She winces. "Well, not the entire truth. But just the *we got married* truth."

Bending down, I press a kiss to her forehead before pulling back. "Sounds good. So, I can expect to see you tomorrow night"—I jerk my chin toward the jersey—"wearing that?"

"And if I don't?" she coos. "Will I be punished?"

"I'd say yes, but I think you'd like that too much," I grumble, already feeling a jolt go to my cock. "So, how about if you do wear it, I'll punish you? Since you seem to be into that."

Licking her lips, she takes a few small steps toward the house. "Night, Watson."

"Night, beautiful," I drawl.

She steps onto the stairs and heads inside. But not before she turns back to give me a smile one last time.

And I think about that smile the whole fucking ride home and when I lie down to go to bed.

20

WATSON

"I still don't get it," Hunter says from in front of me. "You're actually, legally, really, like ... married?" He stops. "Like ... for real, real married?"

"Yep. That's what I told you. Five times now," I mutter as we head into the arena. "Not sure why you can't wrap your mind around it."

"Cade is having a baby. With my sister. You're someone's husband. No, my girlfriend's best friend's husband." He huffs. "Everything is changing."

I hit him on the shoulder. "Sorry, Thompson. But I promise, if we'd had a big wedding, the flower girl position would have been yours. You probably would have had to fight Cade for it. But y'all would have been cute in your white dresses and shit." I jerk my chin toward the ice. "Go warm up and leave me alone, would ya? We've got a game to win."

"Yeah, yeah." He rolls his eyes. "This conversation isn't over though."

He skates away, and I look up to where Ryann is seated next to Sutton. It's good to see Hunter's fake-girlfriend-turned-real-girlfriend back in the stands after she was in the hospital for so long.

Hunter's relationship with Sutton started off as fake, and now, I see how happy they are. Maybe that can happen for Ryann and me too. She definitely doesn't hate me. I just don't know where she stands right now. And that scares me.

If only she wasn't so damn stubborn.

But the other night, in the back room at Peaches and then at the hot tub ... something between us shifted. Well, I guess something inside her shifted.

I've wanted her since I saw her in class for the first time. But she's finally catching up to me.

And it's about fucking time.

I can't help the stupid-ass grin that spreads across my entire face like a moron when I see her in my jersey. And when she smiles at me, before spinning around to show me the back, my heart does some crazy squeezy thing, and my knees feel weird. Which would be fine, but we're minutes away from game time. I need to get it together.

When she turns back around to face me, she blows me a kiss. And I wish I knew if she did it for show, in case someone was watching, or if she did it just for me.

I'm falling in love with my wife. And I know that wasn't part of her plan.

Ryann

"I could literally punch you right now. I'm so mad," Sutton growls. "Who drops a bomb like this at a hockey game? I mean, are you trying to give me another asthma attack? Because, if so, I'll send your ass my medical bills."

I wince. I know this wasn't the right time to tell her about the wedding, but after Watson and I talked last night, we decided we needed to. I'm going to need proof that I actually married Watson for the right reasons—even if that's bullshit. And time is of the essence. Besides, I couldn't keep it from her anymore. It was eating me up inside, and I felt like a terrible friend.

"I'm sorry," I grumble before side-hugging her because it's all our seats will allow us to do. "Forgive me? It just happened so fast."

Being the feisty chick that she is, she shoves me off of her. "Why did it happen so fast, huh? I don't get it. Are you pregnant? Jesus, what is in the water? Remind me to stop drinking it."

"No, I'm not pregnant, I swear," I grumble.

She narrows her eyes to slits. "Something fishy is going on here, and I don't like it. Not one bit." She turns toward the ice before spinning back toward me. "And how'd you get married without witnesses?"

This makes me squirm even more. "Um … we did have witnesses."

Her mouth hangs open. "What?! Who?"

"You remember my friend Zoey, who I used to work with?" I gulp. "And Watson's brother Carson."

"Zoey. The girl who you only hang out with once every few months. She got to be there instead of me? Your best friend." She shakes her head in disapproval. "You're a bitch."

"I know," I whisper. "I'm sorry."

"I don't forgive you," she sasses, ignoring me for a moment. "I will. Maybe. But not right now."

"Okay," I say, nodding. "I understand."

The game starts, and only five minutes later, she's stealing my popcorn and asking for my Sour Patch Kids. Smiling, I gladly hand them over, just happy that she's talking to me at all. I found a friendship in her that I'd really never had before. I love that girl.

I can't tear my eyes from Watson. There he is, completely in his element, blocking shots and dominating as goalie. Handling the pressure like it's absolutely nothing.

I've watched his games before. But now that we're closer, I'm noticing more. Admiring more.

And maybe liking him more too.

Watson

Ryann sits on a bench by the exit, legs crossed, looking at her phone. Her eyebrows pull together as she scrolls mindlessly. Just the sight of her in my jersey gives me a dirty image in my head—me behind her, plowing inside of her while she wears nothing but my jersey. And that alone is making me desperate to steal her away to a restroom or closet right now.

"Hey," I say, stopping just before her.

The stupid-ass grin returns even though I try to play it cool when I'm around her. She turns me into one goofy motherfucker.

Quickly standing, she slides her phone into her back pocket. "Hi to you." She beams. "Great game. Congrats on another win."

"Thanks." I nod toward her body. "Nice jersey. I'll admit, I'm a little jealous of it though."

She looks down, confused. "Why?"

"Because it gets to hang off your body like that."

I wink, and she looks up, throwing her head back.

"Dear Lord, that was cheesy." She rolls her eyes. "Very. Very. Cheesy."

"Maybe that's how I am as a husband. An extra-cheesy one." I shrug. "Chicks dig it. I've seen enough Hallmark shit to know that much."

"*You* watch Hallmark?" She laughs. "Just when I think I'm getting to know you, you throw me a curveball like that."

"Mom likes Hallmark. My brothers were always too cool to watch with her once my sister moved out. Turns out, they aren't all *that* bad. Predictable, but not bad." Holding my hand out, I wonder if she'll even take it or if she regrets hooking up the other night. "Come on, wifey. Let's go celebrate the win."

She surprises me and grabs it instantly. I pull her toward me, kissing her forehead.

We might have won on the ice tonight, and that felt damn good. But this, right now … makes it feel even better.

I'm winning my wife over. And soon, she'll get the idea of divorcing me right out of her head. For good.

Ryann

We dance, and it doesn't even seem weird. I no longer feel like he's a stranger. In fact, I'm completely relaxed in the arms of this man.

I always think that people are hiding their true selves behind a pretty face and a sweet smile. But with Watson, I've learned that what you see is what you get. He's just a good-hearted person. And that's hard to come by.

Deep down, I don't know if I'll ever gain citizenship with my criminal history. Yeah, I was a kid when I stole those things, and I was barely a teenager when I defended my mother from that creep. But it's something that will never go away. It will always be on my record. And because of that, I'm scared this is all for nothing.

What if Watson ruined his first time getting married to save me when it won't make a difference anyway? Guilt strikes me deep in my gut. He's a wonderful man. And I'm using him.

And what if I fall for him, the way I know I'm going to, and then I get shipped back to Canada? Clearly, he's stuck here. He has a spot secured in the NHL.

In an attempt to quiet my own thoughts, I rest my head against his chest, and it feels so natural. And real. Like we didn't commit a major crime. Like I'm not dragging him into my mess to save my own ass.

"Cat got your tongue, Tiny Dancer?" he murmurs against my ear. "You're awfully quiet tonight."

"Somebody's Problem" by Morgan Wallen plays softly at Club 83. To my left, I see Sutton and Hunter dancing. She stares up at him, a certain twinkle in her eye as he talks. And he grins down, holding her like his whole life depends on keeping her safe.

A love so big that it could withstand any storm.

My best friend is so happy. And that makes me incredibly glad. If anyone deserves it, it's her.

"I'm good," I say, looking up at him. "Just tired. It's not easy, you know, being the wife of the infamous Watson Gentry."

It takes him a second, but eventually, he smiles, nodding his head. "Yeah, I suppose it isn't."

"Hey, have you heard anything from Cade?"

His face grows strained. But like always, he tries to hide it. "He can't have any contact with the outside world for the first two weeks of being there." He pauses, like he isn't sure if he should say the rest or not. "Withdrawals can be pretty bad, I guess. And it's part of the rehab's protocol. But honestly, it's probably for the best. If he talked to any of us, it'd likely just make him want to come home that much more, I'm sure. And he's right where he needs to be. Even though it fucking sucks."

"I'm sorry, Watson. I know you're worried about him."

"Thanks. I am. But he'll be home before we know it, and he'll be back to the Cade we all love." He cringes. "The past few months, he wasn't himself. I should have talked to him sooner, but what the fuck do you say in that situation? Like … *Hey, I think you seem high. I'm scared. Maybe you should go to rehab.*" He frowns, shaking his head. "Onto something less depressing … are you busy tomorrow?"

"I just have practice for *The Nutcracker* early in the morning. I'll be done by nine thirty," I say quickly, wanting to spend time with him. "Are you asking me to hang out with you, Gentry?"

"I have something up my sleeve." He winks. "I have to review some game tape first thing in the morning, but that won't take long. After that … I'm free until the following afternoon for practice. I thought … maybe we could sneak away for the night."

"Oh … like, an overnight trip?" I swallow, feeling butterflies going wild in my stomach.

"I still haven't taken you on a honeymoon," he says, half-joking. "Maybe this can count? Until, that is, we take off for a week to somewhere with a white sand beach."

I tense up. He has plans. Big plans. Me? I'm trying to just sort out the fact that we hooked up. Again. And that, if he wanted to, I'd have sex with him right now.

"Ryann, it'll be fun, I promise," he adds, giving me a slight squeeze. "But no pressure if you aren't comfortable going. We can always just do something during the day."

"I'd love to go away with you overnight." I nod. "Sounds fun."

"Hell yes. Let's do it then." He leans down, murmuring against my hair, "Hey, when is this *Nutcracker* show?"

Panic sears through me. Not because of the actual show. But because he's asking about it. If he's asking, he might be thinking about going. Dancing with him was one thing. Dancing in front of him? A whole different story. There's going to be hundreds of people at this show. Yet I'm only scared of messing up in front of Watson.

"It's in a little over a week," I squawk. "Why?"

"Because I want to get my ticket, obviously," he deadpans. "What's your role in it?" He pauses. "Did I say that right? Part? Or ... position? No, that's not it."

"The Sugar Plum Fairy." I chew my lip. "You really don't have to come to it though. It's a long show. You'd be bored."

"Bullshit. Of course I'm coming to support my wife." He scoffs. "I don't know much about this *Nutcracker* business, but I know that role is important."

I smile proudly. Poppy and I have the two biggest roles in the show. Her as Clara and me as the Sugar Plum Fairy. It's not like it's the most important performance I'll ever have. But growing up, I always performed as a background dancer at my town's local *Nutcracker*. This time, I get to be the main person.

Aside from Watson and Sutton, I don't have anyone coming to watch me. But I consider myself lucky to have them because, growing up, whenever I starred in anything, I was that kid who had no one in the stands.

"If you really don't want me there, I won't come," he says, forcing me to look up at him by cupping my cheek. "But I'd really love to watch you do your thing."

"I'm just ..." I stop, looking down as my cheeks heat with embarrassment.

"Hey. Talk to me." He dips his forehead to mine. "Please."

My eyes meet his. "I'm just not used to having anyone there watch me. You know, like solely watching *me*. Sure, I've been in a lot of plays and dances, but I've never had anyone—besides Riley a few times—focus their attention on me." I swallow. "I'll probably mess up."

He slides his hand to my hairline. "Tiny Dancer, you could make even messing up look beautiful. I promise you that." He presses his lips to my forehead. "But something tells me you won't mess up at all. They didn't choose you for that part for no reason. And I'd really, *really* like to see my wife be the star of the show. If it's all right with you, that is."

Inhaling a shaky breath, I let it out before nodding against him. "All right. I'd … I'd love to have you there." Pulling back, I point my finger at him. "But if I mess up or fall on my face, don't you dare laugh."

"If I make you nervous enough to fall on your face, I can't promise anything." He grins down at me.

"You do not make me nervous." I roll my eyes. "It's just … I—"

Sliding his hand into my hair, he kisses me, shutting me up right then. Because we both know he does make me nervous.

And when he pulls me closer to him as our mouths collide, I swear, all is right in the world.

This man is too good for me.

He's too good for a fake marriage and a half-assed wife.

But maybe this marriage … isn't so fake after all. It sure doesn't feel fake. And my feelings, they are real.

Just like moving pieces on a chessboard, things can change in the blink of an eye. It seems that might be what's happening here when it comes to my marriage.

WATSON

"I've never gotten to be a tourist before," Ryann says, gazing around at the streets of Savannah. "I mean, I guess I technically am a tourist, but I've never gotten to go exploring for the day and play the part." She beams up at me, talking a zillion words a minute. "I am so excited. Are you excited?"

"I've actually never been to Savannah before, but I've always wanted to come here." I hold my phone up, showing her all the things I booked for us to do. "I might have gotten a little excited when you said yes to coming away with me, and then I stayed up till two in the morning, watching YouTube videos on the best things to do in the area." My lips form a line. "I'm a nerd like that. I watch videos, and I read reviews. Don't judge me."

She gives me a look, and the panic inside of me sets in. I know that, sometimes, I probably do too much. I've been an overachiever my entire life. And when it comes to her, I'm more than okay with that title.

Before I can apologize for being overkill, she throws her arms around me and buries her face into my shirt. "Watson Gentry, you are truly the best husband a girl could ask for." Pulling back, she looks up at me. "I mean that."

"When I'm married to you, it's not hard. Trust me." I wink before pointing toward our first destination. "Let's go. We're burning daylight."

As she turns slowly, I slap her ass and then give it a little squeeze, making her yelp.

She might roll her eyes like she's annoyed, but the pink in her cheeks tells me otherwise.

I'll be slapping her ass a lot more times tonight. And a lot harder.

Ryann

It almost doesn't feel real. This day. How can it be real when it's been so flawless? Like something out of a fairy tale that happens to princesses in beautiful gowns with the sweetest, softest souls. Not ones like me. Things like this don't happen to girls like me.

But maybe ... they could? I mean, they *are*.

He's made this day perfect. Our first stop was a riverboat ride, followed by a crazy scavenger hunt, where I thought I might actually pee my pants from laughing so hard, and then we stuffed our faces with the most delicious cupcakes.

I've made up my mind ... this is the best day ever.

As we walk hand in hand down the cobblestones that make up River Street, I pull my jacket tighter around myself. It's far from the cold weather, like December in Canada, but now that the sun has gone down, it's cool enough to chill my bones a bit and make my body shiver. And yet I still don't want this night to end.

Gazing up at the buildings, I find myself in awe at the beauty of them. Some look so old yet have held their integrity and truly make this entire street the astonishing place that it is. I could definitely see myself coming back here to visit again.

We walk along until we find a bench near a coffee cart. And once I plop myself down, he walks over to it before returning with a single cup and handing it to me.

"What's this?" I smile, taking it from him. "And where's yours?"

"You know I don't drink that coffee shit that you are so obsessed with." He shrugs before sitting down next to me. "I've heard you order coffee before so I just tried to order that as close as I could. If it sucks, I'm sorry, and please don't spit it out on me."

I bring the cup to my lips, taking a sip of the hot liquid. And even though it's far from my usual back at the coffee shop at Brooks, coffee is coffee. Besides, Watson thoughtfully got it for me.

Leaning back a little, he smirks. "Drink up, Tiny Dancer. You're going to need your energy tonight."

My heart beats faster, and my cheeks heat. I'm already dying from anticipation. I've wanted his hands on my body all day. But I'm glad we spent the day doing real couple things besides just taking our clothes off.

Even though taking our clothes off sounds really fun right about now.

I look at him, and this feeling of comfort washes over me. Like I'm exactly where I'm supposed to be. And where I'm supposed to be is with him.

My husband.

This wasn't supposed to be a forever thing. And the man I was so determined not to care about, I'm falling for.

Scratch that. I've already fallen.

Hard.

"Sweet digs." I whistle, looking around the room. "This is the best fake honeymoon I've ever had."

"Better be the *only* fake honeymoon you've ever had, Tiny Dancer." He stalks toward me, pulling me toward him and kissing me roughly.

Goddamn, he always smells so good. It's like … make you dizzy while making you feel at home with a side of melt your panties off and make you clench your thighs together.

Yeah, that kind of good.

When he tickles me, I giggle, attempting to shove him away.

"Stop! I hate being tickled more than basically anything else in the world," I squeal. "I'm begging you. Cut it out! I'll get grouchy if you don't stop!"

Thank God that after a few more seconds of torturing me, he stops.

This day has been one of the greatest of my life. And not a thing about it felt fake. In fact, I don't know if I've ever felt something so real before.

Watson Gentry is a man straight from the sweetest rom-com. One that makes you feel all warm and gooey inside, like a freshly baked cookie that you can't help but devour. And then, like a light switch, he's a filthy-talking, orgasm-delivering hotshot.

Long ago, the world turned me to stone. And that was good because stone isn't easily broken. But now … I'm slowly crumbling. My insides weakening with every kiss, touch, and kind gesture from this man. And I'm scared that in no time, I'll be nothing but a pile of dust at his feet.

But tonight, I'm not thinking about any of that. Tonight, I'm going to treat this as if it were a real honeymoon. And I'm going to feel my husband's body against mine and show him how much I appreciate everything he's done for me. Or try my damnedest to at least. I don't know if I could ever repay him for the memories we've made today.

I back up a few steps away from him before I slowly glide my fingers to my chest and unzip my jacket, tossing it onto the floor.

His expression grows serious. A familiar hunger swirling inside of his eyes as they remain solely on my body.

This place could catch on fire right now, and I'm convinced it would still be just us. Him and me. And this burning feeling inside of me, making me feel more alive than I've ever felt.

Next, I grab the hem of my shirt and peel it over my head before chucking it to the side. Hearing him hiss, I bite my bottom lip shyly, eager to hear that sound again. The sound that means he likes what he sees. Reaching down, I unbutton my jeans and tug them off, along with my socks. Once I'm only in my blue bra and thong, I slowly stride past him, heading into the bathroom, but not before giving him a small smirk over my shoulder before removing those last two scraps of clothing.

Reaching into the shower, I turn the water on in the astonishingly large walk-in shower and wait for it to get warm.

Stepping into the spray, I let the water pelt against my body. I push my hair away from my face, and when I hear him step into the shower behind me, I don't have time to turn around before his erection is poking against my ass.

"Did you have this planned all day, Ry baby?" he coos against my ear, the stubble of his jaw tickling my flesh. "Just waiting to get me alone so that you could have my cock all to yourself?"

When he runs his tongue down my neck before biting down, I moan, "Yes."

My nipples harden, straining as the water sprays over my body.

Sliding his hands around me, he cups my breasts, grinding his length into my asscheek harder.

"Tell me, Ryann, what do you want?" He pushes my hair to the side and kisses my shoulder. "I'll only give you what you ask me for."

Though my mind is telling me not to say the words, they come out before I can stop myself as I crane my neck around and look back at him. "To be all yours for the night." I hardly recognize my breathy voice. "I'll take whatever you give me."

"Fuck," he groans.

Biting down on his lip, he wraps his hand around his dick. Stroking himself a few times, he spins my body to face him.

"Do you know what good little sluts do?" he growls against my lips. "They get on their hands and knees, and they suck their husband's cock."

Though I don't need his guidance, seeing as I'm already eagerly moving to my knees, he places his hand on my shoulder and shoves me down anyway. And something about that action only drives the monster inside of me madder, so desperately wanting to pleasure this man.

"What I'll give you, Ry baby, is a mouthful of my cum down your throat." He guides his length between my lips before grabbing a fistful of my hair. "You look thirsty, baby. Is that what you want? A mouthful of me?"

I don't answer, but instead, I lean forward and take more of him into my mouth. But it's too much, too quickly. And like an amateur, I gag. Only, instead of being nice and letting me recover, he jerks his hips forward, driving himself further down my throat.

"Good girl. You're taking me so well, baby," he groans. "And when you gag on me? When your throat threatens to close because it's so full of my cock that your body can't take it? That makes me want to fucking come right then. To come and listen to you choke on it."

He feels smooth against my tongue, and I stare up at him, taking him deeper and longer during each pass. Slapping his free hand on the tiles of the shower behind me, he closes his eyes for a second, and he groans.

"Fuuuck," he hisses, along with a slew of other curse words. "It's like your mouth was made just to suck cock." His eyes open again, and he glares down at me. "No, fuck that. These lips were made only to suck on your *husband's* cock. Do you understand me?"

I rear my head back before circling the tip of him with my tongue.

Pulling my hair back, he grits his teeth. "I said, do you understand?" he barks. "When you said *I do*, baby, you were also saying this was the only cock allowed between these plump lips—you know that, right?" He tightens his grip on my hair, forcing my head upward.

Before I answer, I attempt to go deeper. But he pulls me back, driving his length out of my mouth.

"Answer me, Ry baby," he hisses through gritted teeth before pulling me to my feet and cupping my neck. "Whose cock are you allowed to fuck?"

"Only yours," I moan.

I might hate the idea of being controlled in everyday life, but when it comes to this, right here, I crave his caveman like tendencies. Maybe that's not healthy; maybe that's weird. I don't care. When he talks to me like that, I know he's doing it more for my pleasure than anything else. And I eat it up.

"Yeah, that's right." Pulling me to my feet, he reaches between my legs and sinks his fingers inside of me.

As he pumps them in and out, I'm weak in the knees. I grind myself against his hand harder, desperate for him.

Removing his hand from my body, he brings his fingers to his mouth and runs his tongue along them. "The best fucking flavor there is. And soaking wet all from sucking my dick?" He groans. "I promise you, baby, you can have my cock any day, anytime. All you have to do is ask. So, tell me, what do you want now? Or better yet, what do you need?"

Moving his hand between my legs again, he cups me. "Are you throbbing for me right here, Tiny Dancer? Just aching with need?"

"Yes," I whimper. "So much."

Snaking his hands around my waist, he lifts me up. My legs instantly wrap around his body as he pushes my back against the glass of the shower door. He brings me back down, pushing himself inside of me all at once, and I cry out in both pleasure and pain. Yet even when it hurts, I still don't want him to stop.

His mouth is on mine, and his hands are all over me as he moves me up and down on his length. Every time he brings my body down onto his, I press harder against the glass, wondering if it's about to shatter from the impact.

Everything tingles as my orgasm hits. I pull my lips from his, throwing my head back. Moaning, I bite my own lip just as he buries his face against my breasts. His body twitches, and his movements slow.

My brain feels fuzzy, and I squeeze my eyes shut to stop myself from passing out.

Once my soul has returned to my own body, I open my eyes and look at him.

"I hope you don't think that's all for tonight." He kisses me. "We sure as hell aren't going to sleep, Tiny Dancer. I've been waiting to do that all day." He drags in a few shaky breaths. "I've been waiting all day to bury my cock inside of my wife on our honeymoon."

Letting me down gently, he gives me one final kiss before spinning me around.

And then he does something I didn't think any man would ever do for me.

He shampoos and conditions my hair.

Watson

On the couch in front of the fireplace in our suite, Ryann's naked body is draped over mine with a blanket over us. Her ear is against my chest, and we lie here in comfortable silence as I strum my fingertips along the flesh of her bare back.

The thought that this marriage might come to an end eventually is tearing me up inside. That isn't what I want. Not even a little bit. But the deeper we get into this, the more it crosses my mind.

"I had so much fun today." She yawns, turning to gaze up at me. Her face is free of any makeup, and her hair is still damp and a complete mess. But, fuck, she's so pretty. "I don't want to go back in the morning."

"Me neither," I agree. "Wish we could stay here for longer. But we'll come back sometime for sure."

"And do one of those ghost tours?" She smiles. "I actually think that would be kind of fun. I love creepy stuff like that."

"I hate anything to do with ghosts. But for you? Yeah, sign me up," I say honestly. Because let's be real; if she said jump, I'd say, *How high?* It's pathetic, but it's the truth. "Did you tell anyone where we are?"

"Just Sutton. I wanted to tell my sister. And to send her some pictures of our day today because … well, she and I never got days like this, growing up." She stops. "And … I don't know. I don't want her to think I'm over here, living my best life. I don't want her to feel like I've forgotten about her because I haven't." Her voice grows more strained. "I worry about her all the time. But we text daily—a lot since she's a typical teenage girl." She snickers lightly. "Anyway, I'm rambling. What about you? Did you tell anyone?"

"Just Hunter," I murmur. "And I'm sure he told Haley since she lives with us."

"Gotcha. So …" she whispers, patting her hand against my chest. "When do you plan to tell your mom about our arrangement? Or … are you going to keep it from her until …" She stops, and I'm so fucking glad because I don't want to hear the words about us getting an annulment or some shit like that coming from her mouth.

But then she opens her pretty lips again. "Until we, you know … split up or whatever?" She swallows. "I wouldn't blame you if you don't want to tell her, you know. It'll probably just upset her. No point in breaking your mom's heart for nothing."

I try to form some sort of a thought without freaking the fuck out over what she just said. My body tenses, and my jaw tics.

"That what you want, Ryann?" I mutter. "After the hot tub the other night and dancing last night after my game and this trip, that's what your plan is? To just, what, split up?"

She doesn't move. Just continues to have her cheek pressed against my body. "I don't know what the plan is anymore, Watson," she croaks. "I'm so confused now."

Scooching up, I pull her upward so that she's straddling me. "Well, I'm not confused, Ryann. I want you. I want this." I reach up, cupping her cheek and pushing her hair away from her face. "We don't need to stage a breakup. Why can't we just live happily ever after? What would be so wrong with that?"

Tears well in her eyes. "I don't know. I just ... you'll get sick of me. I know it." She looks downward. "And you know, eventually, once I get a real job, my sister will come over here and need a guardian." She gives me a sad look. "Would you really want a wife who had to take care of her teenage sister?" She cringes. "I don't think so, Watson."

"I wouldn't give a fuck if you had ten siblings. Fuck, twenty, and I still wouldn't care." I growl. "Ryann, I can't spell it out for you any more than I already have. I want you. I've *always* wanted you." I stop, dragging in a breath. "And guess what. I think you feel the same way."

"Who wouldn't want you, Watson?" she cries, trying to get off of me but I hold her down. "You're literally perfect."

"Trust me, I'm not perfect." I pull her closer, gripping the back of her neck softly. "I can promise you that."

"You are. And I'm a mess."

After more effort, she grips one of the blankets to her chest and stands up. I can't help but sit up straight, panicked that she's going to do what she always does. Freeze up. Push me away. Run off.

"Watson, you walk around, acting like you won some grand prize when you married me. But do you know why I had to fake my own visa?" She wipes her eyes with the back of her hand, and the fire lights up her tear-soaked cheeks. "It's because I have a criminal history that prevented me from just going out and getting myself one." She gives me a harsh look. "Do you really think your mother will want her precious, sweet, successful baby boy to be with a stripper with a criminal record?" She shakes her head before collapsing onto the plush chair. "Fuck no. Why would she? You're amazing. And kind. And *good*." She signals to herself. "And I'm just me. I don't even know who that is."

Standing up, I walk toward her, sinking to my knees before her. "We can figure it all out, Ryann. I'm sure whatever you did wasn't so bad that you can't get your visa."

"I stole from a local convenient store," she whispers, and I sigh in relief.

"Baby, that's not a big deal." I reach up, brushing my fingers on her chin. "Do you know how many kids do that at some point in their childhood? I mean, Carson stole a fucking soda once because my mom told him he couldn't have it."

"I wasn't a five-year-old who wanted a sugar-filled soda, Watson. I was nearly a teenager," she snaps, but her voice is more embarrassed than it is angry. "And if that wasn't enough to seal my fate, you know what was? When I almost killed a police officer by hitting him in the head." Her eyes float to mine, and her lips form a line. "It didn't matter that he was beating up my mom. Or that he mentioned my sister and I were going to be next. I panicked.

I didn't want him to touch Riley. But none of that matters because even when I told the truth to the police, it was his word against mine back then. And back where I'm from? My word, it's not worth much."

"Don't push me away just because you're scared." I put my palms on her legs. "I hate when you do that."

"And I hate when you try to act like this whole situation is normal," she bites back. "I hate when you look at me like I'm this amazing human being when I'm not." She sits forward, eyebrows pulling together. "And I really, really hate when you pretend like everything is going to be fine!"

"It's better than what you're doing, isn't it?" I snap. "It's better than looking on the fucking dark side all the damn time."

"The dark side is all I've ever had," she hisses through gritted teeth. "You wouldn't know that because you're used to a mom who bakes and gives you fucking cookies and milk before bed."

Standing abruptly, she heads toward her pile of clothes on the floor and attempts to reach for them. But before she can, I pick her up, tossing her over my shoulder.

"Put me down!" she screams.

"Why? So you can run off?" I growl, tightening my grip on her body. "Fuck that. I don't think so."

"I need to clear my head! I need to get out of this room and away from you." She kicks and swats me. "Because I can't think when I'm near you, Watson! I can't think! Or breathe or do anything!"

I drop her down onto the bed, falling right along with her. My nose touching hers, I glare into her eyes. "I fucking want you, Ryann. Okay? Stop fighting me. Stop trying to find a reason to sabotage this. Just let yourself be happy, for fuck's sake." I pause, my voice dropping lower. "And if you can't do it for you, can you do it for me?"

At my words, her body relaxes, and her chest heaves against mine. I know she's on the verge of falling apart. I want her to fall apart so that I can be there to put her back together. I'd spend my life doing that, just as long as I got to be with her.

"Everything feels so out of control," she whispers. "The lies we're telling. The people you're going to hurt when they learn what you've done." A tear spills down her cheek. "It's all turned into a mess."

"Let it be a mess." I shrug. "Let it be a fucking disaster. I don't care. As long as it's you and me in the end, not a damn thing besides that matters to me, Ryann."

Her eyebrows pull together as she stares up at me with her broken eyes. Finally, she leans up and kisses me. Biting down on my bottom lip and making me wince. My cock quickly hardens, begging for her again.

I kiss her back before I push her flat on the bed and climb off of it. I walk to my overnight bag, and her eyes widen when I return with two sets of soft cuffs. One for her ankles, the other for her wrists.

"What do you think, baby? Are you in the mood to let me show you what I'll do if you ever try to run off again?"

Her mouth opens, and her pupils turn huge. Slowly, she nods, already squirming with need.

Taking the cuffs, I'm thankful I booked a room at a place where the bed has posts. And I go right to work, fastening her down. Her legs wide open. Her arms stretched to the sides. And, fuck, what a sight she is.

"You okay?" I ask, and she instantly nods, bringing a smirk to my face. "Good."

Climbing over her, I kiss her lips before working my way to her neck, dragging my tongue to between her tits. And soon, my face is positioned in the sweetest place. Right between her legs.

She can't force my tongue deeper; all she can do is lie there, letting me take control. I've waited so long to have my head buried here, and she's even sweeter than I imagined.

Her moans drive me wild, and my cock aches for a release. But it's not about me right now; it's about her. It's about giving her what she needs, what she wants. Showing her it's okay to not be in control, that she can trust that I'll always have her best interests at heart. No matter what.

I add a finger in, working my tongue and my hand against her before gazing up to watch her face. I know she's close—I can feel it. So, that's when I pull my finger and my mouth from her body.

"Did I tell you that you could come?" I grumble and wait for her answer.

Her lips part before forming a frown. "Pl-please."

"What's that?" I say, bringing my mouth close to her pussy, but not close enough to touch.

I blow a breath against her skin, and her hips rock the slightest bit, attempting to push herself against my face.

"Please," she whispers. "Please, Watson."

"Good girl," I mutter.

And then I dive back in full force. Pushing my fingers in and out, licking and sucking until she screams. As I feel her shaking and my fingers feel her squeezing around me, I just lick harder.

"That's it, baby. Give it to me," I growl. "Give me you. I want to taste you as you come on my tongue."

And she does. So. Fucking. Hard.

And just when I start to scooch down the bed to release her, her voice catches me off guard.

"Now, let me taste you," she whispers. "And don't you dare untie me for this."

Holy. Fuck.

Slowly, I climb back onto her, watching as she opens her perfect lips, welcoming my cock inside. And when I thrust downward, she opens her throat and takes me as deep as she can. I know I won't last long. How can I when I'm fucking my wife's face while she's cuffed to a bed?

Jerking my hips forward and back, I reach my hand around her neck and grip it softly, making her moan against my dick. She sucks harder, drawing me deeper and letting my length slide over her tongue. I push back as far as I can, and she gags, her eyes rolling back. Her throat closes around my head for a split second before she's right back to deep-throating me.

"Ready for a mouthful of my cum, my little slut?" I hiss, and she whimpers before nodding.

I reach back to rub my fingers between her thighs to find she's literally dripping wet.

Yep, that'll do it.

That's all it takes. I fucking lose it. Sending my cum right down her throat.

Right where it belongs.

"Swallow me, Tiny Dancer." I tremble, watching her throat work, doing as she's told. "Good girl," I whisper, pushing my dick down further. "Good. Fucking. Girl."

And she swallows. Eagerly.

And, fuck, doesn't she look beautiful while she stares up at me?

I'm so fucking gone for this girl.

Ryann

Bringing my coffee to my lips, I take a long sip. Letting the hot liquid slide down my throat and make its way into my body to hopefully bring me back from the dead.

After our fight, Watson chained me to the bed—literally—and ate me like I was the first meal he'd seen in weeks. And it was the hottest thing I'd ever done in my life. Well, that was, until he straddled my face and put his length in my mouth. That might have been even hotter.

Obviously, orgasms don't fix the crap we need to talk about. But it felt really good to just put a temporary Band-Aid over that shit for the time being.

But I know things are just going to get more complicated. And the more time that passes, the closer I am to someone showing up to investigate me. Or worse, haul me back across the border.

I have this ache in my gut. This feeling telling me that we're going to get busted. And I'm going to get deported.

I yawn, feeling like a complete zombie. And I'm sure I look like one too.

But we drive along, pretending like everything is fine and normal. Because I don't think either of us has the energy to talk about the hard things.

We both know there's no silver lining. There are no magic words to make everything all better. It just … is what it is.

He continues to drive as we head back toward Brooks. We both have class later even though I'm seriously considering skipping mine.

"Will you see your family for Christmas?" he asks, turning the music down.

"Nah," I mutter. "Riley has no way to get over here, and my mom ... well, holidays have sort of always skipped her mind." I shrug. "I sent some things for my sister, and my neighbor has been holding them until Christmas morning." I chew my lip. "Maybe things will be better for Riley this year though. She thinks my mom is doing better. Apparently, she met some guy a month ago, and Riley seems to think he's decent."

"You don't sound convinced." He states the obvious—my voice must have given it away. "Why is that?"

"You're telling me the woman has dated scumbags her entire life, and now, suddenly, she actually chooses a good human?" I set my coffee in the holder. "I don't know. I just don't buy it, I guess. But for my sister's sake, I really do hope it's true. Riley deserves that."

"Yeah, I don't blame you there. Sometimes, people can change though, right?"

He offers me a tiny smile, and I attempt to nod, but it's hard. I don't trust anything my mom is serving.

"What about you? Is Christmas tough for you all now that your dad is gone?" I ask softly. "That must be so hard for your mom. She must miss him so much around the holidays."

"She does," he answers, keeping his voice soft. "But we have made our own traditions, I guess you could say. And we try to keep Mom busy so that she can't be sad."

Before I can answer, my phone starts going ballistic from text message alerts. Glancing toward me, Watson frowns as I grab my phone from my bag.

"Everything all right?" he utters, and I notice his grip on the steering wheel tightens a bit.

Squinting toward the screen, I read the messages from Poppy one by one as they continue to roll in.

Poppy: Some dude was just here, looking for you. He was terrifying, I'm not going to lie.

Poppy: He was asking me where you were. He even asked me about Watson and if Watson lived here too. I got nervous. I heard a rumor. A rumor about the two of you getting married. And it's clear you two have been spending time together. What kind of mess are you in, Ryann?

Poppy: By the way, I told him I wasn't saying anything. I told him it isn't my place to tell and that I'm not getting dragged into it. I think it bought you some time. I hope anyway.

Me: Thanks for covering for me. I'll be home in an hour. I'll explain everything then.

Poppy: You'd better. See you soon.

Throwing my head back against the headrest, I squeeze my eyes shut. My stomach churns, and I feel like I could throw up. Taking a breath, I open my eyes and stare straight ahead. I try to calm myself down, but it doesn't work. Obviously, Watson would be pulled into this—he married me, for crying out loud. Yet here I am, sick over the thought of him getting in trouble. I don't know what I thought would happen. Of course, if I get in trouble, he will too.

"Ry? What's going on?" Watson's voice is filled with worry. "Who was that?"

I swallow thickly. I don't want to scare Watson. But now that they are asking about him, I can't keep it from him. It wouldn't be fair.

"Poppy said that a man was just there, looking for me." I exhale sharply. "My best guess … it was someone from the immigration office." Nervously, I look at him. "They were asking about you too, Watson. Not just me."

His eyes stay on the road, but his body doesn't tense, like I expected. "What about me?"

"Asking if you lived there." I gulp. "With me."

He's deep in thought, staring at the road and continuing to drive. I don't say anything because honestly … what is there to say? I'm going down, and I'm taking him with me. And I hate myself for it.

And I'm sure he hates me too. He has every right to. I took advantage of him when he offered to marry me. I knew it wouldn't be forever, but I was so desperate to stay here. I knew I couldn't go home to my mom. Too much damage has been done there for me. Maybe Riley can still have that picture-perfect mother everyone dreams of. But me? Forget it. So, I married Watson. And I can't go back there now.

"You know …" He breaks the silence, and I don't know if that's a good thing or a bad thing. "It would be a major red flag for a married couple to *not* live together. Right?"

I look over at him, knowing Watson enough to know what he's going to say. He isn't going to jump ship. He'd stay on this ship until it was hundreds of feet underwater, resting on the ocean floor with no fight left to give. That's him.

"Yeah," I murmur, "I guess so."

Keep digging this hole deeper. You're already halfway buried now, Ryann.

"I'll probably keep my room at the house because I don't want Hunter to think I'm ditching him. Especially while Cade is in rehab. But obviously, that guy is going to come back, and when he does, we need to be ready. So, I'll move some of my stuff into your house. And if it's okay with you, I'd like to stay there sometimes too." He gives me a tiny grin, but I can tell it's for my own benefit. "You know, just to be extra convincing and all."

"You don't think that's taking things, like … too far?" I whisper, chewing my bottom lip so hard that I'm surprised I don't draw blood. "I mean, faking a marriage is bad enough. But living together after knowing each other for such a short amount of time? I don't know. This all … it's just getting to be a lot. And I'm dragging you into it deeper and deeper."

"It isn't dragging when I'm going willingly." He brings my hand to his lips. "We're in this together, Tiny Dancer. Otherwise, I wouldn't have stolen you out of your dance practice and convinced you to marry me. And I for sure wouldn't have gotten down on one knee in the courthouse parking lot and given you a ring." He sets my hand down, giving it one last reassuring squeeze. "I'm in this, Ryann. I said *I do*. And I meant it."

My heart squeezes. I have no idea how someone so selfless could exist. But I'm also not convinced he won't change his mind and want to split. Maybe I should just trust him at this point. He's proven time and time again that I can trust him. But that isn't really the issue. That's not what is making my stomach feel like a ball of nerves, twisting itself into a knot.

No, what's doing that is the reality that he could get into trouble. He could lose everything—including his dream of being in the NHL—because of me.

I care about this man.

No … the truth is, I love this man. And love isn't supposed to be selfish. Yet looking back, that's all I've been.

Before heading to my place, Watson stops at his own house. "I'm going to go grab some of my things. Come in with me," he says, shifting the truck into park.

When I reach for the door, Watson stops me. "I think we should tell Hunter and Sutton the truth, Ry. The truth about you and the immigration officer showing up at your place. All of it." He swallows, a nervous look on his face. "I trust Hunter. And I know you trust Sutton. And if shit hits the fan, if that officer dude goes door to door to our friends, asking for the truth, we're going to need them to know how important it is that they don't say anything to indicate this isn't real." Reaching for me, he brushes his thumb across my lips. "What do you think?"

I sigh the longest sigh. I know he's right. But still, it's scary. It also makes me look like a monster for dragging Watson into such a mess.

"Whatever you think we should do, I'll do it," I whisper, giving him a tiny nod. "Let's do it now since both of their cars are here."

I push the door open and follow him into the house. Right away, my eyes land on Hunter and Sutton, curled up on the couch. Her hair is a mess, and she's wearing his baggy shirt and sweatpants, making it clear she stayed here last night.

"Hey, y'all," Watson says, nodding toward them. "How's it going?"

"She's making me watch the show *Hoarders*," Hunter says with a grimace. "It's gross."

"And intriguing," Sutton adds, pinching his cheek. "Don't lie, babe. You love it."

"I don't know anything anymore," he utters low enough that I barely hear him, still staring at the TV mindlessly. That is, until Watson walks over and turns it off.

"Thank God," Hunter whispers, blinking a few times. "I couldn't stop. It was nasty yet addictive." He shakes his head.

"Rude," Sutton murmurs just as Watson takes a seat in the recliner, pulling me down onto his lap.

"Sorry." He shrugs. "You can go back to watching that weird-ass show shortly." His hand splays on my thigh as he pauses. "We have something to tell y'all. Something that can't be repeated. Ever." He looks from Hunter to Sutton. "You have to swear what we tell you stays here in this house."

"Who did you kill?" Hunter laughs, but then when he sees how serious our faces are, his eyes widen. "What the hell is going on? Did you actually, like … kill someone? I can't keep a secret like—"

"Hush, babe," Sutton says, putting her hand over his mouth. "What is it?" she asks, directing her attention to me. "What's going on?"

We glance at each other nervously, as if trying to decide if telling them is the right thing to do. But finally, we dive into all of the details of what brought us to the conclusion to get married. And I don't think either one of them says a word or breathes until we finish explaining it all.

What I don't add in is the fact that I've fallen in love with my fake husband. Or that now, my biggest fear isn't going back to live with my mother.

It's being pulled away from Watson.

Watson

My eyes sweep around Ryann's room, which is now supposed to be both of ours. I scattered a few of my pictures, some of my hockey shit, and a drawer full of my clothes. Oh, and a brand-new toothbrush she grabbed for me at Target on the way home. I wanted to go in with her, but she told me she had women stuff to buy and I wasn't allowed.

After the realization we needed to move my shit in today, Ryann missed class. But thankfully, it's a class she shares with Sutton. And since Sutton was going there right after we told her everything, she said she'd take notes.

Ryann walks up to me with her hands behind her back. "Before you head to practice and I head to dance ... I have something for you." She blushes, and it's adorable. "It's not much. Especially compared to everything you've given me. But ... anyway, I hope you like it."

She's so nervous, and I fucking love it because, normally, it's me who's nervous, being around her. Not the other way around.

Pulling a frame from behind her back, she hands it to me. Taking it, I look down at the now-framed photo Zoey took of us getting married. Ryann doesn't look happy, but she doesn't look sad either.

She just looks scared.

And me? I look like the luckiest fucker in the world. Because even in that moment, even before we spent time together, I knew I wanted her.

"I figured, you know, what newlywed couple wouldn't have a picture of themselves on their wedding day?" She fidgets with her hands, wringing them together.

"I love it," I whisper, still staring down at it. "Thanks, Tiny Dancer. Really. Thank you."

She might not think it's much. But to me, it's everything.

Watson

Walker attempts to score, only for me to block it—again. And when LaConte announces practice is over, I think everyone is relieved. I pull my helmet off, wiping the sweat from my forehead. Between Walker, Hunter, and Link, I got a fucking workout today.

"Gentry," Coach calls as everyone else heads toward the locker room. "I want to see you in my office after you've showered. Because you smell like sweaty ass and my office is too fucking small for you to stink it up."

"Yes, sir." I nod, following Link off the ice.

"Someone's fixing to get their ass chewed out," Link chimes. "Good luck with that, brother. He's scary when he isn't mad. Let alone when he *is*."

Hunter turns, giving me a concerned look, and I shrug. Whatever it is, I'll find out soon enough. Deep down, I know that Coach likely caught word that I'm a married man now. And, yeah, I'm sure he's fucking confused. And probably nervous that I'll be distracted.

A few days ago, I moved in with Ryann. And even though the investigator hasn't shown up again to question us, I know he will any day now. And I'm ready for it.

No man is going to show up at Ryann's house and take her away from me. No fucking way.

"Close the door behind you, Gentry. This won't take long," LaConte grumbles when he sees me lurking by his door. Pulling his reading glasses off, he sets them on his desk.

Closing the door, I take a seat across from him. "You wanted to see me, Coach?"

"I'm not one for the gossipy shit that comes with coaching a bunch of toddlers. So, I've ignored the whispers about this." He pinches the bridge of his nose. "But once a man who claimed to be an immigration officer investigating your supposed wife showed up in my office today, I could no longer ignore it. And after all the shit with Huff lately, my ol' ticker can't handle much more." He blows out a long, exasperated breath. "Did you run off and get hitched, Gentry?"

I straighten myself in his chair, resting my arms on the armrests. "Uh, yep. Yeah, I did." I nod.

"When?"

"A few days before the fundraiser." I swallow. "To Ryann Denver."

"Why?" he snaps. "Why did you get married when I know damn well you two hadn't known each other before you were paired up? At least, to my knowledge you hadn't. And trust me, boy, I hear more than you think I do."

Coach looks tired. Everything with Cade has taken a toll on him, and I think he blames himself for not drug testing Cade or noticing the signs he was struggling. I don't know how Cade slipped by all of us either. But he was that good at hiding his issues. And he was even better at lying.

This is a man I need on my side. Barren LaConte can make things happen. People trust him, and he can convince them to do as he says. But I also don't want him to be disappointed in me. And if he knew the truth, he undoubtedly would be.

"We were in a class together at the beginning of the school year before I had to switch to the online class." I tell him the honest-to-God truth. "And I've been interested in her since the very first day of that class. Since the very first time I saw her."

"Then, date," he says sharply. "Why get married? You're a college kid, for Christ's sake." He shakes his head. "And why the hell did an immigration officer show up in my office, asking about you?" He dips his head lower, his gaze burning into mine. "I really, really hope you didn't do something stupid, Gentry. Something that could jeopardize your entire future. All for a girl you barely know."

Everything inside of me wants to tell him the truth. But the second he knows the truth is the same time he'll be a part of this … situation we created.

I don't want LaConte brought into this. It's bad enough we brought Hunter and Sutton into it. But at the time, I really thought it would be for the best. Looking back, I realize it was selfish because now, they will be lying too. But it doesn't matter what got Ryann and me to the point we're at right now. Because I'm in love with the girl. And I actually want to be married to her. I want to stay married to her.

Lifting my chin, I look him square in the eyes. And then I fucking lie. I lie to a man I respect more than anyone else on this planet.

"I didn't jeopardize anything. Is Ryann from Canada? Yes, she is. But I married her because I love her. And because I want to be with her. So, whatever they think they'll find, snooping around, they're wrong." I shrug. "We did nothing wrong."

He simply stares at me before dragging his hand down his face. "Jesus Christ, son. I really, really hope for your sake, you're telling me the truth." Jerking his chin toward his door, he huffs out a breath. "Go on then. And, Watson, you make damn sure you don't get wrapped up in something that's going to completely fuck up everything you've worked for." He holds his fingers up. "You're this close, son—*this fucking close*—to all of your dreams coming true. Don't throw that away now."

Nodding, I slowly push myself from the chair. "Yes, Coach. I'll see you tomorrow."

I'm already wrapped up in something that's inevitably going to complicate my plans. But the truth is, I wouldn't trade marrying Ryann for anything. Even my spot in the NHL. I wouldn't trade it because this marriage isn't ending. And she isn't going back to Canada.

When I said *I do*, I meant forever. Whether she likes it or not.

Pulling out my phone, I dial Ryann. Because if the officer paid a visit to LaConte today, that means he's close by. And the last thing I want is him catching her off guard.

RYANN

"I'm sure you're aware by now that when a routine audit was performed at the business"—he looks down at his file—"Peaches, it was brought to our attention that your visa was forged. I don't think I need to tell you how serious of a crime this is, Miss Denver."

I stare at the man before me, who, just as Poppy explained, is indeed terrifying. He's tall and huge. Sort of like Dwayne Johnson, but older and not covered in tattoos. I want to sass him. I want to tell him it's rude to show up at my doorstep, unannounced. But he's right. I committed a crime. So, instead of becoming my feisty self like I probably would have done in the past, I try to keep it together. I'm sure he can see right through me. It wouldn't be hard to notice how nervous I am.

"Officer Hewett, what are you saying?" I ask softly. "Are you going to just cuff me and stuff me in the back of your car and force me back across the border?" I cringe. "Sir, with all due respect, I hope that isn't what you're planning on doing."

He inhales, keeping his sharp eyes focused on me. "Miss Denver, the last thing I want to do right now is force a kid who is the same age as my youngest daughter in my car. And I'm certainly not going to cuff you. As long as you cooperate." His head swivels around, looking for something. Or someone. "Is Mr. Gentry here?" His voice deepens. "Watson Gentry."

"Cookie?" Sutton says, appearing out of nowhere with a plate of cookies. "Ryann made them earlier. They are Watson's favorite." She gives me a sweet smile. "You're so good to that man."

Seeing as Sutton can't bake and neither can I ... I have no idea who actually made those cookies. But if I had to guess, they came from a container, and she perfectly arranged them on a plate.

When Officer Hewett looks from me to Sutton, I give her a *you're doing too much* look. But she simply beams at me before batting her long lashes at the officer and pushes the plate toward him.

"No thanks," he says, but I can tell he's really thinking about taking one. It would probably be considered unprofessional, and Officer Hewett strikes me as a professional type of dude. No time for cookies.

Just then, the door opens, and in walks Watson. His hat is turned backward, and he's wearing his Brooks hoodie and those sweatpants I love so much. Even as nervous as I am, my mouth waters at the sight of him.

Closing the door behind him, he struts in like he actually does live here. I guess the past few days, he sort of has. And I won't lie ... I like it. I don't really want him to leave.

"Hey, baby," he says sweetly, planting a kiss on my cheek before turning toward our not-so-welcome guest and holding his hand out. "Hi there. Can I help you?"

Putting his hand out, he gives Watson's a firm, slow shake before releasing it. "I'm Officer Hewett. Officer Kirby Hewett."

At least his name sounds like he's a friendly elf, straight from the North Pole, I tell myself, sighing in relief that his name isn't as scary as his eyes.

But when his gaze sweeps back to me, it scares the absolute shit out of me, and the image of the adorable elf disappears from my mind. If his job is trained to crack people, he's damn good at it. One icy stare from him has me all but blurting out the truth and begging for forgiveness. But when Watson's hand squeezes my own, I relax enough to keep my mouth shut.

"What can we help you with, Officer Hewett?" Watson chimes like he's the happiest guy in the world, not nervous at all in this moment—even though I know he's worried, judging by his clammy palm.

"Your *wife* is here illegally. At least, she was before she suddenly married a US citizen," Officer Hewett says, completely unfazed. "And even though she is now married to you, a US citizen, I'm not really buying your story, given the timeline of things."

Watson laughs, looking from Kirby and down to me. "Our story?" He shakes his head, still grinning. With his attention on Kirby, he stands taller. "Tell me, Officer Hewett, what's our story? With all due respect, I'm dying to know."

"Miss Denver found out last month that in a routine audit, it had been discovered that her visa was forged." He looks down at his paper, pointing to a date. "And then, miraculously, *two* days later, she's suddenly a married woman." He looks up at Watson, holding his gaze. "Quite a whirlwind, wouldn't you say?"

"First off, it's *Mrs.* Gentry," Watson says boldly. "Second, are you trying to insinuate my marriage is a fraud?" Watson spews the words sarcastically, and they are laced with venom too. Nodding down at Officer Hewett's finger, where a gold band looks like it's cutting off the circulation, he tilts his head to the side. "Because, I have to say, married man to married man ... not cool."

"I'm glad you find this so entertaining, Mr. Gentry," Officer Hewett coos.

He's one of those people I genuinely can't figure out. One second, he seems sort of nice. The next, a dick.

"But I assure you, this isn't a joking matter. This story isn't adding up. And your *wife* will likely be deported in the next few weeks."

"Well, I promise you, our story will add up. We have nothing to hide," Watson says, tipping his chin up in defiance. "I can promise you that. So, dig all you want. You aren't going to find what you're looking for. Not with us."

"So, you won't mind if I look around then?" he replies with a smirk. "For a ... routine evaluation of the place." He shrugs. "Shouldn't be a big deal now that you're married and all. I'm sure there's plenty of proof, right?"

"Go right ahead." Watson shrugs.

"Yes, sir," I squeak. "I'll show you our room."

As he follows close behind me, all I hear is the sound of my heart pounding in my ears.

It's so hot in here. *Is it hot in here?* God, someone must have turned up the heat.

Pushing my door open, I hold my arm out. "Help yourself."

And even though I didn't really have the photo printed and framed in case this happened ... I'm really glad I did it because maybe it'll save our ass.

WATSON

"Watson, you heard him. He's going to be back. And we'll never know when," Ryann whispers against my chest. "He won't stop until I'm back in Canada. I know it."

"I think it's an act," I say. "He has to act scary because that's his job. He can't be a marshmallow; that wouldn't be any good." I tuck her closer into my side, trying my best to make her feel better or somehow ease her nerves. "I'm not going to let him or anyone else take you anywhere, Tiny Dancer. That's a promise.

"Christmas is next week," I murmur against her hair. "I know you have your big performance this weekend, and your schedule has been crazy with that, but it would mean a lot to me if you came home with me. Mom would love it. And you can meet the rest of my family."

Her entire body tenses. "Oh ... I ... I don't want to intrude." She gently shakes her head against me. "Really, I'll be fine here. But you should go."

"If you don't go, I'm not going." I look up at the ceiling, rolling my eyes at how fucking stubborn she is. "So, the choice is yours. You can spend Christmas with me here, just the two of us. Or we can go to Alabama, and you can meet my family." I poke her side. "Maybe take a few pictures to shove in fuckface Kirby's face."

She flips over to look up at me, resting her chin on my chest. "Are you sure you want me there? Christmas should be spent with family, you know?"

"Ryann, you are my family," I say matter-of-factly. "And I don't want to spend Christmas without you."

Ever.

She's deep in thought, but finally, she smiles. "Okay. Yeah. I'll come home with you."

Pulling her upward, I bring her mouth to mine and kiss her. My cock quickly hardens, just like it always does when it comes to her.

And I wish Officer Kirby fucking Hewett could see us now. Because this shit is far from fake.

And if he needs to watch me fuck my wife to realize that, so be it.

24

Ryann

I'm anxious, and that never happens when it comes to dancing. This is just a show we're putting on to raise some money for the dance program and a fun little treat for the public for the holidays. Something for people around the area to bring their kids to, to kick off the Christmas festivities.

And here I am, and I. Am. Shaking.

All because Watson freaking Gentry—also known as my husband—is somewhere in the crowd. I know him; his eyes won't stray from me. They never do. And that right there scares the hell out of me. He makes me nervous. No guy has ever made me feel that way.

"You know, eventually, we're going to have to talk about the fact that I had to learn through the grapevine you were married." Poppy jabs her finger into my side. "Oh, and while we're at it, how about we discuss why that intimidating dude has stopped at our house multiple times, looking for you and poking around about Watson?"

"Nothing to tell, chica." I wink before cupping her cheeks aggressively. "You know, one day, we should do a *Trolls* play, and then you can be Poppy, and I can paint you pink." My eyes widen, and I bring my nose closer to hers. "Oh, and you can sing and smile. And the best part, you can act happy!"

"Ew. No," she says, pretending to gag. "Hard pass."

I release her. Despite some debatable things she's done, I love Poppy. She's sassy and fierce. She's been through more in her lifetime than anyone should have to go through, and in my eyes, she's a warrior.

"You've seemed nervous all day." Her eyes look me up and down, narrowing. "Why is Ryann Denver, queen of the whole *fuck it* motto, nervous for a performance that doesn't count toward anything?" She throws her hand up. "It's just for fun, so why do you look like you're going to piss your leotard?"

"I don't know." I shrug. "Just want it to be perfect, I guess. You know, because a lot of moms brought their kids here. I want it to be good for them. After all, I'm the freaking Sugar Plum Fairy."

She looks past me, and the corner of her lips teases into a smirk. "Ahhh, now, I know why you're scared." She pats me on the shoulder. "It'll be fine. Besides, if you fall and break your asscheek, it's not like he can divorce you for it. Right?" And then she prances off.

I spin around to see what she was talking about, and my eyes land on Watson. Who is now backstage and carrying two huge-ass bouquets of flowers. In a freaking delicious, sexy tux. Looking good enough to eat. Or lick. Or both.

"Sir, do you have clearance to be back here?" the director says, walking toward him like he's about to throw his ass out. When, in reality, the director is smaller than me and Watson towers over him.

Watson looks completely unfazed as he continues to strut toward me. "Sure do. I need to deliver these flowers to someone. Her husband wanted her to have them before the show. And since his wife is the star of the show, it's imperative she gets them before it starts."

The director's eyes widen, and he slowly nods. "Oh, okay. Uh … sorry," he says nervously before walking off.

Looking me up and down, he pulls me toward him and presses his lips to the top of my head. "You look so fucking beautiful, Tiny Dancer."

Tipping my head up, I surprise him when I catch his lips with mine. Kissing him as his free arm is slung around me. Pulling back, I grin up at him. "You look nice too. And I'm really, really happy to see you."

His phone rings, and he releases me, grabbing it from his pocket. Grinning at the phone, he answers it and flips the screen. My sister waves frantically at me, and I'm cursing the fact that I already had my makeup done because there's no stopping my tears from falling.

"Watson got clearance to have his phone on FaceTime for the performance," she yells, basically leaping out of her skin. "I get to watch the entire thing!"

My hand flies to my mouth. Typically, phones aren't allowed at performances like this one. Yet he went and got permission to use his, just so my sister could watch. All without me ever mentioning that, deep down, I wished she could somehow be here. And now, she is.

He's too perfect.

"I love you so much!" I sniffle, looking at Riley. "I'm so happy you get to watch." I wipe my eyes as delicately as I can. "Even though you'll probably be bored out of your mind halfway through because I know you."

"No way," she says, shaking her head. "I'll let you finish getting ready. Good luck. Break a leg!" She pauses, cringing. "Well, not literally. But … you know."

Laughing, I nod. "Bye. I love you so much."

"Love you more! Watson, call me when it's time!" she says before her face disappears from the screen.

"Is there anything you don't think of?" I ask him, in complete awe. "Seriously though."

It's like when God made him, he measured everything perfectly to make him completely flawless. It's as incredible as it is terrifying. Because guys like him? I'm learning they aren't easy to walk away from.

"Trust me, I fuck up much more than you think," he mutters before handing me one of the huge bouquets of the most beautiful red roses.

"Thank you so much. They are gorgeous." Closing my eyes, I inhale the strong smell and sigh. "And they smell *so* good."

Opening my eyes, I frown at the second set of flowers in his hand. "Who are those for?" I nod toward the lilies. "Do you have a second wife here you failed to mention?"

"Nah, my one wife is plenty for me to handle." He laughs before looking down at the flowers oddly. "They are for Poppy, I guess. Apparently, she has a secret admirer. One who wanted her to have these." He shrugs. "Do you want to give them to her?"

I don't see a card, and I don't ask him who they are from because if he wanted me to know, he would have said. But like me, Poppy never has any family in the stands, watching her perform. So, I love the very fact that someone is giving her flowers.

"Sure," I say, reaching for them. "These will make her happy."

"Thanks, beautiful." He smiles. Bending down one more time, he kisses me. "Good luck, Tiny Dancer."

"Thanks," I mumble, now more nervous than ever.

Watson

Nothing Ryann does could ever be boring. If she's involved, I'll always be fully mesmerized by her. She moves with such grace. And as she dances around the stage, it looks so effortless. She makes even the hardest things appear easy. She's that good.

The past week, practicing for this has kept her so busy that she's had to have other dancers cover her shifts at Peaches. And I've been relieved because I really can't stand the thought of her working there. I hate thinking that other men's eyes are on her. And what I hate the most is worrying that she isn't safe. Who knows what kind of scumbags go in there?

For a fairly short girl, she makes her presence extremely known when she's on a stage. She captivates the entire crowd, making it hard for anyone—not just her husband—to look away.

I check my screen every now and then to make sure Riley can still see. What I didn't tell Ryann and what I asked Riley not to mention either is that their mom also wanted to watch the performance. I know Ryann is wary of her mother, but when I called Riley to ask if she wanted to watch through FaceTime, I didn't have the heart to tell her no when she asked if her mom could watch too.

I didn't mention to either of them that we were married. I figured, wrong place, wrong time.

Until today, I had never in my life been to a play or watched ballet—aside from our fundraisers. And I'll admit, if Ryann wasn't in this show, I probably would have left an hour ago. But as long as she's dancing, my ass will be right here in this seat.

I watch her spin around, dancing like the weight of the world isn't on her shoulders.

I'm so in love with that woman. And soon, I need to tell her. It's time to admit that I didn't marry her just to help her get her visa. I married her because I couldn't stand the thought of her leaving the country.

Ryann

Watson closes my door and jogs around to his own. It's cold out tonight, and he jumps in and blasts the heat.

"You fucking killed it tonight, babe," he chants, pulling out of the parking lot. "Your sister told me to tell you, and I quote, 'You were better than everyone else. I love you. Oh, and you should totes wear pink more often because it's soooo your color!'" He raises his eyebrows, glancing at me quickly. "Her words, not mine."

I burst out laughing at his impression of a teenage girl, grabbing my stomach. "Okay, noted. Thanks." I reach over, patting his arm. "Hey, thank you for letting her be a part of it. It felt surprisingly nice to know she was kind of there even though she wasn't." I smile.

He looks uneasy, and that makes me instantly nervous. He's never a guy who seems like he's hiding something. But right now, I get the feeling he's going to drop a bomb on me.

"Hey, so … Riley wasn't the only one who wanted to watch you perform, you know." He looks back at the road, swallowing thickly. "Your mom, she, uh, was watching too."

I feel like his words slap me in the face. But still, it takes me time to form a response. Or even a thought. "Wait, what?"

"Yeah. Your mom and your sister, they both watched the entire performance." He grimaces. "I'm sorry to just tell you now."

His words sting, and I frown. "Did you know that when you came to see me before the show?"

He winces. "Yeah, I did. I just … I was afraid it would make you nervous. I know your mom hasn't been the best mother to you. And the last thing I wanted was to do something to make you feel anxious before your performance. But when I had called your sister this morning to ask if she'd want to watch it, she put me on the spot about your mother. And I just … I wasn't sure what to say." He exhales sharply. "I'm sorry, Ry. I hope you're not upset with me. But if you are, I understand."

While the thought of even receiving a letter from my mother has recently made me a ball of nerves, I can tell that Watson truly is feeling bad for keeping this secret. It's not his fault my sister put him on the spot. I mean, if he had told Riley no … that probably would have made me more upset than my mother watching me perform for the first time.

"Watson, how in the world could I be upset with you?"

"I did something behind your back. And because, in a way, I guess I gave your mom the benefit of the doubt by letting her watch you." He side-glances me. "I don't know everything you've been through. I want to know, but I don't want to push you either." He grips the steering wheel a bit tighter. "But I know enough to know your mom has put you through some shit. And I'd never want you to think I'm excusing her actions. I just didn't want to hurt Riley's feelings. I know how much you love your sister. I see your eyes light up when you talk about her. Or how your face grows sad when you're worried about her. I didn't know what to do."

"I'm upset my mom snaked her way into a performance that was kind of special to me. Because for my entire life, she's never watched me a single time—until today." I sink into my seat. "I want to be mad and curse her out for showing up twenty years too late. I want to scream at her for all the times she dragged home loser boyfriends who would leave emotional scars on both Riley and me. And I really, really want to tell her it's her fault that I can't trust easily in my adult life." I blow all the air from my chest. "I want to, but I won't. Because for once in her life, my baby sister has an actual mother. And I'm not going to fuck that up." I turn my body toward him. "Do you know what I hate my mom the most for?"

"What?" he says so quietly that I barely hear him.

"Thanks to her life choices and always providing the proof that fairy tales weren't real, I couldn't even see what was in front of me for so long. And when I finally saw it, I didn't feel worthy." I sniffle. "I still don't feel worthy of you, Watson. I don't know if I ever will. But for the longest time, I looked at you like you were just another person out to hurt me. But the truth is, you're the one who has put me back together. You're the person who's made me feel like I can trust again." I pause, running my hand nervously over my head. I've never been good at being vulnerable. It's always scared me too much. "And to think … we're just supposed to be fake married. But I don't know, Watson. This just doesn't seem so fake to me now."

His eyes fly to mine before he reaches for me, pulling my face closer to his and kissing me.

"You are worthy of every single thing good, Ryann. It's me who shouldn't feel worthy of you. And I know I'm not. But as long as you'll let me, I'm going to spend my life trying to be."

He said my life. He's thinking about spending forever with me.

"Everything about you—good, bad, embarrassing—I want to know all of it." He cups my cheeks. "And I promise you this: There is nothing fake about us. Never has been either. At least, not on my end."

I'm so close to telling him what I so desperately feel inside. *I love you.* It's only three words. Three tiny words. It should be so easy but it terrifies me. Besides, maybe he doesn't even feel that way back. Who really knows? If he did, he would have said it. He's that type of guy.

"What are you most scared of in this world?" I blurt out. Though I really don't know why.

His eyes travel somewhere else before he speaks. "Having everyone see me as someone who's bound to achieve greatness. And then losing it all." He swallows. "Yeah, I might have a spot in the NHL. For now. But a lot could happen. And I'm scared to let my family down."

"You couldn't let your family down if you tried," I whisper. And even though I'm secretly dreading going home with him, I smile. "And I can't wait to meet them. And to see where you came from. And meet your mom. The woman who brought my husband up."

The second the words leave my mouth, his lips crash to mine, and he slides his hand into my hair.

He's given me everything, and I've given him crumbs. But no more.

I'm ready to go all in. Even if it blows up in my face down the road.

Watson Gentry will be worth the pain.

25

Ryann

It's Christmas Eve, and we're in Alabama. Watson had practice early this morning, but won't have another until the day after Christmas. And LaConte even made it at night. Which means we get to stay here for a few days.

"Thanks for coming back home with me," Watson says as we continue driving. "I talked to my mama the other night, and she's pretty dang excited that one of her sons is bringing a girl home."

"I bet," I murmur, but my stomach sinks further. I feel like I might actually vomit, but I push the thought aside and attempt to seem comfortable.

In my head, a picture plays of him telling his mother I'm his wife. She takes one look at me in my ratty clothes and worn-out sneakers and drags my ass outside and sends me hiking back to Georgia.

And to be honest, I wouldn't blame her.

She's likely never even heard him mention my name, and here I am, showing up at their Christmas as his freaking wife.

And then there's the even worse part—where everyone there will feel bad that they didn't get me a gift because they didn't know I was coming until the last minute. When, really, gifts would make me feel uncomfortable because how the hell would I give them one back? With Watson, it's different.

And maybe that's because he never expects anything in return. That's just another thing about him that sets him apart from most of humanity.

"Do we have time to swing into a mall or something on the way there?" I think about the two hundred dollars in my pocket from my last shift. I know I want to get his mom a gift, but I want to get him something too.

He looks at the clock on the dash. "Oh, yeah, plenty of time. LaConte had practice at the ass crack of dawn to give those of us traveling time to get home. And there's actually a mall just twenty minutes from the house."

"Sweet," I say, looking out the window at the miles of nothingness along the highway.

I have no idea what to get Watson. I don't know what he needs or even likes. But I know his mom loves candles and wax warmers. Maybe Watson can help me choose her gift.

Taking my phone out, I read Riley's message. According to her, my mom is cooking them a nice dinner for Christmas Day, and then they are going to look at Christmas lights. That makes me happy for my sister, but nervous at the same time. Nervous that it won't actually happen. And somewhere in the deep, uglier part of my soul, maybe I'm a little envious that my mom couldn't have decided to be a parent when I was still around. But I shake the feeling off, reminding myself Riley is who matters right now. And if she's happy, I am happy too.

I guess I'm trying to be more like Watson and just be more positive.

My mom sent me a message the morning after *The Nutcracker*. A message that I almost didn't believe could be from her. The same woman who had left me and my sister home alone for three days while her boyfriend at the time took her on a getaway.

In the message, she said how proud she was of me. And how beautifully I danced. At the end, it said, *I love you, Ryann. I hope you know that.*

I didn't know that.

But maybe, one day, I might believe it.

The craziest part was reading that she had sent me a Christmas gift with a letter. My eyes almost bugged out of my head when I read that. I guess I'll have to wait and see if she was bluffing.

For so long, I felt like a plant someone bought that they forgot to water or put in the sun. Dried up and dead. But now ... I feel like I've been brought back to life.

And it has nothing to do with my mother's message. It's all because of the guy sitting next to me right now.

WATSON

With a few bags in my hands, I walk around the mall. The first forty-five minutes, Ryann let me walk around with her. But then she kicked my ass to the curb. And even though I told her not to get me anything for Christmas, I knew that was why she wanted to be alone.

When I passed by one of the many ornament stands, I couldn't help myself, and I got her a personalized newlywed one. It's corny. With two gingerbread people kissing. But it has our names and the year on it with the word *newlyweds* above it. It might scare the shit out of her, but I did it anyway.

Standing next to the giant Christmas tree in the mall, I shoot her a text, letting her know there's no rush, but I'm here when she's ready.

Leaning against a large beam, I slide my phone back in my pocket. This place is packed today. And the mall's a pretty interesting place for some people-watching. Actually, it's sort of one of my favorite guilty pleasures.

"Watson?"

A familiar voice comes from the side of me, and I look to find my ex, Rosie.

Stopping right in front of me, she smiles. "It is you! Hi!"

"Hey," I answer, holding my hand up and doing my best to give her a polite smile.

Years ago, I would have lit up like a Christmas tree to see this girl. Now, it's different.

"How have you been?" She tilts her head to the side in an almost-flirtatious sort of way. "I hear you're a big shot hockey player at Brooks these days."

"I've been good." I nod. "And I don't know about all that."

Touching my arm, she giggles. "Still so humble, I see." She bites her bottom lip. "You look good, Watson. Really good."

Nervously, I drag my hand over the top of my head. "Uh, thanks ..."

For a moment, it's like she's waiting for me to tell her she looks good too. She does look good. She's a beautiful girl. But she isn't my girl.

And honestly, I've never been more thankful that things didn't work out until this moment while I wait for my wife in this mall.

"Well, I should get going," she mutters. "Are you going to be at the tree lighting ceremony later?"

The ceremony is something our town has done every year on Christmas Eve for as long as I can remember. It's a way to bring the town together. They close down the streets to car traffic, play Christmas music, have tons of food, and then they light the huge tree. I haven't put a lot of thought into going, but I don't want to overwhelm Ryann either.

"I'm not sure." I shrug. "We'll see, I guess."

Disappointment flashes on her face. I know that's what it is because when you date a girl for most of your high school years, you get to know her quite well.

"Well, I guess I'll see you if you decide to come." Looking nervous, she suddenly throws her arms around me. "It's really good to see you, Watson," she mumbles into the cloth of my hoodie. "I meant what I said, by the way. You look handsome. As always."

Standing on her tiptoes, she kisses my cheek. And even though every cell inside of my body wants to shove her away from me, I don't want to hurt her feelings. So, instead, I count the seconds until she finally pulls away. And then I sigh in relief.

As she walks off, my eyes land on Ryann across from me, in front of a candle store. She simply stands there, rooted to the floor.

I head toward where she's standing and stop just before her. "That wasn't what it looked like, I swear."

"It didn't look like anything," she says quickly, but I can tell she's stunned. "Are you ready to go? I think I'm all set here if you are." She shifts around on her feet.

"Ryann," I say sternly. "Look at me."

Slowly, her eyes find mine, and she widens them. "Yeah?"

"I didn't want her to hug me. Or to kiss my cheek. I swear."

"It isn't a big deal." She shakes her head. "What was it? Like an old friend?" She shrugs her shoulders. "It's fine."

"That was Rosie," I murmur.

Her body freezes, and she bobs her head up and down once. "Your ex, Rosie?" Her lips purse together. "Oh. Oh, I see. She seemed … nice?"

"I hadn't seen her in a long time." I cup her face, bringing her mouth closer to mine. "You can pretend like you aren't jealous, but if it didn't bother you, you would have walked right over." My eyes narrow. "I find it really fucking hot that you're jealous, Ry baby. In fact, I find it so hot that it makes me want to fuck you right here in front of everyone in this mall. Trust me, the only woman I want touching me is my wife."

She blinks a few times. "I … I'm not—I wasn't—"

Kissing her, I shut her up. Dragging my hand lower, I pull her against me slightly. Hoping my hardening cock won't be noticeable to everyone walking by us.

"You were. But it's fine. If I saw another guy kiss your cheek or hug you, I'd want to kill the motherfucker." I stop, catching myself. "I wouldn't because I wouldn't want to upset you. But, yeah … I'd be pissed."

Kissing her once more, I take her bags from her. "Let's go, Tiny Dancer. It's time for you to meet my mama."

Her eyes widen, and she gulps.

"Okay," she utters. "Let's go."

26

Ryann

I'm going to throw up.
 Yep. We're driving down Watson's driveway, and I'm going to puke. Or pass out. Maybe even die. I don't know. My stomach is turning like it's a washing machine. And my hands are clammy even though my body is trembling and cold.
 What if she hates me? And then what?
 Watson loves his mom. I mean, for God's sake, he keeps the candles she gives him. He brags about her cookies. He freaking buys her ice cream! Of course he'd leave me if his mother hated me.
 I can't bake. Or cook. Jesus, I burn Toaster Strudels. I don't care if my house smells like a batch of fresh-baked cookies; I'm no homemaker.
 This was a terrible idea.
 "I can't cook," I blurt out. "Or bake." I gulp. "And I wash my whites and colors together. And I never use fabric softener because it's expensive." I drag my hand over my face. "What was I thinking, coming here with you? We can't tell your mom the truth. We can't tell her we're married." My lip trembles.
 "Hey," Watson says, reaching over and squeezing my hand. "I don't care about any of that stuff. I know how to cook. I can cook for us. And when it

comes to baking—fuck it, that's what bakeries are for, right?" He looks over at me, smirking a bit. "Besides, if I need something sweet, I'll just eat my wife's pussy." He winks, attempting to lighten the mood. It helps—but only for a second.

"I'm serious, Watson," I utter softly. "If your family hates me ... where will that leave us?"

"It would leave us married with awkward family holidays." He shrugs. "But that isn't going to happen because she's going to love you. They all are." He pauses, cringing. "And ... you'll get to meet my sister. And my niece and nephew. And Jameson too. You already know Carson."

My head flies to his. "Watson! You didn't tell me your sister would be here." I throw my head back. "Your sister will definitely not like me!"

"Why wouldn't my sister like you?" He frowns. "She likes everyone." He laughs. "Well, besides Rosie."

"Not. Helping," I hiss. "Rosie looks like the type of girl who has golden locks curled to perfection and wears pink sweaters to match her perfectly manicured nails. *Everyone* probably likes her! And your sister didn't." I look down at my bright blue nails, painted with my dollar-store polish, and cringe. "I don't feel so good."

"Stop," he growls. "No spiraling today. You're beautiful. I hate the color pink." He stops. "Well, besides when you wore it for *The Nutcracker*, of course. And Rosie's hair is made up with a lot of extensions." He winks. "You're good, Ryann. And you're real. They'll love you."

I look out the window, admiring the land Watson grew up on. So much open space to just ... run. And be a kid. On both sides of the road is nothing but open fields. But off in the distance, near the house, I see a farm pasture. Watson wasn't lying when he said he grew up on a farm.

Parking his truck behind a few other cars in the parking lot, he reaches over and pats my knee. "Ready, babe?"

"As I'll ever be," I mutter, and we grab our things and head inside.

Watson barely gets in the door before a little girl and boy come barreling toward him. Both squealing.

Dropping everything next to him, he scoops them up, one in each arm.

"Uncle Watty!" the boy squeals. "Uncle Watty is here, Mama!"

"You mean, your favorite uncle is here." He swings both of them around before setting them on the floor.

When he kneels down, they both throw their arms around him, tucking their heads into his chest.

"Where my present?" the girl says, stepping back and holding her hands up. Her brown hair is cut into an adorable little bob, clipped in the front to keep it out of her face.

"Phoebe Marie! We don't ask for presents. We've been over this." A gorgeous brunette with long, silky hair walks toward us. "Even if it is just Uncle Watty, we still need to use our manners."

"Very funny, sis." Watson stands, pulling his sister in for a hug. "Ryann, this is Nora. My pain-in-the-ass sister. Nora, this is Ryann."

"I have a friend named Ryan. Ryan is a boy's name!" the boy says, looking up at me. "Are you one of Uncle Watty's girlfriends? Mama says he has lots! But he never brings them to Christmas!"

"Emmett," Nora hisses. "Also rude."

Emmett shrugs. "Sorry, Mama."

Nora looks at me, and even though I'm nervous, the nerves melt away when she gives me a smile. "Nice to meet you, Ryann. This is Emmett and Phoebe. I promise, they have manners. Well, sometimes."

I chuckle and wave. "Nice to meet you, everyone."

"Y'all coming in here, or are you gonna keep me waiting all day?" someone calls before I see a woman with chin-length hair heading toward us. Her kind eyes give it away instantly.

That's Watson's mom.

"Ryann," she says sweetly, throwing her arms around me. "I'm so dang happy you could make it to spend Christmas with us."

"Thank you for having me, Mrs. Gentry," I squeak as she releases me. "You have a beautiful home."

And, boy, does she. It's so light and comfy in here. Like something straight out of a farmhouse Pinterest board. And the scent? Aaaamazing. I wouldn't have expected anything less after Watson has made it clear how much she loves candles.

"Mrs. Gentry is my mother-in-law. That woman, God love her, is a lot. Call me Jeanine. Come in; come in." She begins walking down the hallway, leading us to a living room.

An excruciatingly attractive man I recognize from Watson's pictures struts in the room, his hair wet, like he just took a shower.

"Look who found his way home." Jameson grins, walking over to Watson and slinging his arm around him. "At least one of my brothers came home for Christmas."

Watson frowns. "What do you mean? Carson isn't coming home?"

"Couldn't, I guess." Jameson shrugs. "Guess more food for us."

Watson looks bummed that Carson isn't joining us. And when I gaze at Jeanine, she looks sad. But when she catches my stare, she quickly smiles.

"I sure hope y'all brought your appetites. We'll be having our usual spaghetti tonight with brownie sundaes after. And tomorrow, a turkey and ham dinner with all the fixings. And of course, pie."

That all sounds so good. It's obvious they have traditions they do here, and I feel the envy inside of me swelling. The only tradition I had growing up was the tradition of trying to scrounge for food for Christmas night. I would always save up to buy Riley and me a box of those Little Debbie Christmas trees. It might not have been much, but it always made her smile.

Watson pats his stomach. "You know I did. I don't go anywhere without it."

"Oh, my boy, I'm aware." His mom laughs. "Hey, are y'all planning on going down to the lighting ceremony tonight?"

I have no idea what a lighting ceremony is. Or if Watson planned for us to go. So, I just sit back and watch them all discuss if they are or not.

"No," Jameson mutters, his tone suddenly laced with anger. "All set with that."

"Jameson, you can't avoid Maddy forev—" Jeanine starts, but Nora seems to know that whatever she's going to say will make her brother feel worse, and she cuts her mom off.

"I want to take the kids for sure," Nora says, rubbing her hand through Emmett's hair to smooth it out. "Garrett is calling me around four to FaceTime the kids. But that will leave plenty of time for the ceremony."

I frown, and Watson notices.

Leaning closer, he whispers in my ear, "Garrett is her husband. He's deployed right now."

"Oh." The word comes out in barely a whisper.

It turns out even the happiest-looking families have shit they go through. She and her kids have to spend Christmas away from him while I'm sure she's worried sick for his well-being.

There's nothing light or easy about that.

Watson gives me a strange look, and I know he's trying to tell me something. I widen my eyes and move my head to the side, trying to tell him I'm not picking up what he's throwing down. And that's when he points to my finger.

Wow, I forgot we're both wearing our rings.

I suck in a breath and shrug. I'll never be ready for the moment he likely breaks his mother's heart and I sit here, looking like a villain. But I suppose now is as good of a time as ever.

Nodding once, he squeezes my hand before clearing his throat.

"Uh, guys, Ryann and I have something we want—well, need—to tell you." He glances at me, and I swear my heart stops beating.

"We're, uh … we're not dating. We're actually … married." He stops, swallowing and chancing a look at his mom.

Nora's head visibly rears back; Jameson says nothing, just stares with his icy-cool eyes; and Jeanine is quiet for a moment before she starts laughing.

"Good one, guys." She points at us. "Almost had me for a second."

Nora looks at me and then her mom. "I don't think it's a joke, Mom."

"If my son got married, Nora, I think I'd know about it," she spews. "That would be crazy. And Watson doesn't do crazy. Isn't that right, Watson?"

Watson grimaces, and I know he is scared that he's going to hurt his mother's feelings. When it comes to her, he's a big softy. And I actually love that about him.

"I'm sorry we didn't tell you sooner." Watson's voice grows lower. "It happened so fast. And I just wanted to tell you in person." He glances nervously at me before smiling. "And there's nothing crazy about it. Trust me when I tell you that."

I can't smile back at him because the look on Jeanine's face tells me she's not only shook … but also extremely upset. And when she gets up and walks out of the room, my heart sinks.

My being here is going to ruin their Christmas. And that's the very last thing I wanted to do.

Watson

The cheesy Christmas music plays as people dance and chat in the street minutes before the lighting ceremony. I wasn't sure if I wanted to come here tonight. But after my mom stormed out of the room when we told her we were married, my sister did what she always does in awkward situations.

She talked. Way too much.

And when she was explaining this ceremony, I could tell Ryann wanted to come down and check it out. So, as always, when Ryann wants something, I can't ever say no. And here we are. My mom's somewhere, likely catching up with old friends and hopefully no longer stewing on the revelation that her son is now married.

"I'm sorry. I feel awful that we upset your mom," Ryann says, craning her neck to look at me, her back against my chest as we stand, facing the tree. "My being here might not be the best idea."

I keep my arms wrapped around her but drag her in closer. "Trust me, she'll be fine. I promise." I kiss her temple. "If you hadn't come home with me, I would have stayed at Brooks with you. So, in the end, my mom will be happy you're here. Swear it."

A town official stands before the crowd, giving a small speech about the meaning of the tree lighting ceremony. How it helps us remember the town's values, but also to celebrate those we have lost and love the ones we still have. And soon, the countdown begins.

Ryann smiles, counting down right along with the rest of the town, like she's done this forever, just like everyone else here has. She sways back and forth as she counts, her ass grazing against my cock and making me curse that we're in a public place. And when the countdown stops and the entire tree lights up, her mouth hangs open as she stares up at it.

"Wow," she whispers, and I swear I see tears in her eyes. "It's so beautiful."

I take for granted how good I have it. How good I've always had it. And when I'm around Ryann, I realize that I had it really fucking easy, growing up. I've seen things like a town coming out to celebrate together. That's something I'm sure her mom never did with her and her sister.

That makes my heart hurt, and I nuzzle my nose into her shoulder.

Spinning her slowly, I nod my head toward the sidewalk, where a line is forming fast in front of Jackie's Doughnut Stand.

"You know what would make you feel better? Mini doughnuts." I wink.

Taking her hand, we head toward the stand. But when we get closer, I see Rosie standing in the same line, making me instantly wish we had waited.

Ryann must notice her, too, because I feel her steps begin to slow as I tug her along.

"Will this cause issues? You and me walking over there where she is?" Ryann mutters. "I made a mess of everything at your mom's by being here. I don't want to make issues here too. Especially when everyone here is having such a good time."

"Nah, she isn't like that," I assure her because I've known Rosie long enough to know that she isn't someone who goes out of her way to make waves. At least, she never was when we were together.

As we get in the line, I'm thankful Rosie and a few others I went to high school with don't spot us right away. I have no doubt they'd all come over, and the last thing I want to do is make Ryann feel uncomfortable. Well, more so than she already probably is. When we came down here, I forgot that my entire fucking graduating class would likely be here too.

Rosie and her friends order, and when the lady hands them their boxes, they all turn. Spotting me and Ryann instantly.

"Here we go," Ryann mutters, but I give her hand a squeeze.

Rosie's eyes float from Ryann's to me. I know instantly that she's uneasy, but she plasters on her usual *pageant queen* smile. Just like her mom has always trained her to do.

"Wow, I don't see you for over a year, Watson, and then, *bam*, twice in one day! Now, this is a record," she says sweetly, but I know she's trying to make a point of making sure Ryann knows she's already seen me today.

"Yep, I'd say." I nod before tipping my chin up at Gavin, another classmate, who stands next to her. "How's it going in Alabama?"

"Oh, it's going." He grins. "You know how it is. Always on the go."

Gavin went to Alabama to play baseball. And from what I hear, he's a pretty big deal there.

"This is Ryann." I pull Ryann closer to me. "Ryann, this is Rosie, Gavin, and Sylvie."

Sylvie has always been Rosie's best friend, but I've never cared for her too much. She's always acted like a spoiled brat. Truth be told, Rosie did too.

"Hey, Ryann." Rosie waves, tensing up just enough for me to notice.

"Sup?" Gavin nods, taking a bite of his doughnut. "What's a pretty girl like you doing, slumming it with this guy?" he jokes.

Ryann laughs, wrapping her arm around mine. "You know, I'm not quite sure." She beams up at me, giving me a wink. "But I suppose it could be a lot worse."

"That's funny," Sylvie says, hiccupping. "Not long ago, it was Rosie slumming it with good ol' Watty boy. Now, it's this chick with a boy's name." She giggles, and the way she sways around on her feet, I know right away that she's been drinking.

Rosie's eyes widen. "Sylvie, stop." She turns her attention to Ryann. "Sorry. My friend had one too many glasses of wine with dinner tonight."

"It's fine." Ryann gives her a tight-lipped smile.

"Not too many to forget you telling me how delicious Watson looked at the mall earlier," Sylvie squawks. "And I have to tell you, I don't blame you for wanting to hook up with him tonight." She looks me up and down, blinking slowly. "You, sir, are like a fine wine." She snorts. "And as you can see, I'm a lover of all wine."

"Sylvie, I'm begging you to stop," Rosie hisses in warning just as I start to step around them.

"This has been fun and all, but, uh, we're next to order." I nod. "Have a good night, guys."

"See ya, Gentry," Gavin says, taking Sylvie's hand to steady her before walking off.

But unfortunately for me, Rosie doesn't go anywhere.

"I'm really sorry about my friend. She gets like that when she drinks." Rosie shrugs nervously at Ryann.

"It's fine. I live in a house with three other bitches. I get it," Ryann tosses back before looking at me. "Ready to get our doughnuts?"

I nod, but when Ryann releases my arm to step up to the window to order, Rosie stands directly in front of me.

Placing her hand on my abdomen, she looks up. "It was *really* good to see you. If you're in town for a few days, maybe we could get coffee."

"No." The word comes from my mouth before I have time to stop it and say something less blunt.

I open my mouth to speak again, but Ryann glares at Rosie, a hand on her hip.

"If you could refrain from touching my husband's abdomen, I'd really appreciate it," she sasses. "I get it; his abdomen is insanely hard and hot. And obviously, you're still obsessing over your high school days." She waves her hand toward my stomach. "But ... don't."

Looking down at her own hand, Rosie yanks it away from my body. Her eyes are as wide as saucers.

"Y-you ... you're married?" she stutters, looking up at me, her eyes filled with tears. "To her?"

"Yep, I sure am." I step away from her and closer to Ryann. "It was great catching up, Rosie. But if you could excuse me ... I promised my wife Jackie's famous mini doughnuts. And that's what she's going to get."

Once she's gone, I suck in a breath. "I'm sorry."

Ryann squints toward the menu, ignoring me. "Hmm ... mini éclair doughnuts? Or mini strawberry cheesecake doughnuts." She taps her fingers on her chin. "That's a tough one. I can't decide."

"What can I get y'all?" Jackie, the owner, says from inside the booth. "Watson! I haven't seen you since last year's ceremony. How have you been?"

"Hey, Jackie." I wave. "I'm good. Hey, we'll take an order of the éclair ones and an order of the strawberry cheesecake ones." I look down at Ryann. "Did you want anything else?"

She can't fight the smile that breaks across her face. She might have been annoyed from the Sylvie and Rosie stuff, but it's easy to see she's not that mad.

"You got it, sweets," Jackie says, taking my money and getting to work on our order.

Stepping to the side, Ryann folds her arms over her chest. "What do you think—that you can make me not grumpy with food?"

"Pretty much." I shrug. "Worked, didn't it?"

Rolling her eyes, she giggles. "You're annoyingly swoony, Gentry."

"And you're adorably jealous." I wink just before Jackie hands us our order, making Ryann's eyes widen.

"Oh. My. God. Those look good," she whispers.

And when she brings one of the doughnuts to her lips, before her tongue darts out, licking the creamy filling, a jolt goes right to my dick. I know I'm never going to look at a doughnut the same.

Because I know exactly how good her lips feel when they are wrapped around my cock.

"Keep it up," I warn her. "Keep it up, and I'll have you on your knees, swallowing down my cum instead of that cream you seem to be enjoying so much."

Licking her lips again, she gives me an innocent look. "I don't know what you're talking about, dirty-minded boy." She puts another mini doughnut between her lips, this time lapping the strawberry topping off of it. "I'm simply enjoying my doughnuts."

"You'll be enjoying something else real soon, Tiny Dancer," I growl against her ear. "That's a promise."

27

Ryann

I stare down at the message from Officer Hewett. It's Christmas Eve, for fuck's sake. Why is he sending me this shit today?

> *Officer Hewett: Hello, I understand it's unorthodox to be in contact the night before Christmas, but I've been left no choice. It's imperative that you call me ASAP.*

It's after eight thirty at night. I have no idea what can't wait until I return to Brooks. A part of me wants to ignore the message. Maybe if I ignore it ... it'll go away.

Yeah, right. More like you'll go away in the back of a cop car.

We just got back home a few minutes ago, and Jeanine rushed inside to get the board games ready. Apparently, it's another tradition of theirs.

On the drive home, she finally started to warm up to the idea of us. Though she still hasn't mentioned the whole marriage thing. But maybe it was seeing us together. Perhaps it was Watson's private chat with her. I don't know. But whatever it was, I'm thankful for it.

"I've got to make a quick call to my sister." I smile. "I'll be back out in a few."

" 'Kay, babe. Hurry along so I can kick your ass." Pressing a kiss to my forehead, Watson heads toward the table where everyone has now gathered. Turning around, he winks. "You're going down."

Though I grin at his playfulness, I can't stop the feeling of dread that's filling my body, knowing what phone call I actually have to make. If Officer Hewett needs to talk to me on Christmas Eve, it can't be good.

Walking into Watson's room, I close the door behind me and sit on the edge of the bed. Bringing Officer Hewett's contact up on my screen, I hit the Call button.

"Hello, Miss Denver," he answers on the second ring. "Merry Christmas Eve."

I roll my eyes. "It's Mrs. Gentry actually," I correct him.

"I'm going to get straight to it. Despite how you feel about me, I'm not a complete monster. And while I think your marriage is a sham and I believe you wrongfully came into the United States and need to return to Canada, I don't believe the man you claim is your husband deserves to be brought down with you."

That has me sitting up straighter, my heart lurching into my throat. "What do you mean? Why would he get brought down?"

"Ryann ... your visa was forged. Your marriage is fake. It's time to pack your bags and go home." He pauses. "Go home before you ruin that man's life. Because from what I can see, he's got a lot to lose."

"I don't know what you're talking about," I bite back. "We got married because we love each other."

"No, you didn't," he says, completely unfazed. "You got married because you found out you were going to be deported, and you conned him into marrying you to save your own ass. The way I see it, you have two choices. One, you continue doing what you're doing and fight tooth and nail—alongside Watson. You both get dragged to court, and it becomes an entire legal mess. Only for you to lose. You'll be taken back to Canada immediately. And Mr. Gentry will stay here. He'll be here, alone, facing criminal charges, and he'll inevitably lose his spot not only at Brooks, but his future position in the NHL as well."

There isn't a cell in my body that can make me form a word. I'm just ... numb. I'm not taking Watson down. He's too good of a man for that. Everything he does, he does to make others happy. He's selfless. And I refuse to ruin his life. Well, more than I already have.

"Two, and I personally really like this one," he says, stopping for a second, "you confess to using Mr. Gentry to gain citizenship. Sign an annulment. And go home to Canada. Watson will likely come out with a slap on the wrist, and we'll leave you alone. If you don't try to illegally cross over to the US again, that is."

The entire room spins. I feel like I'm going to be sick. I know what I have to do. I mean, what other choice do I have? It's one thing to ruin my own future, but I'll give up everything before I ruin his too.

"When?" I whisper. "When ... when would I need to go back?"

"That's another reason for my call. I just got word an hour ago that next Friday, at nine a.m., you'll have a hearing." He sighs. "And if it goes the way I think it's going to go ... you'll be escorted back to the border after."

"I'll be there." I sniffle. "I'll do whatever I have to do. But Watson needs to be kept out of this."

"Good choice," he mutters. "Merry Christmas, Miss Denver."

That time, I don't bother to correct him that it's Mrs. Gentry. Because soon, I won't get the honor of having that last name.

And for a girl who didn't think she even wanted to date a guy like Watson Gentry, my heart is breaking inside of my chest at the realization that, in no time, I won't even get to be his wife.

Watson

"What if someone hears us?" Ryann says as I'm tearing her shirt over her head. "Your mom finally doesn't hate me. I don't want to disrespect her by ... you know ... in her house."

"The only other bedroom on this side of the house is Carson's. And as you can see, he isn't here. My sister went to her house for the night, and I promise you, no one can hear us."

Pushing her backward, I yank her jeans and thong off, throwing them to the side.

"All fours—now," I demand, dragging my own shirt over my head. "You thought it was funny to tease me earlier with those doughnuts, but now ... you can crawl to me and show me how sorry you are."

"Wat—"

"Fucking. Crawl," I hiss, and a strangled whimper escapes her lips.

Doing as she's told, she crawls to the end of the bed. Pulling my jeans down, I palm my cock, giving it a few strokes before I shove it right between her lips.

"Suck." I give her the command, knowing my good girl will do exactly what she's told.

Right away, she goes to town, sucking my dick, reminding me how much I love that fucking mouth of hers. Gripping her hair, I push her back and forth aggressively before pulling out of her mouth.

"Enough," I growl. "Turn around and face the other way. But don't you fucking dare get off all fours."

Spinning around, she gives me a clear shot of her beautiful ass. And, wow, what a fucking sweet sight that is.

Putting my knees on the bed, I give her ass a spank. Climbing over her, I bring my fingers to her mouth. "Open," I mutter.

Her lips part, and she drags my fingers between her lips. Letting her suck on them like she would my cock, I pull them out before shoving them between her legs. I work them in and out of her, and she moans, quickly trying to quiet herself.

Grabbing my shirt from next to me, I thrust it in her face. "Bite this. Muffle those slutty moans with my shirt, you dirty fucking girl."

When she bites down on the fabric, her moans are quieted, but loud enough for me to hear them the slightest bit. Making me even harder.

Replacing my fingers with my dick, I thrust inside of her at once, filling her so beautifully full and hitting her so deep that I know it won't be long and I'll be seeing stars.

Grabbing her wrists, I pull her upward slightly and pin them behind her back as I continue fucking her over and over again, listening to the sound of her muffled moans, mixed with my hips smacking against her asscheeks. Her asscheeks that look so fucking gorgeous from behind. Practically begging me to explore.

I release her hands, flattening her out on all fours again, and drive into her. She's close—I can feel it. And when I reach around, brushing my thumb across her most sensitive spot, she withers beneath me, squeezing the life from my cock as she comes so hard, dripping all over my length, just like I wanted her to.

"Good girl," I growl. "But now, I'm going to come all over this ass."

Pulling out, I grip my cock, putting it against her ass while giving it a few strokes. My movements grow jittery as a shiver runs down my spine, and I drip my seed down her ass.

Bending forward, I bring my lips to her ear. "Your ass looks so fucking hot, covered in my cum."

And it does. It really, really fucking does.

WATSON

"**U**ncle Watty! Uncle Watty! I love it so much!" Phoebe squeals, pulling the backpack I got her for dance class to her chest.

I found it on some crazy online store that basically customizes anything and everything you could imagine. It has a little ballerina with brown hair, like hers, with her initials under it.

Running toward me, she throws her tiny arms around my neck. "Thank you, Uncle Watty."

"That's not as cool as the monster truck he gave me," Emmett mutters, but his sister ignores him. "You can't play with that. It's boring."

"You're welcome, little lady." I give her a squeeze. "Did you know Ryann is a ballerina?" When she steps back, I take my phone out and pull up some pictures from *The Nutcracker*, zooming in on Ryann. "Look, there she is right there."

I glance at Ryann to find she's blushing but grinning at me.

Phoebe rushes over to her, showing her the backpack. "Do you have one of these too? Did Uncle Watty get you one but with your color hair instead?"

"I don't have one, but I sure wish I did," she says, admiring the backpack and giving my niece a sweet smile. "Uncle Watty only got that for his very favorite girl." She shrugs. "How lucky are you?"

"Soooo lucky," Phoebe says, her eyes growing wide. "Can I come and watch you on one of those big stages sometime?"

"Of course you can!" Ryann smiles. "I'll give Uncle Watty the schedule of shows left for the year, and he can give it to your mom."

"Hey, did you look inside of it, Phoebe?" I nod my head toward the bag in her hand. "Might be something inside. You never know."

Squealing, she quickly unzips it, pulling out the two new leotards I got her. I had to ask my sister what the hell size she'd be and what color, but since she seems to be loving her ballet class, I thought it would be a fitting gift.

"I love them!" she yells, holding up the sparkly pink and baby blue leotards. "Mommy, can I put one on right now?"

"Why not?" Nora laughs. "Live your life, girlfriend."

Giving me one last squeeze, Phoebe disappears into the bathroom, followed by Nora.

"What a big softy you are," Ryann coos, scooching closer to me. "Who knew Brooks goalie did things like order leotards and custom dance bags?"

Throwing my arm around her, I kiss the side of her head. "Full of surprises, babe. Full of surprises."

"That's how I know I raised my boys right." My mom smiles at Ryann before pointing to Jameson and me. "They might have all given me some gray hairs over the years, but they are good boys. Even Carson—even though I could kick his ass for not being here."

Ryann looks at me, her smile reaching her eyes. "This one is a good one for sure," she says softly.

Though my brother is missing and Christmas morning has never quite felt right since my dad died, this Christmas is one of my favorites. Because Ryann is here. And she fits with my family so easily. Last night, we all played charades and card games. This morning, Jameson and I cooked breakfast while she hung out, sipping coffee with Mom and Nora. My sister, of course, made sure to share some embarrassing stories of me when I had been a kid.

It all seemed so perfect.

If the immigration officer could see us now, he'd leave her alone. He'd understand that this is real. And it's genuine.

But I have a feeling in my gut that it's not going to be that easy.

Ryann

Phoebe hugs both of us good-bye, still wearing the adorable leotard Watson gave her. Something about a man who isn't afraid to show his sweet side ... is hot.

Really hot.

Jeanine throws her arms around Watson before moving to me. "I'm sorry for being so cold to you when y'all told me the news that you were married. I was just in shock. My boy, well, he's never been one to jump into something so serious. Usually, he's my patient one. My boy, who overthinks and waits until every duck is perfectly in its spot in the row before he makes a move." She looks from me to her son. "I know that he must have felt strongly about you though. Because for once, he thought with his heart." Her eyes find mine again. "And I can tell not only that you really love my Watson, but adore him too. And that right there is enough for me to love and welcome you into our family with open arms."

An odd expression passes over Watson's face, and I feel my heart sink.

Way to blow my cover, Jeanine. Here I thought, I was playing it cool.

I do love her son. Of course I do. But I can't tell him that. Especially now that Officer Hewett has told me basically my only choice is to sign an annulment and leave Watson. Forever.

Releasing me, she raises her eyebrows. "That being said, y'all don't be strangers, you hear? Come visit an old lady from time to time."

A lump lodges itself in my throat, making it damn near impossible for me to talk. My heart breaks because I know I'll likely never make it back here. And that this Christmas was the closest thing to a real one I'll ever get. A house that felt more like any home I've ever known, but one I'll never return to.

But slowly, I force myself to nod. "We sure will. Thank you for having me." I attempt to smile, but it's next to impossible. "I really, really loved being here for the holiday."

"Thank you for the candles and wax warmer." She winks. "You already found the way to my heart."

I wish I really were this woman's daughter-in-law. I wish that Nora was my sister-in-law too. And the tiny humans hugging Watson and my legs? I'd give *anything* to watch them grow up. And to introduce them to Riley even though she always says she hates little kids.

No one could hate these two kids. There's no way.

Giving his sister one last hug, Watson grabs our bags and looks at me. "Ready to head back?"

No, is what I want to say. I want to stay here, in this bubble where nothing can hurt us. Where no one is waiting to tear us apart.

But that's not how life works. Life doesn't care if it hurts you. Life just moves on to the next person like nothing ever even happened. And I … well, I'm no stranger to pain. But something tells me that losing Watson Gentry might just bring a whole new agony I haven't felt.

And to be honest, I'm scared.

But it doesn't matter. Because when we get back, I need to cut him loose. Before he loses everything.

Because losing just me is far better than losing everything he's worked for.

WATSON

Ryann and I have only been back home for a day, and something has already shifted. And not in a good way either. I felt it on the way home from my mom's. Well, to be honest, I felt it a little bit on Christmas Eve after she disappeared to talk to her sister. I guess I tried to push it aside, telling myself I was just being insecure and that everything was perfect.

I should have known with Ryann to never ignore the signs.

I stand under the spray, washing off the sweat of today's practice, hoping the scorching hot water will ease my aching muscles and melt the negative thoughts away from my brain. Everything in my world now revolves around Ryann. And that'd be fine, but she's so fucking unpredictable at times.

Even this morning, when she was leaving for dance, I could just sense something was off. And when she hugged me, I felt her sigh, and I swear it was like she was trying to live in that moment a little longer. Almost like … it wasn't going to happen again.

My back teeth grind together. No, I can't fucking think that way. We're past her *trying to leave* type of shit. I know we are. We aren't the same couple we were back in Savannah when she was trying to bolt. We're solid.

I can tell myself that over and over, but my mind won't stop reeling. Maybe taking her home for Christmas was too much. No, that can't be it. She played with my niece and nephew. She hung out with my mom and Nora. And her smile? It was a real, honest smile.

Stepping out of the shower, I pull my towel around my waist and head to my locker. Link stands at his, pulling a shirt over his head.

"Well, if it isn't the married man himself." He grins. "How's married life going?"

"It's, uh … it's going good." I toss back, nodding. My voice doesn't sound nearly as confident as I planned it in my head.

Link picks up on everything. The dude is observant. I guess as our team captain, he has to be.

"Really good."

Closing his locker, he sits on the bench and pulls his socks and shoes on. "You hesitated."

"I did not," I say, quickly shaking my head.

"You did." He bobs his head up and down. "Don't worry; I get it. Women are fucking crazy."

By now, it's just us in here. He and I stayed back to run over a few things after practice ended, just like we always do. Link is a lot like me, always feeling like he could give more, even when he's giving well over one hundred percent. He's never satisfied with his performance. And what an aggravating feeling that is. I'd know.

"It's just … Ryann is so stubborn sometimes; it drives me crazy. It's like … just when I think she trusts me, she gets weird and then shuts me out once again." I blurt the words out, unable to even stop my mouth from spewing them. "I don't know why I'm telling you this. Sorry, man. I gotta get going."

Standing, he grabs his duffel, hiking it over his shoulder. "Nah, it's all good. I understand. Do you know how long of a road it's been for me and Tate to get to the place we're at? And trust me, I know stubborn. She literally ran away just because I was a hockey player and she told herself she'd never date an athlete. I get it." He chuckles lightly before shrugging. "But I also know I'm a pain in her ass. Always have been. But you know when it's worth it. When you don't want anyone else even if someone else might be less stressful."

He laughs harder, shaking his head. "You know, Coach always tells us the things in life that are the hardest often come with the highest level of reward. I don't know, man. I think he's onto something. After all, he's one smart dude." He hits my shoulder. "If it's worth it … if *she's* worth it … you've gotta stick it out. Pain in the ass and all."

Leaving Ryann has never even crossed my mind. I could never do that. I fucking love the girl. Now, her getting spooked and leaving me? That's a fear I have every day. At the end of the day, I married her because I wanted to. And knowing that we would never have been in this situation if she hadn't needed a visa is a hard pill to swallow.

"Thanks, man." I grab my duffel bag, following Link out of the locker room and toward the exit.

When we get outside, both heading toward our trucks, I stop. "Hey, Sterns?"

"Yeah?" he calls back, tipping his chin up.

"Was it hard for you to put the pros on hold and stay at Brooks another year?"

I've always wondered. When it came time for him to go, Tate still had another year in college. One day, he decided the NHL could wait for him because he wasn't leaving his girl. At the time, I really didn't get it, and I thought he was one insane motherfucker.

Now, well ... now, I think when it comes to Ryann, I'd do the same thing.

He seems surprised by my question, but then a grin spreads across his face. "Not one bit," he says. "You know why?"

"Why?"

"Because, pussy as it might make me, I'd put the pros off forever if it kept me with Tate." Turning, he holds his hand up and waves. "See you tomorrow, Gentry. Go home and fix your shit." Getting in his truck, he rolls the window down. "And remember, whatever it is ... just say you were wrong and she's right. Have some make-up sex. Move on." He shrugs. "Easy-peasy."

He pulls away, and I lean against my truck. A feeling in my chest tells me whatever is going on with Ryann, it's not going to be that simple.

Ryann

I move around my room like a zombie. My face feels chapped from crying, but I've lathered it with moisturizer in hopes of hiding it from Watson when he gets here. I feel like I'm going to throw up as I gather his stuff up before he gets back from practice. There's no other answer. There is absolutely nothing I can do to keep him. If I do, we're both going down. Making him think I don't want him—it's the only way we won't both go down in flames. This way, it'll just be my ass to the fire. Just like it should be.

When Poppy got the mail today, I had two items in the stack. One, a letter from my mom. The second ... the annulment papers. Sent from Officer Hewett himself.

I have yet to read the letter from my mother because, let's be honest, today sucks enough as it is. No need to pile onto the shitfest.

As I put his things in a neat pile, my bedroom door opens. I don't turn to look right away, but I don't need to. I already know it's him without looking over. I feel it. I feel his gaze. His presence. I even smell his bodywash; the scent that usually makes my mouth water has me wanting to cry.

I'll miss that smell. So fucking much.

"What the fuck are you doing?" His voice is deep, but more hurt than mad. "What is this? Why is my shit in a pile?"

I need to keep myself together. If I cry, he'll know that this isn't what I want.

Of course I don't want this! I love him.

He's my person. But if he finds out that I'm doing this strictly to save him, he wouldn't accept it. He'd go down with me without flinching. That's who he is, but I refuse to ruin his life. He's too good of a guy for that. He's worked his whole life to make his dreams come true. Now that he's so close, I'll be damned if I take that from him.

"I'm so sorry." I look down. "I ... we need to talk."

"Talk about what? The fact that you packed my fucking shit up while I was at practice? You waited for me to kiss you good-bye, and then you went to town, making sure to unravel everything we've built?" He steps closer, and there's no mistaking the pain in his eyes. "What the hell is going on, Ry?"

I know what it's like to work so hard for something and have it gone in the snap of the fingers. The difference is, he's actually a good guy. An angel even.

When I don't answer, he grows frustrated. "Fucking speak, Ryann!" he roars, making me flinch, and I can tell he instantly regrets it. But I don't blame him for yelling. I'd yell at me too. "Don't be scared of me, baby. I'd never hurt you. I just don't understand."

A tear rolls down my cheek, and my throat burns so badly that it hurts to swallow. "I know you'd never hurt me, Watson. I've always known that."

He waits for more, watching me and anticipating what will come from my lips next. I'm putting him through hell. I hate that I'm putting him through hell.

"This is too much for me." I force the words out, feeling a stabbing pain in my chest as my heart betrays me. "I'm really sorry to do this, but—" My voice threatens to crack, so I swallow thickly, pushing through. "I need you to take your stuff. To take it ... and go."

"No," he growls, stepping toward me. "I'm not fucking leaving. I don't know where this is coming from, but I know it's not what you want. So, just tell me—what the hell happened between Christmas and now?"

Finding the words in this moment is like trying to find a needle in a haystack. It's impossible, useless, and exhausting. But for him, I have to do it. I have no choice.

"I just had a change of heart, okay?" I look down at my hands because I can't look him in the eyes. "I appreciate all you've done for me and what you did to save me, but I just can't let this go on any longer."

Walking toward my dresser, I open the top drawer and pull the papers out. Stepping toward him, I gently push them toward his hands.

Glaring at me, he eventually snatches the papers from my hand. His face pales as he reads through it. And when he sees my signature at the bottom ... his jaw tightens.

"An annulment?" he hisses. "Between Christmas and now, you had annulment papers drawn up?" He holds the papers in the air, his face twisting with pain. "This is bullshit. And guess what. I'm not signing it." He moves closer to me, just a mere inch from my body, and the anger radiates from him.

Holding the papers in front of my face, he rips them down the center.

"I'm not signing anything. So, it looks like you're stuck with me till you get your head out of your fucking ass and quit playing games." His chest heaves. "Just when I think you're coming around, you pull something like this. And how stupid am I? Because like always, I stand here, unable to let you go." His hands turn to balls at his sides. "I'm fucking pathetic when it comes to you."

There's no single tear coming from my eyes now. No, they all come at once, completely unwelcome. Not just because of how badly everything inside me hurts. But also because I know how much pain I'm causing him. Causing this man who has walked across fire just to be by my side. Who would do just that if I just let him. Over and over, he proves how loyal he is. And I have to hurt him. Like I always do.

"You have to understand, this just can't work," I say as he cups my cheeks, lifting my eyes to meet his. His stare breaks me, making me want to collapse in a pile at his feet, so instead, I squeeze my eyes shut to say what I need to say. "We got married to save me, Watson. But I'm going back to Canada now." I swallow. "I want to be with my sister. It's time for me to go home."

Finally, I pry my eyes open, looking right in his. "Thank you. For being a friend when I needed one. For being patient with me when I didn't make it easy. For marrying me just so that I could maybe stay here. And for taking me home so that I could meet your family."

I swallow back another lump in my throat. "I want to go home now. Please respect my wishes."

"No. I don't fucking believe you," he says through gritted teeth. "Don't shut me out. Just talk to me. For once in your fucking life, Ryann, tell the truth!"

"I guess I didn't realize you took me for a liar." I narrow my eyes, pulling away from him.

Stepping around him, I walk to my door and open it wider. "Please, Watson, leave."

His eyes hold so much pain inside of them. And his body slumps.

I can't give in. I can't let him see how much this is fucking *killing* me.

I didn't want to sign those annulment papers. And I certainly don't want to go back home. My sister is happy with how things are with my mom right now, but some things are just hard to repair. And the relationship between my mother and me ... just seems unfixable.

"Ryann, please." This time, his words come from his mouth in a tortured whisper, and when I dare to look at him, I see tears streaming down his cheeks. "Don't do this. You don't mean it."

A man the entire campus sees as tough ... I've broken. I've ruined my husband.

Wiping my own tears with my sleeve, I suck in a breath. "I'm so sorry, but I do." It comes out as more of a squeak. "Leave. Or I will."

And then he does something that I know I pushed for, but it hurts as much as I imagine burning in hell for eternity would.

He grabs his things ...

And he leaves.

Walking out of my room and halfway down the hall, he turns slightly, glancing over his shoulder. "I'm not signing anything. So, I guess you'll need to lawyer up." The words come out so cold.

And then he disappears, slamming the front door behind him.

I can't breathe. I can't breathe, and everything hurts. And I feel like I might die. Even though I know it's impossible to actually die from a broken heart, right now, it feels very possible that it could happen to me.

I cry. Uncontrollable sobs rip through my body, and my entire face is soaked with salty tears.

What is this kind of pain? I've never felt it before.

My door creaks open, but I don't even look up to see who it is. I keep my face buried in my pillow, dragging in shaky breaths that don't fill my lungs.

PERFECT BOY

The bed shifts with weight, and I feel a small hand on my back.

"I saw Watson leave. If you want to talk, I'm here." Sutton's voice is soft. So soft that I barely hear her. "And if you don't ... I'm still going to be right here."

That only makes me hyperventilate more. I sniffle and try to calm myself down, but nothing works. This is the most impossible situation. But this is the only solution.

Love isn't supposed to be selfish. *Ever.* And yet, until this very moment, selfish is all I was.

"I—can't ... breathe," I cry, my chest heaving and my lips trembling. "I can't breathe, Sutton."

"Shh," she says, running her hand over my hair, then brushing the strands stuck to my soaked cheeks away from my face. "Slow, deep breaths, okay? In through your nose, out through your mouth."

I do my best to focus on what she's telling me to do. Listening to her and doing what she says to calm myself down. I have no idea how long it takes for me to be able to form a thought, but when I finally do, I know I need to tell her the truth. She's my best friend, and I need her to know I'm not leaving her just for the hell of it. That, in this case, I don't have a choice.

"It was the only way," my voice rasps. "Making him leave ... doing what I had to do. It was the only thing I could do," I whimper. "To save him."

"What do you mean, Ry?" She keeps her voice soft, though I can hear the confusion in it. "Why was kicking him out the only way?"

"Because I'm going back to Canada." My teeth clatter, though I'm not even cold. "And he'll be here."

"What?" she cries out. "Why?"

Sitting up, I wipe my eyes. "Because if I don't go to my court hearing and admit to a judge that I tricked Watson into marrying me just for citizenship and go back to Canada, he's going to get dragged down with me." I begin to sob like a baby yet again. "I love him, Sutton. I can't let him take the fall for this." I shake my head lightly. "I would never forgive myself."

She's silent, her eyebrows pulled together.

"How many days?" she croaks. "How many days until your court hearing?"

"Tomorrow," my voice barely squeaks. "At ten in the morning."

"Fuck," she whispers. "Fuck."

I nod slowly before another sob rips through me, and I crash my head against her chest. "Yeah. I know."

I'm not just saying good-bye to my husband. I'm saying good-bye to my best friend too. To all my friends here at Brooks.

This girl right here has become like a sister to me. And I can't imagine life without her.

Watson

After driving around for hours, I finally head home. When I pull into the driveway, I see Haley is the only one home. And seeing as all she does is go to class and sleep since she got pregnant with Cade's baby, I'm not too worried about running into her. I hope I don't anyway. The last thing I want to do is face anyone. Especially her since I can't openly be a dick to Haley. Because, I mean, she's Haley.

Heading inside, I quietly close the door behind me. And when I see her curled up under a blanket on the couch, I curse inwardly, knowing I can't possibly walk by her. She's too sweet, and she's been through a fuck ton of shit lately. I can't be a dick to her even if all I want to do is bolt to my room.

She looks drained, emotionally and physically—something I've noticed about her since Cade went away. And to be honest, I think she's absorbing Cade's pain and dealing with her own.

"Hey." Sitting up slowly, she gives me a small smile before she frowns. "Are you okay?"

How bad do I look if she's asking me that after a few seconds of seeing me? Jesus.

"Yeah, I'm good." I give her a nod. "You?"

"I'm all right." She shrugs, and I can tell she needs someone to talk to.

I'm sure, sometimes, it's hard to talk to her brother, Hunter, about everything. After all, she got pregnant by his best friend and kept it a secret at first.

"I ... I, uh ... sent a letter to Cade with his parents when they went to visit him." She chews her lip. "I just worry about him every single day he's in rehab. I'm sure he's fine." Quickly, she shakes her head. "Anyway, I'm just hormonal. I've been crying a lot lately. So ... ignore me."

Haley and I have built this friendship, and since Cade's been gone, it's gotten stronger. But I've been so preoccupied with Ryann and spending all my time with her lately, I really haven't checked in with Haley as much as I should.

Taking a seat next to her, I throw my arm around her shoulders, pulling her against my side. "He's okay, Hales. And I bet you he'll send you a letter back any day now."

"I don't know if he will. I'm not going to get my hopes up. But if he did ... it would make me so happy. Even if he told me he hates me. I just want to hear something from him. Anything to tell me he's still ... Cade."

She stops, looking up at me. "Watty, are you sure everything's okay? You seem a little off. And you look … sad."

I swallow, looking straight ahead. "I'm not right now, but I will be." I pause. "I hope anyway."

Who am I kidding? I'll never get over Ryann. She'll forever be a ghost haunting me.

"Do you want to talk about it?" she says softly.

"Nah. Not yet." I shrug.

I can't talk about it. I don't want to even say the words out loud. Partly because I feel like an idiot. And also because I know once I say it out loud, it's out in the world.

And I can't imagine a world where Ryann Denver moves back to Canada and I don't see her again.

30

WATSON

Link scores on me—again. But judging by the look on his face, he's not happy about it. He looks concerned and a bit annoyed. Hunter doesn't say anything because I'm sure, thanks to his girlfriend being my soon-to-be ex-wife's best friend, he already knows what's going on inside my head. And Cade isn't even here to cheer me the fuck up because he's still in fucking rehab.

"Are you sleeping out there or what, Gentry?" Coach roars. "If you play like this at this weekend's game, you'll find yourself on the bench. That's a promise."

Normally, I'd say sorry. Usually, I wouldn't even have to get threatened to ride the bench in the first place. Because before Ryann Denver, hockey was the only thing that mattered.

Then, suddenly, hockey came second to her, my fake wife.

I'm in the world's worst mood.

Practice this morning sucked because all I could think about was the fact that my so-called wife is going back to Canada and I don't even know when. And she signed her name. She fucking wrote out her signature on the annulment papers. Pretty much saying our marriage doesn't mean shit to her.

Why should I be surprised though? She's proven time and time again that she doesn't feel the same way I do. I should have taken a hint the first time when I walked up to her in class and she bit my head off for speaking to her.

While the team prepares to run through another play, I squirt some Gatorade in my mouth just as LaConte makes his way over to me.

Great.

"Everything all right, Gentry?" he says, tucking his clipboard under his arm. "Because no offense, but you fucking suck right now. Have all damn practice."

"All good," I answer quickly.

"Out of this entire team, Gentry, you've always been one I didn't have to worry about letting the outside world affect your ability to show up and just play hockey." His eyes widen, shooting me some sort of warning. "I hope that hasn't changed."

"No, sir." I shake my head. "I'll do better. Sorry."

He gives me a pointed look, and his voice lowers as he says, "I asked you not long ago if you had gotten yourself in a mess. I don't know what the hell is going on with you today, but I sure hope you weren't lying to me when you swore you hadn't."

I say nothing because I don't want to lie to LaConte, but I also don't feel like diving into the truth either. He gives me a long stare, as if seeing if I'm going to tell him what's going on, and eventually walks off. And we resume practice. And even though I still suck, I try my best to keep it together.

If I lose my starting position and my wife all in one week, I might just lose my fucking mind too.

Walking into the house, I waste no time beelining it for the stairs. But before I can make it there, I notice Sutton sitting on the couch. Hunter pulled in right behind me—usually, we ride together, but today, the thought of talking to anyone made me pissy, so I drove by myself.

"Watson?" Her voice is small and soft, and even though I really don't feel like talking, I stop.

"Yeah?"

"I'm sorry about everything with Ryann." She sighs. "Just know that this is hard on her too. Okay?"

I turn toward her, unable to stop the glare that sets deep in my eyes. "Hard on *her*? What exactly was hard on her, Sutton? Packing my shit while I was in practice? Or signing the papers to get our marriage annulled without even talking to me first?" I breathe out a resentful breath, shaking my head.

"Don't let her fool you. Nothing about this is hard on her. She's just selfish and really fucking stubborn."

The shock is clear on her face, followed by anger. I don't wait around to hear what excuses she makes for her friend's behavior. Instead, I turn my back to her and head up the stairs. Only it must be my unlucky day because she fucking follows.

"That is so not true!" she says, barging into my room behind me. "And also, watch your tone. This shit isn't my fault!"

Pacing around, she rakes her hand through her hair. "Ughhhh. I could kill her for telling me what she did. Because now, I have to lie—or not lie—and just watch you practically sulk around and be a jerk to everyone." She squeezes her eyes shut, rubbing her temple. "Damn it, Ryann. Why would you put me in this position!"

I stare at her. "What the fuck are you even talking about?"

She opens her eyes, dropping her hand from her head. "I shouldn't have said anything." Slapping her hand on my wall, she throws her head back. "Fuck! I hate this!"

Walking toward her, I look down, narrowing my eyes. "Sutton, what are you fucking saying? Talk. Now."

Taking a breath, she cringes. "The immigration officer ... he told Ryann that if she didn't admit to the judge that she'd tricked you into marrying her and that this was all her fault and that you had no knowledge she was using you to get a visa ... your future would be ruined." She pauses, covering her mouth for a split second, like she can't believe she let the words slip out. "She isn't selfish, Watson. She's trying to save you." She shakes her head, her voice growing much softer. "You can't possibly think that she wants to go back home after she's worked so hard to be here in the first place?"

She reaches up, putting a hand on my shoulder. "That girl loves you. And because of that love ... she's taking the fall for this entire thing. And throwing away her own dream just so that you don't have to give up yours." She pauses, and then her voice is hardly a whisper as she says, "That's not selfish ... that's love."

Opening my mouth in an attempt to talk, I'm stopped when Hunter walks into the room, looking at Sutton and me in utter confusion.

"So, this is weird," he says, shaking his head.

Both of us ignore him as Sutton steps away from me and tips her chin up higher. "Her court hearing starts at any minute. And then ... she'll be sent back across the border." Her eyes widen. "And seeing as it'll take fifteen minutes to get there ... you'd better haul ass."

I blink a few times, my mind realizing what I have to do. I quickly kiss her forehead. "Thank you, Sutton! Thank you!"

"Now, you're kissing my girlfriend's forehead," Hunter mutters. "I don't get it. This day is fucking strange."

Without another word, I bolt out of my room and down the stairs, heading straight to my truck.

I might lose my future spot in the NHL, but I refuse to lose my wife.

If she's going down, well, so am I.

RYANN

My knee bounces, so I cross my legs in hopes of stopping it. That helps, but then it's my hands that are shaking. I sweat, but the sweat just makes me shiver. Every ounce of me is scared. I know my fate, but that doesn't make this easier to accept it.

I've made friends here. I've found a job.

I got married.

After I told Officer Hewett that I accidentally lost the annulment papers, he printed a new one, and once again, I signed on the line. It hurt just as bad as the first time. I couldn't tell him the truth—that Watson tore them in half. He'd think I was just lying in a last-ditch effort to prove something, I'm sure.

The judge reads me everything I've done wrong. Fake visa. Marriage for citizenship, yada yada. Only in their fancy terms that I don't really understand. And when it's my turn to talk, I don't have anything to say.

I hear the double doors push open and turn around. When my eyes take in the sight of Watson rushing into the room, my heart squeezes inside of my chest.

I can tell he's fresh from practice. The way he's dressed in his gray Wolves hoodie and sweatpants tells me he came here as a last-second decision.

Which means someone had told him I was here. And by someone, I mean, my traitorous best friend.

Damn it. He's going to make this even harder than it already is.

"Excuse me, son! You can't just barge on in here!" the judge calls out, clearly angered by Watson's actions. "Can't you see we're in the middle of something?"

"Well, seeing as I'm her husband, shouldn't I be here too?" he says, tipping his chin up. "Y'all had those annulment papers drawn up, but did she tell you what happened to them?"

"Yes, Miss Denver said they were lost," Officer Hewett huffs out.

"Nah, that's bullshit. I tore them in half when she tried to get me to sign them." He holds his hand out, pointing toward me. "And her name isn't Miss

Denver. It's *Mrs.* Gentry. Because she is my wife. We aren't getting an annulment."

"Save it, son. She's already admitted to using you in an attempt to gain citizenship. So, while I appreciate what you're doing … you're just digging a hole for yourself," the judge says matter-of-factly. "But while you're here, you can do yourself a favor by signing the papers." He looks over his glasses. "The *new* papers. The ones that aren't ripped in half."

"I told you, I'm not signing shit," he says, his voice sharp. "I did marry her to make sure she stays in the United States. That is true." His eyes find mine. "Because I'm in the United States. Because my future is in the United States. Because *her* future is here. In. The. United. States. And the thought of her being in another country? No. I can't have that." He shakes his head. "That right there is the truth." He steps closer to me. "If you send her back across the border, I'll just follow her there. Hell, if you try to send her to the moon, I'll build a rocket to follow her there." The corner of his lips turns up a bit. "I love this woman. I have loved this woman for a long time now. We might fight, and she might drive me absolutely insane at times." He laughs. "Okay, a lot of the time. But guess what. That's a marriage. In its truest form."

He's close enough to touch me, taking my hand in his. "I love you, Ryann Gentry. And I meant what I said. I'm not signing those papers." He narrows his eyes. "And you can't make me either."

Tears stream down my face, and I smile at him just as he cups my cheek and kisses me.

"I love you too." I nod slowly. "I love you so much."

The judge's voice pulls me back to the present at our scary, harsh reality.

"That's nice and all, but you're leaving out the part that she came here illegally."

We both turn toward him.

"Miss—Mrs. Gentry, you forged your visa. I don't think I need to tell you what level of offense that is."

I swallow, looking down briefly. "No, sir. You don't. I know it's bad."

"And if her mother or the police hadn't failed her, she would never have had to do that," Watson barks out. "The events that took place for those charges to be there in the first place? They were a life-or-death situation for her. As a judge, one of the highest positions within the law, how could you not see that?" His face grows sad. "Have you even looked at her file to know that?"

"I've seen her file, Mr. Gentry. And that wasn't up to me to decide, son." The judge's voice grows softer. "The law is the law."

"I understand," I whisper. Looking at Watson, I dip my forehead to his. "I'm so sorry. I just … I was so scared you'd lose your future."

"Ryann, you *are* my future. The NHL, it's a career. And, yeah, I want it. But none of that matters if it's not you next to me through it. None of that matters if I can't cheer on the shows you've choreographed." He shakes his head, the emotion thick in his voice. "I'd follow you to Mars just as long as you wanted me there."

I blink the tears away from my vision, aware that there are people—important people—watching us. But if this is our last face-to-face conversation, I don't care if the president of the United States is watching.

"You're the only one I'd live on Mars with," I say, attempting to laugh but only crying harder. "Thank you, Watson. For making me realize that I am lovable. And worthy."

Officer Hewett's voice surprises me when he speaks next, making Watson and me both spin around and face him.

"Judge Martinez, with all due respect, I'm glancing back at these criminal charges, and … I think Ryann needs a lawyer." He looks at me and back to the judge. "I don't think it's fair to pull a college kid from their school year until we know exactly who is at fault. These charges, well, we might be able to get an expungement order for them."

He turns toward me, dropping his voice. "All that means is, we could get the charges dropped from your records." He pauses. "If it went your way."

His eyes soften. "I know I've been adamant to get you back to Canada, but I can see now things are not so black and white in your case. I want to help you, Ryann."

Judge Martinez looks confused, but then he squeezes the bridge of his nose. "That's all well and good, but are we going to ignore the fact that she came into the United States with a forged visa?" He shakes his head. "Officer Hewett, I don't make the rules. But I do have to enforce them."

"I understand. I do," he answers. "But I've looked through her college transcripts. I've spoken with her professors. This isn't a criminal. It's just a kid who had a rough start to life. A kid whose dream was to come here and make her own way." He looks at me, giving me the smallest smile. "To be honest, I think Ryann Den—Gentry is the type of citizen we need more of."

The judge's eyes find mine. "I'll tell you what. We'll appoint you a lawyer, okay? And if these charges can get sorted out and you can get a real visa, I'll do my best to forgive the charge of the false visa. Okay?"

My heart pounds, and I nod erratically. "Yes. Yes, thank you. Thank you so much!"

Holding his hand up, he stops me. "Don't thank me yet. There's still a lot of work to be done." Nodding toward the door, he gives me a tight-lipped … smile? "You are excused for now. Officer Hewett will keep in touch."

Watson's fingertips lace with mine, and he leads us outside. Once we're on the steps and away from everyone else, I leap into his arms, unable to stop myself. His arms wrap around my body, and I breathe him in. So happy I get to smell his intoxicating scent for another day.

"Thank you," I say, pulling my head back and kissing him. Because I know that if it wasn't for his speech, I'd be in the back of a car, headed for the airport by now.

Watson Gentry, my husband and knight in shining armor.

"I love you, Watson." I kiss him again, over and over. "And I don't want to annul our marriage. Ever."

At my words, he lifts me up, forcing my legs to wrap around his waist. The judge could walk out right now, and I wouldn't care.

He spins me around, sliding one hand in the back of my hair. "I'm taking you home now, Tiny Dancer. And I'll show you exactly how much I fucking love you over and over again."

As he carries me down the stairs, I feel his erection quickly growing harder against my body.

And the truth is, I don't think I can make it home without jumping my husband's bones.

31

Ryann

"You're, like … glowing. In an annoyingly beautiful way," Sutton says next to me, pushing her hair back. She glances over at Haley. "And not in the way Hales is glowing. Which is in a *creating life, baby growing inside of her* type of way. This is different." She moves closer to me. "You totally got railed by your husband before this game!"

"Indeed, I did. Though I was the one doing the railing, considering I had to do all the work." I gaze down at the goalie, feeling my heart flutter. "Couldn't let my man be tired for tonight's game."

Because of everything that's happened this past week, I can't get enough of him. I jump his bones every single time he walks through the door. I don't even try to contain myself.

"No fair." Sutton pouts. "I tried. Hunter basically ran away from me." Her face brightens. "But he promised the second he's out of this arena … he's going to let me ri—"

"Please, I beg you," Haley cries, "do not finish whatever you're about to say about my brother and you and whatever you will or won't be doing." She cringes. "I am already nauseous. Don't make me puke all over you."

"My bad." Sutton shrugs. "I can't help it that your brother is, like"—she fans herself—"really, really hot."

"Not. Helping," Haley hisses. "I love you. But please stop talking about my brother."

"Fine," Sutton mutters, glancing at the huge bag of Nerds Clusters Haley is currently inhaling. "I feel like your baby might come out asking for those if you keep eating them. Goddamn, girl."

I swear Haley might actually start crying, and Sutton must see it, too, because she quickly stumbles over her words, trying to take them back.

"But you're pregnant! So, yeah, eat away!" She reaches in the bag, taking one for herself, nodding her head. "Live your life."

Haley's lip pokes out. "Cade used to buy these for me."

I shoot Sutton a glare, and she widens her eyes, shrugging. God love the girl. She's just a tad abrasive at times when she shouldn't be. Especially with the poor girl whose baby daddy is in rehab.

Moving my attention back to the arena, I watch Watson stretch his body against the ice.

Except this time … I don't even try to pretend I'm not.

Finishing up, he stands, skating back toward the goal. And when his helmet lifts and his eyes meet mine, my legs go to jelly.

God, I love that man.

WATSON

A win is always fun. But a win on a night my wife is in the stands, wearing our last name and my number on her back? That's a fucking victory.

I shower quickly, already hating that I'll be stuck in interviews for too long when all I want to do is go cuff my wife to the bed with her wearing nothing but that jersey and make her come until the sun comes up. I guess all in good time, but, fuck, it sucks to wait.

Changing quickly, I head out of the locker room, surprised when I see LaConte outside his office and not already talking to the press.

"Got a second, Gentry?" he asks, and I'm instantly nervous.

"I do," I say with a nod, following him into his office.

"I owe you an apology, son." He sits down behind the desk and rests his hands in front of him, his eyes fixed on mine. "As a man who's been married for too damn long to remember, I shouldn't have questioned your marriage with Ryann. I'm sorry for that." A look of concern crosses his face. "I hope it all goes her way in court and you two are able to move past all of this shit that you've had to work through." He tilts his head to the side. "Remember, sometimes, it's things like this in life, the things that are the hardest ... well, more often than not, they are the same things that come with the highest level of reward."

He pats his hand on his desk. "Go on and get out of here, boy. Get those interviews done so you can go see your wife." He sighs. "I know I'm ready to see mine."

Slowly, I stand. "Thank you, Coach." I nod. "Really. For everything, thank you."

"Anytime, Gentry."

As I walk out of his office, I know that not long ago, I lied to him when he asked me for the truth. But the truth is, I loved Ryann then just like I love her now. And it won't matter if the court goes her way or not; nothing will keep us apart. Moving to Canada and joining the pros over there isn't anything I ever imagined doing. But if it was between the New York Rangers or Ryann, I'd choose her. I wouldn't even have to think about it.

RYANN
SEVEN WEEKS LATER

"I love it here," I say, gazing up at the never-ending buildings that somehow seem to reach the sky. I've always known they'd be tall—I mean, they aren't called skyscrapers for nothing. But still, nothing could have prepared me for them. Or to be standing here, in New York City, in complete awe.

Sounds of honking horns and the sulfur-like smell that fills the air are welcoming. To some, I'm sure it would turn them away. To me ... I feel like I'm home.

For so many years, I've waited for this very moment. To be in the Big Apple, in the city that never sleeps. And I love it.

"Whatcha think, Tiny Dancer? Is it everything you dreamed it would be?" Watson says, wrapping his arms around my waist and pulling my back to his chest. "And more importantly, are you happy?"

"It's more than I ever imagined," I whisper, letting my eyes roam up one building and down another. "It's ... beautiful."

"I love you, baby," he murmurs against my neck. "But the smell is not beautiful. Why does it smell like a dumpster?"

Spinning in his arms, I grin up at him. "I like the smell."

"No one likes that smell," Sutton mutters from behind us, and when I glance over my shoulder, shooting her a glare, she shrugs. "What? They don't." She points to her chest. "Visiting you when you live here is probably going to give me an asthma attack. You know what that means? You should probably stay in the South with me. Forever."

"Babe, you're my Southern girl. And I love it," Hunter says, throwing his arm around her shoulders and pulling her against him. "But not everyone is like that, you know?"

"Y'all suck." Sutton pouts.

When Watson releases me, I walk over to Sutton and pull her against me. "I love you. And I'll be at Brooks until I graduate. So, you're stuck with me for two more years, babe." I inhale. "But, yeah ... down the road ... I am going to move here. And you're going to have to pack your inhaler, get on the damn airplane, and come and smell the shitty air of the city. Because if you don't, I'll kick your ass."

She sighs. "Fine. Two years is a long time. Maybe you'll change your mind by then." She gives me her big puppy-dog eyes. The one that Hunter literally loses his mind for. "One can hope, right?"

I press my forehead to hers. "Nothing will ever keep us apart, not even living states away from each other. You're my sister. You're my person."

Tears form in her eyes, and she sniffles. Sutton's a tough chick who rarely shows her emotions. A childhood like the one she had will do that to you. One where you dance and compete, even when your toes are bleeding and your entire foot is screaming in pain. She never got sympathy, and now, she spends her time trying to be tough.

"You're my person too," her voice squeaks, and we squeeze each other one last time before stepping back, both wiping our eyes. "And I'm so happy that everything worked out for you in court. Because if I had to hide you in a secret room just to keep you in the US, I would have done it."

"I know," I say, nodding slowly. "Now, let's go see the school you dropped out of to go to Georgia, shall we? I need to check this place out for myself."

Rolling her eyes to the sky, she huffs out a breath. "You're never going to let me live it down that I left Juilliard for Brooks, are you?"

I shake my head quickly, my lips forming a line. "Not a chance, babe."

I turn toward Watson, and his hand finds mine as we start to walk with Hunter and Sutton close behind us.

"I thought I was your person," Hunter grumbles. "I feel lied to."

I can't help but giggle.

"You are my person." She laughs. "You're the person who I love. Who makes me smile—"

"Who gives you the best orgasms?" he mutters a little too loudly.

"Yes. That. And the one who makes me happy and so on and so on. So, yes, you are my person. But then there's also my *person*. The type you can call if you just killed someone and you need some help to dispose of the body in a way that will not make you go to jail for the rest of your life." She pauses. "And that is Ryann."

Watson stops, spinning around, his eyes shifting from me to Hunter before finding Sutton's. "Uh … got something to tell us, Savage?"

"Well, not literally killed someone, you weirdo." She looks at me, smirking as she raises a brow. "But if I did, best believe my girl would help me bury the body. So, y'all better not piss us off."

Hunter's eyes grow huge, and Watson frowns.

"Uh … well then," Watson utters, "remind me not to piss the pair of you off."

As we all start to walk again, I hear Hunter ask, "Okay, but, like … Little Bird, am I still the main person? Like … your *person*, person. Right?"

"Yes, Hunter." She giggles. "Don't be jealous of Ryann."

"I'm not. I'm … fine," he grumbles.

"Good job, wifey," Watson whispers. "You've made Thompson pout."

I grin up at him as we stroll along the sidewalks of New York City. And it's the most surreal thing in the world. I have friends. And a husband. I'm in the city of my dreams, and tomorrow, I get to go with Watson to check out the New York Rangers hockey arena, where he'll be playing professional hockey after he graduates.

A few months ago, I assumed my ass would never get the chance to chase my dreams in the United States. And now, I'm a true US citizen. My record has been cleared. And the annulment papers were torn up long ago. When I dreamed my big dreams as a girl, it was missing the most important thing that is now my reality.

It was missing Watson.

After a long talk with Ginger, I decided not to go back to Peaches. While I appreciate all she did for me and she was a wonderful boss, my heart was no longer in it. But I did, however, get a job at a local ballet studio, teaching lessons a few nights a week. The pay isn't nearly as good, but it's so fulfilling that it makes it all okay. And Watson and I found an apartment to move into in a few weeks. So, all in all, life is good.

I never thought of myself as marriage material. Honestly, I never even cared to have a husband. But then I married Watson, and he spent day after day making me fall not only in love with him, but with us too.

And I can't wait to see what our future might hold.

Watson

"Whose house is this?" Sutton scowls, looking at the random house I just drove us to. "Are you going to kill us all off now? I'll have you know, I'd make a very scary ghost that would come back and haunt your ass. Daily."

After we went to the Rangers arena and checked out where I'd be playing pro hockey, I had a surprise for Ryann. One that I'm hoping will earn me some major sexy time when we get back to the room later.

"Just trust me, would ya?" I call back to Sutton before opening my door. "Come on, guys. You don't want to miss this."

Ryann's voice stops me. "Babe, what the hell are we doing at this random-ass house?" She looks from the blue house and back to me. "You're creepin' me out, dude."

Jerking my chin toward it, I give her a grin. "Trust your husband. Have I ever steered you wrong?"

She gives me a look like she's thinking before she laughs. "Fine. You have a point there."

Getting out of the truck, Ryann follows my lead, and hand in hand, we head toward the front door with Sutton and Hunter trudging behind. Both undoubtedly with confused looks on their faces, much like my wife's.

When I knock, a middle-aged woman with auburn hair opens the door, smiling at us. "Watson! You made it."

"We did. After five weeks of emails and calls, I'm finally here to pick up my package." I laugh. "Thank you, Judy. For holding it for me this long."

"Oh, it's no problem at all." She grins at me before her eyes move to Ryann's. "I think your husband here is about to get hubby of the year." She opens the door wider. "Come in, guys. Come in."

The second we're inside, I can sense Ryann is stiffening next to me. She's never been huge on surprises, but I know this one will be an exception. And when we head into the living room, there he is, sitting on the couch next to Judy's husband, Tony.

A dog. No, a French bulldog.

Ryann's hands fly to her mouth, and she looks at me. "You remembered?" she cries.

Pulling her to my side, I give her a look. "Of course I did. I remember everything when it comes to my wife." I kiss the top of her head. "I take it, you want to take him home then?"

Her head bobs up and down, and she cranes her neck to look up at me. Kneeling down, she makes a kissing sound, and the dog jumps from the couch to the floor and runs over to her. Jumping up onto Ryann's legs, he kisses her face.

"I love him," she sobs. "I love him so much."

Sinking down so that I'm at their level, I rub my palm over the squirming pup. "This is Wilson," I tell her. "If you still think that name sounds domesticated, that is."

"Wilson." She sniffles. "I love Wilson." She leans in, kissing my cheek. "And I love you." Turning her attention back to Wilson, she wipes her cheeks with the back of her hand. "I finally have a pet."

I nod. "Yes, baby. You do."

And the way she looks at me, it's priceless. There's nothing I wouldn't do to continue seeing that look for the rest of my life.

33

Watson
Three Years Later

From the balcony, I look down at the hundreds of seats below me. Red seats, each and every one of them filled with a body. A person who paid for a ticket to tonight's show. But when I look around at the huge-ass section currently occupied by a bunch of hockey players and their families, I can't help but laugh to myself. Never did I think I'd be the type of dude sitting at a Broadway show. Yet here I am, alongside so many others, all here to support the same person.

Ryann.

She did it. She really, really did it. She became a choreographer for Broadway, just like she always wanted to. After being here for a year and working some of the other positions here to work her way up the ladder, she finally landed the job of her dreams. And I couldn't be prouder.

"How cool am I, Isla?" Cam grins, winking at his daughter. "Scored you tickets to a debut Broadway show."

"Daddy, I love you. But ... Watson got us tickets. Not you," she says, patting his arm when he instantly frowns. "But thanks for having cool friends." Her smile grows when she looks at her dad. "And, yes, you are cool.

Kind of. Except when you blast Taylor Swift in the school pickup line and roll your windows down." She cringes. "That? Not cool."

"You didn't ..." Addison groans. "Didn't you learn when she was going through her JoJo Siwa phase and you pulled up to a birthday party, singing along to one of those annoying songs, that eight-year-old girls do not like their dads to do things like that?"

Cam looks genuinely hurt, and he literally pouts. "But we always listen to T. Swift on the way to school. She's your favorite, I."

Isla pats his shoulder, giving him a smile while scrunching up her adorable nose. "Yes, Daddy, she is. But not in the school pickup line." She stops. "Or at birthday parties."

Rolling his eyes, he crosses his arms over his chest. "Fine."

I feel a large hand clasp my shoulder, and when I look back, I find Brody grinning at me.

"Where're the snacks?"

"Seriously, I swear all you do is eat," Sutton gripes before she moves to the other side of me. "Ignore my brother and his constant need for food. Can we instead talk about how freaking amazing it is that my best friend choreographed a Broadway show?!"

"Rude," Brody says before turning to his wife, Bria. "Can we go find snacks? I'm hungry." He jerks his head up and down, wiggling his eyebrows. "Maybe you should have a coffee. You know, we're kid-free for the night. Bow chicka wow wow."

He thrusts his hips, and she laughs, covering her reddening face.

"Ew! Stop talking!" Sutton glares at her brother. "TMI. Unless you want me to start talking about my plans with Hunt—"

Covering his ears like a toddler, Brody quickly heads toward the stairs, no doubt looking to hit up the concessions.

"Ew, I agree with Brody. I don't need to hear about my brother and you. Or anything you do." Haley grimaces, resting her hand on her very round belly. "Ever. Also, why do I always have to remind you of this?"

"I mean, clearly, you know people have sex," Sutton teases her, shifting her eyes down to Haley's stomach. "Cade keeps putting babies in you after all."

"Damn right I do." Cade grins proudly. "My swimmers are basically the next Michael Phelps."

"That's ... actually gross," Sutton says, wrinkling her nose just as Hunter steps beside her.

"Babe, what did you say to your brother?" He looks around, completely confused. "He just glared at me when I walked by him."

She shrugs. "Nothing. He's just a big baby."

"True that." Hunter nods before handing her some Twizzlers and a soda. "Sorry, babe. They didn't have Sour Patch Kids. Closest thing was Twizzlers."

"Tell me about it. I almost cried when Link told me that. I mean, who doesn't have Sour Patch Kids?" Tate, Link's wife, groans before holding up her own soda. "At least there's Diet Coke though."

Addison nods, smacking their cups together. "For real. Thank God for that."

Link stretches in his seat, eating his M&M's. "You know, I've never been to one of these shows before. In my head, I did not think they let you eat in your seat at a Broadway show. Then again, I figured everyone would look like they had a stick shoved up their ass and use those weird little glasses things you hold up to your face like you're in the olden days." He gazes around, sighing. "What a pleasant surprise that only, like, five people—including that dude over there currently glaring at us for being loud—look that way." Link shrugs. "I don't get it. The show hasn't started. Why is this guy's balls in a twist already?"

Tate shakes her head before snuggling against him. "You're so weird."

When I hear a familiar voice, I turn to find Ryann's sister and mom walking toward me with my mom following close behind. I stand, heading to greet them, and Riley throws her arms around me.

"I can't believe I'm at my sister's Broadway show! Can you even believe it?" Tears flow from her eyes as she looks up at me. "She made her dream come true."

The corner of my lips turns up. "She sure did." I nod before she releases me.

Her mother doesn't hug me, but gives me a wave and a smile. "Hi, Watson. Nice to see you again."

"You too." I nod. "How was the trip here?"

"Not too bad," she says softly. "I'm so thankful for the invite."

"She'll be happy you're here," I tell her, and I know that Ryann really will.

Years ago, maybe she wouldn't have extended the invite to her mother, but finally, they are in a good place.

I don't know if Ryann will ever fully trust her mom. And I know she'll forever carry the trauma from her childhood even though she tries to pretend like she doesn't. But her mother has proven that she's a different person now. A better person. And I know a lot of that is due to her husband, Randall. Randall really stepped in to be a father figure for Riley. He tries with Ryann too. But she lives too far away. And she's too independent now. But she likes him, and they get along.

"What'd you leave the old man at home?" I ask her, looking around for Randall.

"No, this one gave him a list of wants from the concession stand." She laughs, looking at Riley. "He'll be out at any minute."

"Oh good. Well, sit anywhere." I step around her, giving my own mom a quick hug. "Thanks for coming all the way to the big city, Mama," I drawl. "Whatcha think? You ready to move out here?"

"Boy, you know the answer to that already." She laughs, swatting my arm as I release her. "Too crazy here for this old biddy." She turns to face the stage, a smile spreading across her face. "I'm so proud of Ry." Tears fill her eyes. "Your daddy would be so proud of the husband you are and the wife she is. You two … you're what it's all about." She waves her arm around. "This is what it's all about. Supporting each other. Loving each other. *Believing* in each other." She nods, cupping my cheek. "You and Ry girl definitely do that."

"Thanks, Mom." I inhale. "She makes it pretty easy though."

"So do you." She winks. "I'm going to go find my seat. I can't wait to watch my mastermind daughter-in-law's debut show."

"Me too," I say softly. "Me too."

As I take my own seat and look around at everyone here to support her tonight, I feel like a pussy when my heart flutters. Not all that long ago, she felt like she had no one. And now, all of these people came out just for her. Just like she deserves.

If someone had told me before I ever met Ryann that I'd marry her the way that I did, I would have told that motherfucker he was crazy. But the truth is, the moment her path crossed mine … I never had a chance.

And I wouldn't take a single thing about how we became *us* back.

Ryann

The show ends, and the sound of applause resonates in my eardrums, but it doesn't really register in my brain that I'm a part of the reason why people are clapping. The dozens of uber-talented performers absolutely killed it on the stage tonight. Each one was handpicked by me. And let me tell you, not one of them disappointed. Along with the producers.

But this … this was my show. I choreographed it. I know the entire thing like the back of my hand. In a way, it feels like my firstborn child. Each step, each movement, was thought about over and over, jotted down before ever being put on the table. But it doesn't seem real. It can't be. I must be dreaming.

From behind the stage, I stare up at the crowd, and my heart swells inside my chest because I know my husband is up there. Supporting me, rooting for me. Just like he always does.

And just like I know he always will.

I can't fathom how I—a girl from a small town, who grew up smuggling school snacks and milk cartons into my backpack at the end of the day, just so that I'd have something to feed my sister when I got home—could be here. When I forged my way into this country, this was the reason why. I wanted this. Something deep inside of me wouldn't stop until I got it.

And now that it's here, I know that if I didn't have the man in the crowd, waiting to kiss me and tell me how proud he is of me, his wife … it wouldn't be worth a damn.

God, I love that man.

"Nice work, Ryann," my coworker Cora says, patting my shoulder. "It was beautiful. Congratulations."

"Thank you," I whisper. "Thank you so much."

And then I wait not so patiently for the building to clear out. Because I … well, I have something up my sleeve. Something I've wanted to do for a long damn time.

In an almost-empty theater, now moved to the first few rows, my family and friends chat among themselves—that is, until they see me heading toward them.

Every one of them stands, clapping their hands. Cade whistles loudly, giving me a dimpled grin, while Link holds his drink in the air, and Tate squeals. I don't have time to look at everyone else before my eyes land on my mother.

We might never have those moments when I run to her and she holds me tight, telling me how proud she is and that she loves me so much. But we're in a good place now. And even though she isn't my safe space, like I so long ago wished she could be, I do love my mom.

"That was incredible, Ry." The words come from her lips with such emotion, and her brows pull together snugly as she looks into my eyes. "Ryann, I. Am. So. Proud. Of. You." Each word is bold and emphasized, hitting me like a ton of bricks. Here I didn't think we would have this moment … and it's here. Right now.

My throat grows dry, and the tears spill from my eyes before I can stop them.

Wrapping her arms around me, she pulls me against her. "You, my daughter, are my hero. You did this. All on your own. You made this happen." Kissing my forehead, she pulls back. "I know that I messed up on a lot of things, and for that, I'm so sorry. But the fact that I am your mom?" Tears well in her eyes, and her lip trembles. "I'm the luckiest human alive. I love you, my strong, beautiful, talented girl. I know I wasn't there for you like I should have been. But I am a lifetime's worth of proud."

Kissing me on the forehead once more, she gives me a smile and steps back. "I know a certain tall, handsome man just dying to see you. I'll let you get to him."

When she starts to turn, I catch her hand in mine and stop her.

She looks down, and there's no hiding that she is stunned when she sees me holding her hand.

"Thank you, Mom," I whisper. "I love you. I really do."

Sobbing, she nods, her eyes squeezing shut. "Thank you."

I release her hand slowly, and she makes her way back to my sister, who I know is likely champing at the bit to hug me. But before she can, Watson struts toward me, and his entire face lights up when he sees me looking at him.

The one thing I've loved about that man since day one ... I've never had to wonder how he feels about me. He makes it very, very clear.

"Quite the show you put on, Mrs. Gentry," he drawls, throwing one arm around my lower back and pulling me against him. His nose touches mine as he grins down. "I'm quite impressed."

"Why, thank you," I murmur against his lips before pushing my mouth to his. "Glad you enjoyed it."

"I did. I would have loved it more if you'd dusted off your ol' ballet slippers and joined the others, but ... it's all good." He throws his other arm around me, holding me tightly. "I'm very proud of you, baby. This was your dream. And you didn't stop until it came true."

"Thank you." I sniffle, brushing my tears against his shirt.

"Did you just use me as your own personal hanky?" He frowns.

"It was tears, not snot, wiseass." I poke my finger into his chest. "Can you come with me for a second?"

Wiggling his eyebrows up and down, he smirks. "Ooh, a little quickie action to celebrate?" He thrusts his hips playfully against mine. "Yeah, I'm game for that, baby."

Swatting him, I can't help but giggle. "No, jerk. Get your mind out of the gutter. I didn't say anything about that." I shake my head before stepping out of his hold and grabbing his hand. "Come on, ya big perv."

He follows me, and I lead him onto the stage. And when everyone sees us up there, it grows seemingly quiet.

Turning my body so that it's partially facing him while still turned toward our friends and family, I smile.

"Over four years ago, a boy did the most selfless thing in the world and offered to marry a girl just to save her."

When the words leave my lips, Watson's body freezes as he hangs on my every word.

"The girl was stubborn and, truthfully ... a bit bitchy. But the boy was an angel. And he overlooked all of that and saw something else. Something the girl had never seen inside of herself. Something she didn't think could possibly be there." I blink the tears from my vision, inhaling. "Little by little, the boy taught the girl not only that she was capable of loving ... but that she also was worthy of love herself." I look down for a split second. "And with his love, she finally felt like she had a place on this earth."

I'm a blubbering mess now, but it's fine because so is Watson.

Taking both of his hands, I rub my thumbs against his.

"Watson, on the day we got married, you said that you knew you weren't the man of my dreams. That day, you selflessly vowed to love me forever even though I gave you nothing in return."

I move my body closer to his, staring up at him. "You are the man of my dreams, Watson. You're my whole world. My safe place. My person. My best friend. Every single part of me begins and ends with you." I sniffle.

"That day, you chose me. And you've continued choosing me every day since." My face is drenched with my own tears now, but I'm not done saying what I need to say. "I choose you, Watson. I will choose you for every single day of my life. I know our love story is unlikely and insane, but I don't care. Because our story saved my life. Our story ... is the best thing that has ever happened to me." I take one hand and cup his cheek. "*You* are the best thing that has ever happened to me. So, marry me again. This time in front of our friends and family."

"Really?" He sniffles. "You'd marry me again?"

"A million times over." I nod. "I love you."

Turning quickly back toward the crowd, he takes his hands and cups them around his mouth. "Guess what y'all? Ryann asked me to marry her. And this time, we're having the whole damn fam there!" He grins, making that dimple come out. "And since our friends are our family, that means y'all have to come watch us get hitched. Again."

Everyone erupts into cheers, and when I look at his mom, she's crying because she's so happy. I know it killed her that she didn't get to watch Watson say *I do*. Now, she can. Only this time, it'll be so much more meaningful. Because this go-around, we'll both be all in.

He spins me back toward him, and suddenly, his lips are on mine, kissing me and making me taste the tears dripping down our faces. Quickly, he lifts me up and twirls me around. "I fucking love you, Ryann. So much."

Burying my face into him, I do what I always do. I inhale, bringing my greatest comfort into my nose.

I'm far from Cinderella. But it turns out, even the non-Cinderellas sometimes find their own Prince Charmings.

Watson chose me before I knew how to choose myself. And for that, I'm really, really thankful.

THE END

You didn't think it was really over, did you? We can't leave Brooks University just yet. Not before Walker and Poppy have shared their story. Preorder *Last Boy* now.

Feel like crying? Check out Cade and Haley's story. But first, grab the tissues! This one's an emotional ride. Read it now!

Uh-oh, did you miss Hunter and Sutton's story? Read it now!

Curious about the other puck boys of Brooks University? Check out their stories.

Missing Cam Hardy? Did you know he also appears in the entire Florida East series? (For better or for worse.) Binge the entire Florida East series!

Other Books by Hannah Gray

NE UNIVERSITY SERIES

Chasing Sunshine
Seeing Red
Losing Memphis

READ IT NOW!

BROOKS UNIVERSITY SERIES

Love, Ally
Forget Me, Sloane
Hate You, Henley

HEAD TO THE BROOKS UNIVERSITY FOOTBALL-VERSE!

FLORIDA EAST UNIVERSITY

Playing Dane
Stealing Bama
Catching Kye

BINGE THE SERIES TODAY!

THE PUCK BOYS OF BROOKS UNIVERSITY

Puck Boy
Broken Boy
Filthy Boy
Chosen Boy
Lost Boy
Perfect Boy

MEET THE OTHER PUCK BOYS NOW!

acknowledgments

To think, up until about a month or two ago, this was going to be the last book in the series. Watson would have been the perfect one to end on, no doubt. But I just wasn't ready to let the puck boys go. Not just yet anyway. But even so, it was fun to end this story by bringing back the whole gang and giving them a scene all together.

The characters who have insecurities and hide their pain behind jokes or, in Ryann's case … bitchiness toward men, those are the ones I connect with. Real life is not perfect. And it certainly isn't a fairy tale. But this story was as close to a fairytale as I've ever written. It's about choosing love. And deciding that, even when it's scary, to follow your heart. I loved that Ryann did that. And I love that Watson made it his life mission to make her happy.

Right off the bat, I need to thank my readers and bookstagrammers. I have been completely blown away and overwhelmed with the love you have shown me in this community. I have never felt so loved and appreciated as I do by you all. It is truly because of you that I get to do what I love for a living. Because you are the ones who believe in my stories and get the word out there. Thank you. So much love to you all.

My kids continue to show me so much grace when it comes to my writing. They understand that I have deadlines. They cheer me on along the way. And when I cross the finish line, they are there with the sparkling cider. So, for Charlotte, Carter, and Ava … thank you for being the reason why I choose to believe in myself. And to push myself to do better.

My husband, who has to listen to me brainstorm randomly and gives his input, even when he knows I won't take it. He talks me down when I read a bad review and convince myself that I'm the world's worst writer. Thank you for reminding me to not give up. And to not let the negatives take away all I've accomplished.

I could never write enough words to thank my mom the way she truly deserves. Because without her answering my minimum ten phone calls a day, I don't know how I'd make it through this life. I never have to question if you're proud of me. You make it known every single day.

I owe my dad a huge thank-you for showing me that if you want something, you have to work for it. And if it doesn't come easy, work harder. Even on the days you feel like quitting, dig deep and push yourself more. Thank you for teaching me that humor can be found, even in the hard times. And that a joke or a laugh can go a long way.

For my Autumn. Thank you is never going to be enough for the work you've put in to help me reach the goals that I have reached. I never foresaw being an Amazon top 100 seller. Or having an audiobook company purchase the rights to my stories. And I certainly didn't expect for my books to be picked up by foreign publishers. You have helped me do all of those things and so much more that I cannot even grasp. All while being a friend too. You don't always tell me what I want to hear, and you know what? Thank you for that. Because it's made me a better writer. Love you.

This is the fifteenth book baby that Jovana Shirley and I have brought into the world together. Without you polishing these stories and helping me craft them into their full potential, I wouldn't feel as confident as I do when it comes time for pub day. Working with Unforeseen Editing has been an absolute dream, and I will never go anywhere else. You're stuck with me.

Thank you, my beta readers, Tatum Hanscom and Candice Butchino. The two of you are also two of my biggest supporters. You're always an ear when I need to talk something out. Or to be talked off of the *this book sucks; I should trash it* ledge. I truly cannot put into words how much I appreciate you guys.

For Sara Stewart for getting my TikTok up and running. Lord knows I'm too scatterbrained to make those gorgeous videos the way you do! And thank you for always being such a supporter of me. I'm so happy that we found each other!

Thank you, Jaimie Davidson, for constantly dropping everything to be an extra set of eyes. I appreciate all you've done for me since the very beginning, and I'm so dang happy to have you!

For my model cover designer, Amy Queau with Q Design, thank you. Thank you for always being so easy to work with. I love that I tell you my vision and you waste no time to bring it to life.

Sarah Grim Sentz at Enchanting Romance Designs, thank you for the beautiful alternative cover! Every single time I work with you, I fall in love with your artwork more and more. Thank you for sharing your gift with the world.

Thank you for the gorgeous photograph, Mark Mendex at mcmpix. You made the perfect Watson.

about the author

Hannah Gray spends her days in vacationland, living in a small, quaint town on the coast of Maine. She is an avid reader of contemporary romance and is always in competition with herself to read more books every year.

During the day, she loves on her three perfect-to-her daughters and tries to be the best mom she can be. But once she tucks them in at night—okay, scratch that. Once they fall asleep next to her in her bed—because their bedrooms apparently have monsters in them—she dives into her own fantasy world, staying awake well into the late-night hours, typing away stories about her characters. As much as she loves being a wife and mom—and she certainly does love it—reading and writing are her outlet, giving her a place to travel far away while still physically being with her family.

She married her better half in 2013, and he's been putting up with her craziness every day since. As her anchor, he's her one constant in this insane, forever-changing world.

Printed in Great Britain
by Amazon